LAMAN LIBRARY
3 7910 50221519 4

D0282910

PAID IN FULL

PAID IN FULL

A Quint McCauley Mystery

D. C. Brod

Five Star
Unity, Maine

This novel is a work of fiction. Names, characters, places, and incidents are either the product of the author's imagination, or, if real, used fictitiously.

Five Star First Edition Mystery Series.
Published in 2000 in conjunction with Tekno Books and Ed Gorman.

Cover photograph by Jason Johnson.

Set in 11 pt. Plantin.

Printed in the United States on permanent paper.

Library of Congress Cataloging-in-Publication Data

Brod, D. C.
Paid in full / by D.C. Brod.
p. cm. — (Five Star standard print mystery series)
ISBN 0-7862-2673-0 (hc : alk. paper)
1. McCauley, Quint (Fictitious character) — Fiction.
2. Private investigators — Illinois — Chicago — Fiction.
3. Chicago (Ill.) — Fiction. I. Title. II. Series.
PS3552.R6148 P35 2000
813′.54—dc21 00-030847

PAID IN FULL

Chapter 1

Why do the moments in your life that you'd most like to forget revisit you like past-due notices on your soul, while reminders of the really good ones seem scarce as refund checks?

I pitched in the minors for a few years until my shoulder went south and my ERA north. My first year in class A, I pitched a no-hitter. I was on fire—throwing better than I knew I could. My fast ball left batters shaking their heads as they tossed their bats and retreated to their dugout. In the twenty-some years since that game, not once has a new acquaintance said, "Hey, weren't you the guy . . ."

A year and a half ago, I had an ill-advised assignation. Well, almost. Since then I've lost track of the number of times it has tainted what otherwise might have been an evenly-matched encounter. It was about to come back at me again like a runaway train.

A year-and-a-half ago Ellie Carver and I shared a brief, albeit intense history. I was new to Foxport, a far west suburb of Chicago, living out of a motel on the east edge of town that was next door to a small tavern with the dubious name of the Dive Inn. A squat, brown prefab building with painted-on windows trimmed in Christmas lights, it used to be what the locals referred to as a "gentlemen's club" until a women's group bought space in the paper and started publishing the license plates of cars parked on the lot. Patronage dropped off fast. Now, posters of Olympic swimmers and divers plastered the walls and customers called it a water sports bar. From the outside, the bar looked like it drew a tough crowd; in reality, the Dive Inn and most of its clientele were too tired to be tough.

I had been sitting at the bar nursing my third Scotch, feeling sorry for myself. A number of things had driven me from Chicago, not the least of which included losing my job and my girlfriend at almost the same time. While it was not a high point in my life, I knew I just had to put some days behind me. A couple drinks helped. Sometimes the magic number was three.

I wasn't aware of anyone in my vicinity until a husky, feminine voice beside me murmured, "Can I bum a cigarette?"

I turned and saw a small, pretty woman with large, liquid blue eyes sitting on the stool next to mine. She wore her blond hair piled up on her head in a haphazard style with a few tendrils falling down over her forehead and ears.

I said sure and pushed my pack toward her. She made a face and muttered something about preferring menthol but took one anyway, then waited for me to light it. As she shot the stream of smoke up at the ceiling, I saw something in the way she looked—the hair, pale pink lipstick, blue eye shadow—that took me back to my senior year in high school where I wasn't even in the running for most likely to succeed, but all things were still possible. Sitting on the hard bar stool, that appealed to me mightily. I offered to buy her a drink.

She nodded like she expected no less and said, "Vodka gimlet." I wasn't surprised.

We talked about things, none of which I recall, and after another drink there didn't seem to be any question that she'd go back to the motel with me. The bartender, a heavy-set guy with a craggy face and serious bags under his eyes, had been giving me wary looks as I talked to this woman. I figured he had a thing for her, and since she didn't seem to notice, I refused to let it bother me.

In the yellow light of the motel room, I saw she was older than I'd thought—at least my age which, on an optimistic day, hovers around the midpoint of my life. I wondered what the light did for me. Her kiss was cool and tasted like lime. She pushed away from me and walked over to the bed, pulling her blouse out of her short, black skirt. Standing there with her eyes closed and her chin lifted, she seemed to be trying to superimpose a more compelling image over this one. I couldn't blame her.

She sat on the bed and kicked off one high heel with the toe of the other while unbuttoning her blouse. It was high-necked with white lace. We'd used up all our conversation in the bar and neither of us bothered with the pretense. We just wanted to get our clothes off.

That never happened. Someone pounded on the door so hard the room shook, as a loud voice announced, "Police. Open up." I tried to figure out what I'd done to get busted. My companion's reaction was curious. At first her eyes widened, but then the corners of her mouth twitched—a gesture which, in the short time I'd known her, I'd come to recognize as a preface to a smile. She left her top three buttons undone, crossed one leg over the other and planted her hands beside her, palms down, on the bed. Then she waited for me to open the door.

When I did, two men burst into the room like they were spearheading a major drug bust. Neither was in uniform but they both had the moves. The larger of the two shoved my face against the wall and patted me down. Satisfied I wasn't carrying, he flipped me around, grabbed my collar and thrust the barrel of a .357 under my chin. I couldn't swallow.

The cop had a ruddy complexion and narrow, close-set

eyes that were a muddy shade of brown. Apparently he'd tried to mask the smell of gin with mint, but it wasn't working.

"The lady is off limits," he said. "You got that?"

I nodded.

"What's your name?"

I hesitated, then decided I didn't want him groping around for my wallet. "McCauley. Quint McCauley."

"Well, McCauley, if you're ever seen with this woman again, you're getting more than a warning."

Now was not the time to ask her name.

The other cop watched her, keeping his distance as she collected her purse and sweater. She didn't seem scared or even alarmed. Maybe a little annoyed. Before she left, she stopped and gave me this sad little smile and said, "I'm sorry."

Had I known she was married to the chief of police, I might have left town in the morning. But, ignorance works in strange ways. By the time I learned Ellie Carver's name, I had decided to stay in Foxport for a while.

In the eighteen months since then, I had opened a detective agency, gone into partnership in a small import shop with my landlady, Louise Orwell, and moved into an apartment above her house on the Fox River with a border collie I'd adopted. My life wasn't perfect, but I didn't need three Scotches at night anymore. Ed and Ellie Carver had separated. No surprise there. The woman who'd left me in Chicago, Elaine Kluszewski, had come back into my life and we had tried again, but failed. Fortunately, the parts that had nothing to do with passion were still intact and we managed to remain good friends. Elaine was now living with Ed Carver. Irony is no stranger to my life.

Which brings me back to the present. I was sitting in my

office wondering why one of my clients, a local-hero-turned-investment-wizard, hadn't bothered to pay me. It had been three months—time to mobilize the collections department. I hated making these calls, but I hated getting them even more. Then the phone rang. Giddy with relief, I lifted the receiver.

"Hi, Quint." The voice rendered me speechless.

"Quint?"

"Ellie. How's it going?" I managed.

"Not bad. Not good, but not bad. I need to talk to you. Actually, I think I need to hire you."

"What for?" I lit a cigarette.

"I'd rather talk in person. Can you meet me at the Dive Inn? You remember where that is, don't you?" I thought I detected a smile in her voice. "Seven-thirty?"

I hesitated. "Why me?"

She sighed. "I went through my whole list of people, and you're the only one who might be able to help me who I think I can trust." Then she added, "Kind of sad, isn't it?"

I didn't think that was an intentional slam.

"Will you be there?" she asked.

"Sure," I finally said. "Seven-thirty."

Three seconds after I hung up, the phone rang again. I should have known better than to answer. Bizarre occurrences tend to enter my life in pairs. But I'm nothing if not a slow learner. This time it was Elaine.

"I have a big favor to ask." Elaine didn't believe in couching her requests. I admired that about her. Usually.

"I'm listening."

"I'd rather ask in person. You know, so I can tell what you really think."

"Don't worry. I'll tell you what I really think."

"All right."

Silence. "I'm listening."

"Well, I don't know if you're aware of this, but," she drew in a deep breath, "Ed is allergic to cats."

It took me all of three-quarters of a second to figure out where this was heading. "Elaine—"

"Let me finish." She kicked her delivery into overdrive. "Now, I don't know if this is going to work between Ed and me, you know. But I want to give it my best shot. And I know it's not going to work if he's sneezing and blowing his nose twenty-four hours a day. But, just in case it doesn't work, I don't want to give McGee away. You understand, don't you?"

"I think so. You're fostering out your cat on the presumption that your relationship with Ed Carver isn't going to be permanent."

"I'm not sure that 'presumption' is the right word, but I'll give it to you."

"Does Ed know this?" If he didn't, I wanted to be the one to tell him.

"He doesn't need to know." She paused. "Besides, McGee is a neat cat. It would be easy to find a home for him. Even you admit he's okay."

"As cats go." I guess I'm too lacking in self-love to want an animal who is going to spend the day sleeping, eating and ignoring me. I need a pet that is something of a sycophant. Peanuts, my border collie, fits the bill nicely.

"Look, I don't want to make light of this commitment you and Ed have, but do you know how long it's going to take to decide whether it's working?"

"Never mind. Forget I asked." From the way she clipped off her words, I knew my attitude annoyed her, but evidently not enough to hang up.

She had me cornered. If I said no, she'd have to give up either McGee or Ed. If she gave up the cat, she'd be hurt. If she gave up Ed, my motives would appear sus- pect. I really believed she deserved better than Ed Carver. But then, I also thought she deserved better than me.

I rode out the silence for another ten or fifteen seconds, and then I sighed. Real deep so she'd hear. "We'll see how it works. Peanuts isn't used to sharing me, you know."

"That's okay. McGee ignores you anyway."

"I know."

"Don't take it personally, Quint."

"I'll try not to."

"I really, really appreciate this."

"I know."

"When can I drop him off?"

"Why don't I come by your place? I've got a few errands to run anyway."

"You sure?"

"Yeah. Is two okay?"

"Great."

I hung up and ground the cigarette into the brown plastic ash try, adding its crumpled white carcass to the half dozen others. The window air conditioner droned behind me. Absently, I hoped it lasted the summer.

Why didn't I just let her bring the cat to me? I finally admitted that I wanted to see how Elaine filled the spaces in Ed's apartment. I also wondered what he was doing these days since losing his job as Foxport's chief of police. He'd been ousted in the spring thanks to some political finagling. Once the smoke cleared and reason returned to everyone involved, they'd offered him his job back. He said no. I had to admire his resolve, which, in the face of survival is pretty scarce these days. I just hoped he didn't hang up his shingle and become my competition. Foxport wasn't big enough for both of us.

The detecting business was down. If it weren't for the income from the Jaded Fox, I'd be in bad shape. It was just too damned hot to get riled up about anything enough to hire a detective. Spouses who suspected their mates of cheating on them were either grateful for the respite or had taken to the idea themselves. More likely the latter. Libidos tend to run high during August heat waves.

I lit another cigarette, noting how lousy it tasted, muzzled my dignity and punched in the delinquent stockbroker's number.

Chapter 2

I slammed the phone down. Hell, on a good day Kurt Wicklow made ten times what he owed me. If the guy could afford to take the day off, he could afford to pay me twenty-five hundred bucks. When I'd asked his assistant where I could reach him, she informed me that she couldn't give out that information. I could tell by the way she said "I'm sorry," sort of wallowing in it before she moved on, that she wasn't.

Time for a tactical adjustment. I don't usually bother clients at home. But there was no reason to be discreet about the work I'd done for him. I'd left three messages at his office and he hadn't bothered to return any of them. Maybe he'd respond to an attack on his castle.

I pulled his record and noted his address put him among the big, expensive homes surrounding Foxport's country club: 39W265 Tammi Hill. As I punched in the phone number I figured the residents should count their blessings. The developer could have had a kid named Benny.

A woman answered on the third ring and in response to my request to speak to Wicklow, told me he was out of town.

"When is he due back?"

"Any time. Today perhaps. Tomorrow." From the sound of it, Wicklow wasn't on a tight schedule. "This is Gina Wicklow. Can I give him a message?"

He probably ignored the messages he got at home faster then the ones he got at the office. In spite of the odds, I went ahead and gave her my name and phone number.

After a brief pause during which I assumed she was writing this down, she said, "Will he know why you're calling?"

"He should." Then, I added, "He owes me twenty-five hundred dollars for some work I did for him."

"He does?" She sounded both surprised and confused. "I-I'm sorry."

The little stutter deflated me. "It's probably a misunderstanding," I offered. "Would you make sure he calls me?"

"Of course, I will. I'm sorry you had to call."

I mumbled something about that being all right and hung up, secure in the assumption that Wicklow wouldn't respond to this message either. His wife sounded sincere enough, but I didn't think Wicklow took her seriously. He had once referred to her as a "professional hobbyist."

I glanced at my watch. Just after eleven. Since it was early for lunch and I felt ornery, I decided a stop at Wicklow's office might prove interesting. His assistant, Karen Lassiter, didn't care much for me. It hadn't always been that way. She'd been real friendly and helpful when Wicklow first hired me, and she even invited me to join her and some friends at her parents' cabin in Wisconsin for the weekend. I declined. Being trapped for forty-eight hours with a bunch of strangers sounded like a bad idea. (I learned later that she liked to lure unsuspecting pagans such as me up to the cabin where she and her church friends tried to show us the light.) After that, the pit bull aspect of her personality blossomed. From the hoops I had to jump through just to talk to Wicklow, you'd have thought I was the IRS trying to audit his records instead of a guy hired to save him from a lawsuit.

Karen and I jousted, we parried, we slung thinly veiled insults at each other, and when I nailed the guy trying to sue Wicklow, it must have ripped her in two. I kind of enjoyed the game, though I'm not sure Karen did. It had occurred to me that Wicklow might not be the one sitting on my check.

Like many of Foxport's businesses, Wicklow's office was in a refurbished home. It had probably housed a fairly well-to-do family when it had been built back in the twenties. If it fit the typical scenario, after going through several owners, it became a rental property, eventually falling into disrepair until Foxport's rebirth in the seventies. Then a savvy investor snatched it up and sank some money into it, restoring it to its former stateliness. A wooden sign hanging from a lantern-topped post listed the occupants. On it, Kurt Wicklow, Investment Counselor, separated a lawyer from an aromatherapist. I love this town.

I parked on the street behind Karen's red Cavalier and walked up the curved, stone path to the building. That was when I noticed a man on one of the top rungs of a ladder, painting the detail in the eaves. He wore cutoffs and a sleeveless T-shirt and his shoulders had turned a bright red in the scorching sun. The house was a pale shade of blue and most of the accent trim a darker blue. Using a small brush, he added gray- brown strokes to the scrollwork. As I watched, he pulled a white rag out of his back pocket and wiped off a few inches, dipped the brush in another pint-sized container and painted over the smudge. I couldn't see any difference in the color, but that kind of attention to detail was typical of property owners around here.

Just standing there watching him made me sweat harder. I climbed the steps, anticipating the air-conditioned cool.

Karen looked up from her desk as I opened the office door. When she saw me, her mouth twisted into an annoyed frown. "I should've known you'd find your way here."

I shrugged. "Just wanted to make sure you were duly impressed with my circumstances."

"Oh, I am." She didn't so much smile as gloat. "But he's still not here."

She wore a yellow jacket over a plain white blouse and no jewelry except for a diamond-studded silver cross around her neck. As her gloat faded, she tucked a lock of light brown hair behind her ear. If she wore makeup, it wasn't obvious. She was around thirty and had an odd face—her features were slightly out of proportion—nose too long, eyes set too close and her mouth too wide. Picasso might have found her interesting.

Bracing my hands on the edge of her desk, I leaned over it. "Now, I seem to recall you signed the check for my retainer. Why can't you do the same for the balance?"

She rested her chin on her fist. "Because it's for more than five hundred dollars."

"All you do is stamp his name on it."

"Can't." She smiled. "Sorry."

"You're not."

"You're right," she agreed, adding, "If, as you insist, you weren't paid, I'm sure Mr. Wicklow will compensate you."

A phone rang, sparing me the pressure of repartee. It must have been Wicklow's private line, because the ringing came out of his office.

Karen glanced over her shoulder into the open office door. "Why don't you go now?" She pushed back her chair. "I'll be sure he gets the message."

As she covered the distance to Wicklow's office, I saw that she wore jeans instead of a skirt. Now I was certain that Wicklow wouldn't be in today and Karen knew it.

I had no intention of leaving. Not yet. Though I tried, I couldn't hear her as she spoke into Wicklow's phone. After a few seconds she placed the receiver in a paper-filled basket and went to a file cabinet on the back wall of his office. I pretended to be studying the watercolor hanging on the wall above the side of her desk. While I did, I dropped my gaze to the desk top, scanning it for anything interesting—a letter from Wicklow, an address, a ransom note. Anything. I spotted a thin, brown leather book under a pile of unopened mail and decided an appointment calendar might prove enlightening.

Karen returned to the phone carrying a file. I shoved my hands into my pockets and tilted my head as though trying to get a new perspective on the painting. I could almost feel her scowling at me. A second later the door to Wicklow's office clicked shut.

I slipped the book out from under the mail, flipped it open and paged ahead to August. Busy month. Up to a point. Prior to this week there wasn't a date without a note, a name or a time on it. But this week and the rest of the month were blank, with the exception of a dried coffee ring and something scribbled in for next week. Squinting at the page, I saw she had an appointment with "R.S.!!" on August 20th at 9 a.m. Week after next, nothing. I closed the book and replaced it. A moment later, Wicklow's door opened.

Karen's expression clouded as she looked from her desk, to me and then back again. Then she unbuttoned her jacket, shrugged off the shoulders and let it slide down her arms. "Why are you still here?" She hung the jacket over the back of her chair. Her blouse was sleeveless and I guess I was a little surprised to see the muscle definition in her upper arms. Apparently Karen took her body-sculpting classes seriously.

"Just admiring this painting." I made a concentrated effort to examine it. The watercolor depicted a cabin set back in the woods. I wondered if it was the infamous Wisconsin getaway. A wide porch ran the length of the cabin and on one end a bench swing hung from an overhang support. The wind had yanked a curtain's edge out an open window, and it fluttered like a woman's lace handkerchief. With the shade from the trees and the motion of the wind, I got a nice, cool sensation looking at the painting.

"Oh," she said, unimpressed. "Mrs. Wicklow did that." She sat in her chair and pulled a gray legal pad out of a drawer.

"Well," I said, "you be sure to tell Kurt I stopped by. You think he'll be back today?"

"He might." She gave me a curious look as she closed the drawer. "I don't know why, but I really thought you were better off than this."

"What do you mean?"

"I thought you made pretty good money."

"Actually, I do. And when I don't have to chase down deadbeat clients I live that way."

She arched a thin eyebrow. "Don't you think it's kind of pathetic? You coming around here begging for money."

I shrugged. "You get used to it."

I decided to drown my shame in a sandwich and a beer. My finances weren't so bad I couldn't afford lunch at the Tattersall.

The Tattersall Tavern has the look and feel of an English pub—from the bottles suspended upside down behind the dark wood bar, the mullioned windows lining the wall, to the menu, which features delicacies such as fish and chips, shepherd's pie and ploughman's lunch. Sammy even has haggis on the menu, mostly for show. The one time someone ordered it, he'd cut up some liver and onions, tossed them into ground beef, called it authentic, and hoped the guy didn't ask to see the sheep's stomach it was supposedly cooked in.

Fortunately, the Tattersall also offered sandwiches less inclined to adversely affect one's cholesterol rate. Hell, I smoke, I drink, I enjoy a steak char-grilled medium rare. My nod to my doctor's suggestion that I have a death wish was a healthy lunch.

I killed an hour at the pub, nursing my beer and chewing my smoked turkey slowly. As I stared out the window watching the heat rise off the asphalt, I thought about Kurt Wicklow.

He'd hired me when he was sued by some guy who claimed to have ruined his back when Wicklow's brand new Lexus rear-ended his ten-year-old Thunderbird on icy pavement after an early spring ice storm. Wicklow thought the guy was faking. After looking into the man's financial situation, I had to agree. The guy would have settled—in fact he was dying to settle. It had taken a while, but I finally got a photo of the plaintiff scaling a rock wall up in northern Minnesota. He had quietly dropped his suit.

I washed down the last bite of my sandwich with a final swallow of beer. Kurt Wicklow wasn't one to settle.

Outside, the air felt thick with heat and humidity. It was like living in a plastic bag. All summer our weather had been coming from the Texas gulf and, with damned few breaks, the heat just kept pouring up here. As I walked the three blocks back to the office, feeling the sweat slide down between my shoulder blades, I decided I'd pick up a couple things, then go home and let Peanuts out and try to explain to him about the cat. I turned the corner to my office and saw a woman crouched in front of the door, slipping an envelope into the mail slot.

My office is in the back of the Jaded Fox, the shop I own with my landlady. It's on the corner of Foxport's most popular shopping street. The town works hard to maintain its reputation for small-town charm and the shops that line the streets draw a healthy tourist business. Since being a private detective isn't all that charming, I try to keep a low profile. The entrance to my office is around the corner where all that suggests what lies behind the door is a sign that reads: Quint McCauley, Confidential Investigations.

The woman seemed to be having a little trouble keeping her balance as she pushed the envelope through the slot with one hand and maintained her hold on a huge, leather portfolio with the other. I stopped on the walk a few feet from her, admiring the way her dress draped her backside and asked, "Can I help you?" a second before the envelope slid through and the flap clinked back into place.

She turned her head and peered up at me from beneath the wide rim of a straw hat which sported a red ribbon tied around its crown. All I could see of her face was a small, sharp chin.

"Are you Quint McCauley?"

"I am."

As she straightened, she shook some of the wrinkles out of her pale denim shift which almost touched her ankles. The dress was sleeveless and a narrow bra strap, stark white against her tanned skin, had slipped about an inch down her shoulder.

"I'm Gina Wicklow. Kurt's wife." She gestured toward the door. "I dropped off a check for what we owed you."

"Thank you." Then I added, "You didn't have to make a special trip."

"You've been too patient. Most creditors aren't, you know."

I shrugged. "It's been a tight month."

She nodded like she understood. "I had business in the area. It wasn't any trouble."

Large sunglasses obscured much of her face, but from

what I could see, she was a small-boned woman, probably early thirties, with short, feathery brown hair. As though responding to my wishful thinking, she removed her sunglasses, blinking into the afternoon light for a second before her eyes found mine and held them with an intensity I wouldn't have expected from a wealthy woman with time on her hands.

"I apologize for the delay. You saved him money." With a shrug that was more matter-of-fact than apology, she added, "What can I say? He's not always as grateful as he should be."

Then she turned her head slightly and I saw that she had sort of a Brando nose with a bit of a hawk-like bend at the bridge. But it was in proportion with the rest of her features and it worked on her.

She put her sunglasses back on, tucking them beneath the wisps of hair. I wondered if she hadn't been relieved to find the office empty and now hoped for a hasty retreat. I nodded at the portfolio as she shifted it from one hand to the other. It came up to her waist, making it awkward for her to carry.

"Is that your business?"

"Yes," she said.

I stepped off the narrow walk, giving her room. "Thanks for bringing the check."

As she walked past me, the rim of her hat brushed my chest. When she reached the sidewalk, she stopped and looked back over her shoulder. "Do you like art?"

"Sure do," I said, adding, "I once traded two tickets to a Bears/Packers game for tickets to the Monet exhibit." I didn't tell her that I had the flu on the day of the game and was desperately trying to impress a woman I'd just met whose business card featured a water lily below her fax number.

She smiled, and I had the feeling she saw right through me. "I'm going to have several paintings on display at the

Campbell Street Gallery. I paint as Gina Montague. Come by some time if you can."

"I will."

I watched until the wife of my deadbeat client disappeared around the corner. With some effort, I turned away and tried to shake some sense into my head as I dug for my keys. Don't go there, Quint.

Chapter 3

When Ed answered the door, he didn't look happy to see me. Not unusual. But, today I was removing a blight from his existence. He could have forced a smile.

Undaunted, I nodded slightly and said in a deadpan, "I've come for the cat."

Ed sneezed and followed through with a hearty snort into a wilted handkerchief, which he then stuffed into his back pocket.

From somewhere within the apartment, I heard Elaine's laugh and the low tones of a male voice.

Sighing deeply, Ed rolled his eyes up toward the ceiling, as though someone up there might actually be disposed toward helping out a guy who scowls at Salvation Army bell ringers.

He stepped back from the door and let me walk past him into the hall leading to the living room. Then he shook his head in a resigned gesture, and I realized he wasn't so much annoyed as he was tolerably amused. I had seen Ed amused before. Once or twice. But there had never been any subtlety to the emotion. Now, he reminded me of a parent amused by some stunt his kid played, but reluctant to endorse it by laughing out loud.

Puzzling over his behavior, I walked into the living room where a large man stood in front of the couch, arms outstretched as though showing off the size of the one that got away. "And then," he was saying, "Eddie and Danny come marching into the dorm carrying these Mars lights. The head resident's standing there right by the elevator. Danny's scared shitless, white as a ghost, but Eddie just says 'scuse me' and pushes the 'up' button, looking as nonchalant as someone with a sack a' groceries. The resident pulls back, looks at the two of them—Danny's wishing he could turn invisible—then at the lights and asks where they got 'em. 'Crap game' Eddie says, not batting a lash. The resident looks like he's taking forever to compute all this. Finally he says, 'Those are from a squad car. A police car. Do you know that?' Eddie shrugs and says, 'Hell yes. Who d'you think I won 'em from?' " Smiling with satisfaction, he dropped onto the couch and reached for a beer bottle.

I glanced over my shoulder. "Eddie" stood, arms folded over his chest. At first I thought this guy must have finally crossed the line, but then the corner of Carver's mouth twitched, his face split into a smile and he started to laugh.

I've got to admit this behavior threw me. Ed has a stoic, humorless way about him. It's his trademark. If life were Star Trek, Ed would be a Klingon. But here he was, laughing until his eyes glistened. Not only that, but someone had called him "Eddie" and was getting away with it. I felt like I'd crossed over into an alternate universe.

Elaine sat cross-legged on the floor. She wore a T-shirt over shorts, and her auburn hair was pulled back and captured in a wide clip. She rocked forward, letting her laughter spill into her hands which covered her face.

The guy on the couch started chuckling again as some thought amused him. He shook his head. "Poor Danny spent so much time in over his head, I'm surprised he didn't come down with the bends."

When I looked at Ed again, his smile had dwindled and his eyes looked flat.

At that point, Elaine saw me standing there. She glanced at her watch and jumped up from the floor. "Oh my God, I didn't realize how late it was. I'm sorry." She came over and kissed me on the cheek.

"I've come for the cat," I said.

Placing her hand on my arm, she replied in an appropriately solemn tone, "I've prepared him."

Without releasing my arm, she continued. "First you have to meet someone. Quint, this is Brewster Plunkett. He and Ed went to college together."

Brewster stood, transferred the bottle to his left hand and shook my hand with his right. His grip was moist. I'm just over six feet and, despite the apologetic slouch, he had a good four inches on me. Deep lines bracketed a gap-toothed smile. "Nice to meet ya." The pale blond sideburns and mustache seemed to go with the drawl.

"This is so strange," Elaine began. "You and Brewster are both private investigators."

I took another look at Brewster. "Where're you from?"

"Cape Girardeau, Missouri."

I nodded. Although I have few opportunities to meet others in my line of work, I had absolutely no desire to pull him aside and share experiences with him. Actually, I felt kind of awkward.

"C'mon," Elaine said, taking my hand, "I think McGee's in the study." We left Ed and his friend to revel in memories.

She led me through the dining room toward the back hall and I reflected on this side of Carver I'd never seen or even imagined existed. As we passed the dining room table, I saw evidence of another bizarre aspect to his personality. When Elaine and Ed moved in together at the beginning of the month, it was his apartment they chose because it was larger. Though she never told him, Elaine had been reluctant to give up her place. She was the sort of person who started settling in as soon as the movers hauled the first piece of furniture over the threshold, and it went from "apartment" to "home" in less time than it took to unpack. She loved the place. I wouldn't have thought Ed sensitive enough to understand that, but there on the dining room table sat a bouquet of flowers—white roses against splashes of pink and red. Protruding from the center of the bouquet was a stick clutching a card in its tiny, plastic fist. I couldn't look at the flowers and not read the words on the card: "Welcome home, Elaine. Love, Ed."

She saw me eyeing them.

"Nice," I offered. What else could I say?

"He can surprise you."

We shared a laugh when we found McGee in the corner of the closet, curled up on Ed's overcoat which had slipped from its hanger. "Bad kitty," Elaine said without a trace of reproof as she gathered the feline into her arms. He was a big cat with brown and black markings.

"I bought lots of canned food and enough of the soft stuff to last a month. I leave hard food out for him all the time." She kissed his head. Sublimely unmoved, he blinked at me. "I've got a big bag of litter. I want to subsidize his upkeep, Quint. This is a huge favor you're doing me."

I scratched his chin. "Don't worry about that." Hell, I'd just deposited a check for twenty-five hundred dollars. We could both eat tuna.

"He's a little quirky about his water. He won't drink out of a bowl. Don't even bother to put one down for him." While she explained this, she cuddled the cat, stroking his neck and cooing between instructions. "He likes to drink out of the tap. Bathroom's fine. He'll let you know when he's thirsty."

"You're joking, right?"

"Really. Isn't he a character?" Then to McGee: "You're a

regular scamp, aren't you?" He batted her nose with his paw.

"You're telling me that if I put a bowl of water down and refuse to play his little tap game, he'll die of thirst before he touches the bowl?"

"Of course not. When I'm gone, I just leave the toilet seat up." Smiling, she added, "That shouldn't be a problem for you."

She finally pulled her attention from the cat. "If you have a few minutes, why don't you stay for a beer?"

Back to Ed. Though the request sounded offhanded, I knew how much she wanted Ed and me to get along.

"Yeah, sure."

When I'd agreed to take care of the cat, I believed it was for the short term. I figured their relationship didn't stand a chance. When I left an hour later, I took with me a slightly altered opinion.

While Brewster did most of the talking—he was one of those natural born storytellers who could make a trip to the drug store sound like high adventure—Ed and Elaine acted amused and attentive, but never lost track of each other. I sat in a chair off to the side wondering where I'd been when all this had happened. I tried looking at Carver like I was meeting him for the first time. I supposed a woman might find him attractive if her taste ran toward tall, dark, square-jawed men. But he was getting a little thick around the middle and, I noted with some satisfaction, his hair had thinned some. I come from a family of thick-haired people. Although we did nothing to deserve it, we are inordinately proud of the fact that most of us die with a full head of hair. It's become a point of discussion at funerals, which probably makes us a little strange, but then every family has its quirks.

"Eddie," Brewster was saying, "you remember the time Danny streaked through O'Banyon's physics class? Didn't you bet him a fin he wouldn't do it?" I figured in the early stages of their acquaintance, Ed probably spent a lot of time correcting Brewster, ("It's Ed, not Eddie.") and he'd finally succumbed to the moniker in much the same way most of us have gotten used to automated answering systems.

As I listened to Brewster, I found myself admiring him in the way I do people who have a way of walking into a room and owning it. When they leave a room, the space never quite gets filled. I tend to disappear in a crowd—a useful trait for a private detective but hell on your social life.

Brewster drank a lot of beer, preferring a long-necked bottle to a glass. Once, when he stopped for breath, I asked what brought him to Foxport. "Just blowing through town and decided to harass an old friend," he said, moving onto another tale before I could ask what business blew him through Foxport.

Mostly I marveled over the change in Ed Carver. Sitting there with one arm resting on the back of the couch, drinking his coffee, he looked more relaxed than I'd ever seen him. Had all this happened since Elaine moved in with him? Could one person make that much of a difference? If that person were Elaine, then I guess she could.

Behind the annoyance and the bad feelings, I always felt kind of sorry for Carver. Anyone that bereft of emotions couldn't find much pleasure in life. If some gypsy had told me there'd come a day when I'd envy him, I'd have told her it was time to use some Windex on that crystal ball.

I was thinking of graceful exit lines when Brewster made a big show of standing and getting everyone quiet—like anybody else had been able to get a word in. Clutching the bottle by its neck, he raised his arm. "I'm proposing a toast." After an elaborate bow toward Ed and then Elaine, he continued, "To Eddie, my good buddy who I've known forever. Let's keep in touch. And to Elaine, who I barely know but who may be the best thing that ever happened to him." Elaine caught my eye as I raised my bottle with the rest of them. She smiled.

When I left, Carver helped me take McGee's paraphernalia out to the car while Elaine got the cat into his carrier and said her good-byes. As I slammed the trunk lid down on the litter box and bags of food, I looked to the door of the apartment, hoping Elaine wouldn't take long. Not only was it hot, but neither Ed nor I were any good at small talk.

But then he cleared his throat and said, "Ah, thanks."

I turned to him.

He was rubbing the back of his neck and looking past me. Finally he dropped his hand to his side. "For taking the cat. It's hard for her to give him up."

"I know."

"This way it's easier on her. She knows you'll take good care of him."

"You do the same for her."

His jaw tightened and for a second I thought he was going on the defensive. But then he relaxed and nodded. "I know a good thing."

He didn't exactly say that I didn't, but he might as well have.

When I pulled into the long driveway leading to the green house on the river, my landlady, Louise Orwell, was sitting in a chair on its tiny back porch. Ours was as close to an ideal landlord/tenant relationship as I could imagine, which probably explained why our business relationship worked as well. I'm the silent partner—Louise was the buyer and the seller. I had it easy.

She waved to me as I maneuvered my car around hers so it was adjacent to the single flight of stairs leading up to my apartment. Her chair had some bounce and she rocked slightly while fanning herself with a pink and purple fan.

Louise was probably in her seventies, though she seemed younger. She walked a couple miles every day and worked out with weights. If she weren't thirty years older than me, I'd ask her out. Who was I kidding? If Louise were my age, she'd have better things to do. In the year and a half since we first met, I'd never known her to be without a gentleman friend. I'd come to the disturbing conclusion that Louise probably has a more active sex life than I do.

I came around the car and set the cat carrier on the drive while I opened the trunk. Louise stopped rocking.

"Quint, is that a cat you've got in there?" I loved what her clipped English accent did for my name.

"I'm afraid it is."

Once I had the litter box and the bags with McGee's food out of the trunk, I walked over to the porch and raised the cat carrier so she could view its contents. "Louise, this is McGee. McGee, Louise."

She leaned forward and squinted into the metal grating, then reached her hand up to him. The white tip of his paw poked out, batting at her fingers.

"Goodness, he's a handsome fellow, isn't he?"

"I guess."

"Is he Elaine's?"

Louise was Elaine's biggest fan and, though she never came out and said it, she thought I was an idiot for ending the relationship. I never told her it was as much Elaine's idea as mine. Why spoil the image?

"Yeah," I said. "Ed's allergic to cats."

"A pity." She drew her hand away. "Does Peanuts know about this?"

"What could I tell him?" I shifted the carrier to my other

hand. "It's probably for the best. Ever since that group with nothing better to do came out and said border collies were the smartest thing on four paws, he's been impossible to live with."

"Is that a fact?"

"He finishes the crossword puzzle for me. I hate that."

She chuckled. "You two may take to each other. I find cats quite soothing."

I turned the carrier so I could see McGee. He hissed at me. "Yeah, well, I think we've got a ways to go."

I set the cage on the grass so I could gather the rest of his belongings. Louise resumed fanning herself.

"Why aren't you inside enjoying the air conditioning?" I asked.

"Albert's picking me up. We're going to try the senior special at that new spot north on 41. I'm not so prone to new experiences in cuisine these days, but he assures me I can still have my glass of wine."

"You two are quite the item, aren't you?"

She frowned as though considering her response. "He's persistent. These days I find that a rather appealing trait." Then she added, "Although, I suppose all the ones who are still alive at Albert's age are persistent."

There was that. I heard the crunch of gravel under tires and picked up the litter box. "Well, you and Albert have a nice dinner."

Even as I spoke and tried to make good on my escape, Albert announced his arrival with a polite toot of the horn. I glanced over my shoulder and saw his knobby little head peering over the Bonneville's steering wheel.

Albert had a large nose which would have dominated his face were it not for the thick-lensed glasses that made his eyes look like pale gray saucers. He wore his plaid pants high and never went out without a sports jacket over his knit shirt. His walk reminded me of an egret—all legs and neck with a torso that threatened to throw him off balance. I'd have bet when he was young Albert was a geek. Now, as he cruised through his ninth decade, he had a shot at the former prom queens. If I only live that long.

"Quint, it's good to see you." He waved as he climbed out of the car. "How're things going? Insufferable weather, isn't it? They say we should be looking at some rain by the weekend."

I didn't know which question or comment to respond to, so I just mumbled a greeting.

"Louise and I are going up to Burlington's for dinner. Chicken fried steak special, I hear. Care to join us?"

"No thanks, Albert." I held up the carrier. "I've got to tend to my new roommate here."

"Ah, well then." He turned to Louise. "You're looking lovely today, my dear."

As I climbed the stairs to my apartment, I mulled over my impression of Albert. He tried too hard. Maybe I shouldn't fault him. That's probably what got him Louise. Before I knew it, I was thinking about how easy and comfortable it gets when you're letting life slide by instead of going for the brass ring. An image of Gina Wicklow popped into my head, but I only had a few seconds to enjoy it before Peanuts discovered what I'd smuggled into the apartment.

Chapter 4

Meeting Ellie at the Dive Inn meant leaving McGee and Peanuts on their own for the first time. I thought they'd be okay. So far, no major skirmishes had erupted. Peanuts spent a lot of time near my feet, nervously looking around for the cat. McGee, on the other hand, had taken to the top of a bookshelf in the living room. I didn't know whether he felt safer up there or if he figured, being as short as he was, that was the place to be if he wanted to look down on everyone.

As I pulled into the lot of the Dive Inn, I was nearly overwhelmed with relief that I didn't need the place anymore. Early on a Thursday night, the lot was less than half full, but then I didn't ever recall the place being packed.

The sun was on its way down, leaving behind the oppressive humidity, taking just enough of the heat so you think it'll be cool enough to sleep. You're wrong. When I was a kid, on nights like this my five siblings and I would take our sleeping bags out to the backyard and count stars until we fell asleep.

Stepping through the door to the Dive Inn tossed me back a couple years. Same mercifully dim light- ing. Same grimy, wooden floor. Same pinball machines. Cool, but muggy. The place had the feel of an indoor swimming pool only it smelled like smoke instead of chlorine.

I was about five minutes early and I didn't see Ellie so I sat at the bar. Same hard stools.

The bartender broke away from a conversation with a guy

wearing a denim shirt with its sleeves torn off and a cowboy hat. The cowboy squinted his right eye at me as he exhaled a plume of smoke, then went back to his beer.

"What can I get you?" The bartender dropped a Miller Lite coaster on the bar in front of me.

Déjà vu hit as I stared at the bottle-lined mirror be- hind the bar. The desire for a Scotch washed over me. With some effort, I said, "What kind of beer have you got?"

He rattled off about eight brands and I went with a lager. Too hot for Guinness.

I didn't recognize this bartender, but figured some things had to change in two years. I hoped I was one of them.

"Quiet night," I said as I watched him pour the lager down the side of a glass.

He glanced up at me as he righted the glass, letting the beer's head build a little.

"It's early." He released the tap, tipped off some foam, added another half inch and then set the beer down in front of me. "You've been here before?"

"Not for a while."

He extended his hand across the bar. "Mick Jensen." He was probably around my age with a high forehead and a narrow face. Thinning, frizzy red hair went with the pale complexion. His eyes, buried under bushy red brows, were set close together. If it hadn't been for a pleasant, unassuming smile, he'd have looked kind of crazed.

We shook and I introduced myself.

"How long have you been working here?" I asked.

"Just a couple months."

His T-shirt had an acoustic guitar on it. Printed in a circle around it were the words, "Abel County Folk Music Society."

"Here for the festival?" Foxport had one of the Midwest's

biggest folk festivals every Labor Day weekend.

He glanced down at his chest, then smiled a little sheepishly. "What can I say? Old hippies die hard."

I nodded. "What do you play?"

"Martin twelve-string."

"Nice."

"You play?"

I shook my head. "No, but I've got a brother who does." I glanced over my shoulder at a small stage that occupied a corner of the room. I didn't remember it being there a couple years ago. "Do you sing too?"

"Not here." He laughed. "That's for Karaoke night. Some guy loans us his machine on Wednesdays."

"Damn, I just missed it." The night I climb on a stage and sing "Feelings" to a roomful of drunks is the night before I join AA.

Mick excused himself and went to fill another order, and I was left to wonder if I were forced, through circumstance, to sing along with a machine, what song would I choose? I had it narrowed down to something by Dylan or Prine when a raspy voice said, "Hey there."

Ellie Carver moved in between me and the empty stool to my right. She didn't sit. If she hadn't said something first, I might not have recognized her. Her hair wasn't piled up on top anymore. It was chin length with bangs that grazed her eyebrows. It looked more contemporary, but I kind of missed it the other way. She had traded in the high-collar Victorian style blouse for a short, sleeveless dress that showed off everything the blouse had covered.

Smiling like she couldn't imagine I'd be anything but impressed, Ellie glanced down the bar and had no trouble at all catching Mick's attention.

With a smile and a nod, he mixed her a gin and tonic. Although her choice in bars hadn't changed, her drink had. He handed her the glass and she responded with a big smile. "Thank you, Mick." I pushed a ten toward him.

"And thank you." She took a sip as Mick brought me my change. When she lowered the glass, there was a bright red smear on its rim.

"Should we get a table?" I collected my money, leaving a couple singles on the bar.

"Good idea."

We selected one toward the back. As I settled into a chair, I noticed something else that hadn't changed—"Rocket Man" was still on the jukebox.

"How've you been?" she asked.

"Okay." I drank some beer. "How about you?"

"Better." She nodded, agreeing with her assessment. "This divorce is really for the best." Removing the plastic straw from her drink she tapped a drop off its end before setting it on the table. Then she took a sip as though checking to see if the drink tasted the same without the straw in it. "Of course, I am getting tired of Ed flaunting this new friend of his in front of me." She scrounged up a brittle smile. "He'd better remember that both signatures have to go on the bottom of the paper." Lowering her gaze, she added, "Sorry. I forgot. You and that woman used to date, didn't you?"

When I didn't respond, she was silent for a moment, and then giggled. "Don't you find it kind of weird? Ironic, I guess."

I knew where this was going, but let her finish.

"I mean, first there's you and me. We almost get together. We were that close. You nearly get run out of town and I—" She took a quick drink. "Well, let's just say that I had hell to pay. And now my husband and your girlfriend are living together." She shook her head. "Crazy world, isn't it? Crazy, stupid world."

"It can be."

"What is she like?"

"She's nice." I hadn't come here to discuss Elaine. "So, why are we here?"

"Divorce can be liberating, you know."

"It can be overrated too." I lit a cigarette and put the pack within her reach.

"I suppose." She stared down at the pack and I wondered if she'd stopped smoking. If that were the case, I didn't want to be the one to corrupt her.

For a lot of reasons, I felt awkward. She seemed inclined to make small talk when all I wanted to do was get to the point. Maybe if I hadn't already had a few Scotches that first night, I would have felt awkward then too. None of this would be happening. "What are you doing these days?"

"Working." She finally drew her gaze from the cigarettes. "Taking some time for myself." Then she added almost as an afterthought, "My kids."

"Where do you work?"

She picked up the straw and began fidgeting with it. "Foxport Memorial. I'm a nurse."

"That's right," I said, although it roused no memories.

"How are the kids?" I couldn't for the life of me remember their names.

"They're fine. Takes some adjusting, of course, but kids are good at that, don't you think?"

"Sure." What did I know about kids?

"I've been seeing someone."

She sort of blurted it out and I hoped we were moving in the right direction. "That's good."

"He's really nice." She paused. "It's funny. We dated a few times in high school. He was real popular."

"Ed knows him?"

"They were friends in high school, went to college together, but haven't had much to do with each other since then. Ed's not in his league." Chewing thoughtfully on the tip of her straw, she continued, "In high school I never dreamed we'd get together."

I didn't quite know what to say, but went with, "I'm glad you're happy." Although she hadn't said she was.

"He's married." She hurried to add, "I'm not proud of that, but I won't apologize either. I mean, right now I'm not looking for the complications involved in a committed relationship. You know?" She dropped the straw on the table. One end had been gnawed beyond recognition.

I waited.

"He and I have a nice understanding. It works really well." She rested her elbows on the table and clasped her hands beneath her chin. "I feel freer than I ever have."

"Okay," I started, "why do you need me?"

She released her breath abruptly. "I'm worried. I was supposed to meet him Tuesday at this restaurant in Richton up near the Wisconsin border. Beaumont's. He didn't show. That's not like him. Even when, you know, family things happen, he always manages to call me." She picked up the straw again, then dropped it and took one of my cigarettes. I lit it for her.

"Are you sure you didn't get your signals crossed?"

"We always meet at Beaumont's. Usually on a Tuesday."

"Where does he live?"

From the way she pulled in the smoke, closed her eyes, and exhaled in a protracted sigh, I guessed that this was the first she'd had in a while. That plus the fact that she didn't bitch about them not being menthol. "Here in Foxport." She opened her eyes. "But he's been staying at this house they have in a town right on Lake Geneva called New Berne."

I nodded.

"I'm worried sick and I don't know what to do." She tapped an ash off her cigarette and continued, "For obvious reasons I can't go to the police."

"So, you want me to find him?" Someone had to say it.

"Would you?" From the way her eyes lit up, you'd have thought that idea had never occurred to her. "Really, would you? I just need to know if he's all right. Can you see if you can find him? No one will wonder about a man looking for him. Just say you're a friend or something." She had this all worked out.

I drained my beer. This didn't sound difficult. I'm good at finding people. That wasn't why I hesitated. I was trying to work out if there was anything unethical about my looking for the married boyfriend of the woman who was divorcing the guy who was living with my ex-girlfriend. My head spun.

Ellie said, "A small problem. I can't afford to pay you right now." She quickly added, "I will pay you. I'm not asking for a freebie or anything. Our money—Ed's and mine—is all tied up in the settlement. But the divorce should be final in September—I'm sure—so I can pay you then." She must have sensed my reluctance because she quickly added, "If you find my friend, he'll pay you. He's quite well off."

When I didn't give her an answer, she leaned forward, and placed her hands on the table. I noticed she still wore her wedding band. "Please, Quint. It would only take a day or so. I'm sure someone up there knows where he is. It's probably something simple. But I can't ask and it's making me crazy."

"What kind of message do you want me to give him?"

"Just tell him I was worried. Tell him to call me. That's all."

"Where is this place on Lake Geneva?"

She squeezed my hand, then reached into her purse, rummaged around and finally retrieved a scrap of paper. She squinted at it before handing it to me, then continued to dig through her purse.

I glanced at the address. "What's his name?"

She handed me a photo. "Kurt Wicklow."

Shit. Kurt Wicklow, all six-feet-three or so inches of him, leaned against the fender of his Lexus with a sports jacket tossed over his shoulder. With the jet- black hair, his pale, lightly freckled complexion, and the mile-wide smile, he looked like a model for Irish Spring. I must have scowled.

"What's wrong?" she asked.

"You and I had better work out the terms right now. I know for a fact that this guy doesn't pay on time."

Chapter 5

I left for New Berne first thing in the morning with Peanuts in the back seat of my Accord. From the way he bounded down the steps, glancing over his shoulder, I think he was glad to get away from the cat. As a border collie, he's got these instincts he can't ignore. But, when he tried to herd McGee, he got batted in the snout for his efforts. It was a real pity my dog couldn't see the innate humor in attempting to herd a cat.

I'd taken Peanuts with me before when I was working and he'd never been a problem. He's got good manners and knows when to keep his mouth shut.

The air was muggy already, and Friday promised to be another hot one as I headed north up route 41. I hoped it was cooler over the Wisconsin state line by Lake Geneva but wasn't optimistic. I don't get along with the heat and I actually like rain. Every summer I think about moving either to Oregon or Ireland.

We passed through Richton, a small town just south of the state line, where it seemed like every other shop name had the word "Antique" in it. Beaumont's, the restaurant where Ellie was to meet Wicklow, took up a corner of the main street.

For some reason, crossing the Wisconsin border reminded me of Ed Carver. Probably the cop connection. Wisconsin police pick off Illinois speeders for sport. As I eased up on the accelerator, I pondered the change I'd seen in Carver since he and Elaine had gotten together. True, he no longer had the pressure of being Foxport's top cop, but I couldn't believe that alone accounted for the new, improved Carver. Flowers, no less.

New Berne was a tiny, picturesque town on the north end of the lake with the requisite stone churches and shops selling T-shirts and real estate. I had some trouble finding the tourist center, finally locating it in an adjunct to the post office. Since it didn't seem prudent to ask for directions to Wicklow's place, I figured I'd need a map. The woman working there looked down her nose at Peanuts and informed me that dogs weren't allowed in the building. I left him outside with his leash tied to the porch railing.

Kurt Wicklow's summer house was embedded in an area where the lake-front homes had large, wooded lots and long, winding drives. The sun filtered through the trees so that the road resembled a leafy mosaic. A steady stream of cars accompanied me. Every now and then someone would merge in from one of the side roads. I had figured the heavy traffic would hold off until mid afternoon, the unofficial beginning of the summer weekend, and wondered if the hot weather had convinced some people to start early.

I turned off the main road and onto Arrowhead Drive. Every road I came to had an Indian name. I wondered what tribe, if any, had called the area home. Steering with one hand, I propped the map against the wheel with the other. I counted four roads leading to the lake before I came to Wicklow's. Each was marked by a small, obscure sign attached to a thin pole.

As I approached Wicklow's turn, a white Chevy S-10 pulled out of the gravel road. I wouldn't have thought much of it, except I'd noticed one in my rear view mirror on the way up. Probably a coincidence, but I jotted down the plate number as it drove off in the opposite direction. I couldn't read the state, but the colors—dark letters on white—were different from both Illinois and Wisconsin.

The Wicklows' residence was less than a quarter of a mile down the road. Like the places surrounding it, this vacation home was nicer than what most people lived in year round. The long, curved drive led to a two-car garage attached to a stone "cottage"—a ranch with a deck that wrapped around it.

As I pulled into the empty driveway, I wondered if finding Kurt Wicklow might be as easy as ringing his doorbell. It had occurred to me that Ellie might have misread his absence at the restaurant. Maybe he didn't want to see her anymore and that was his way of break- ing the news. I knew the guy was a deadbeat. I wouldn't put being a louse past him. Although, most of Foxport's citizens would have disagreed with that conjecture.

Wicklow had earned the town's undying affection in high school when he was named All-State tight end both his junior and senior years. He could have stopped achieving at that point and not slipped a notch in popularity. But Kurt Wicklow continued to excel. After college, the Bears made him their third- round draft choice, but he played for only one year before a knee injury did him in. He had a good head for business and didn't mind trading on his name and connections while he established himself as a stockbroker and financial advisor. He married a hometown girl, the daughter of a prominent family. They appeared to be as close to an ideal couple as you could get—prosperous, sociable churchgoers, not to mention photogenic. When his wife died in a hiking accident, he maintained his eligible-but-grieving status for a number of years before remarrying. The guy could do no wrong.

It was going on eleven when I attached the leash to Peanuts' collar and we got out of the car. I rang the doorbell and listened to the chimes echo within the house. No answer. I rang again. Still nothing. I tried the door and was surprised to find it unlocked.

I knocked, then pushed it open. The heat poured out in a wave. "Kurt? You there?" Not likely, I thought. Not only did the house feel empty, but who could stand living in a sauna? On the other hand, I didn't smell bodies festering in there either.

A gravel path skirted the porch, and Peanuts and I followed it around the house, passing tall, narrow windows facing west, their curtains wide open. That probably added ten or fifteen degrees to the house's temperature. Once we got around to the back, the pine-tree studded yard dipped down to the lake—an expanse of about fifty feet where a short, wooden pier jutted out into the calm water. No boats were moored to it. The air was heavy and still, and when I looked out onto the lake, I didn't see any sailboats, but I did hear the drone of motor boats. If he had a motorboat, Kurt might be out there. Peanuts pulled at the leash as he tried to persuade me to go back up the hill toward the house. I decided I couldn't resist the temptation of an open door. If Kurt were out in his boat I'd hear him return.

When I opened the door, I called his name again. Nothing. It felt empty. While it was possible he'd walked next door for a beer with a neighbor, the temperature in the house implied that no one had been there for a while. I went on in.

Peanuts' claws clicked against the rust-colored ceramic tiles that spilled out from the entryway, past the living room and into the kitchen on the right and down a hall on the left. As I walked toward the hall, a painting over the couch caught my eye. It was a watercolor of a rocky, rugged coastal scene that reminded me of Scotland. I walked up to it, leaning over the couch to see the signature. Gina Montague.

The living room had a vaulted ceiling, skylights and glass doors looking out on the lake. Except for Gina's painting, the walls were bare. While the furniture looked expensive —leather couch and chairs, marble coffee table with matching chess set—I didn't see anything in the way of personal touches. The place seemed sterile—like my place, only pricier. The way I figure, if sterile is the look you're going for, might as well do it on the cheap.

I checked out the kitchen next, going straight to the huge, stainless steel refrigerator. From its size and prominence, I expected to find it stocked with gourmet products, but it held only the bare basics—bread, milk, lunch meat, frozen dinners. Déjà vu again. The cheddar looked a little stale but it hadn't turned green yet. The milk was dated yesterday and the ham had been purchased seven days ago. Wicklow's taste in frozen dinners ran toward the low fat, high salt variety. Again, I related.

A wine rack built into the cabinets stocked some impressive labels. French white wines with words like "Premier Cru" and "Grand Cru" on the labels. That probably meant "expensive" and "really expensive." A larger selection of reds. When I pulled out a bottle of Opus One I wondered, briefly, if he'd miss it.

A door in the corner of the kitchen led to the two-car garage. A silver Lexus, license plate BROKER9, took up half the area. Its hood felt cool. On the other side, a bicycle hung from the wall above a motorcycle. Apparently Wicklow liked variety in transportation. An elaborate weight gym occupied the rest of the garage. I wondered where Mrs. Wicklow parked her car.

By this time a bored Peanuts was pulling on his leash, trying to drag me back into the house. I took one more look around the kitchen and saw an expensive, modern room—professional-looking stove, granite countertops, butcher block table—with no personal touches. No fingerprints marring the stainless steel appliances. Except for mine. I wiped these off the refrigerator with my handkerchief. A stiff, dry washcloth draped over the sink tap implied some use.

Peanuts led me down the hall. In the first room on the right, a half bathroom, I found a used bar of soap in a brass dish and a white towel hanging, unfolded, on a brass rack.

The next room appeared to be an office—bookshelves, a large desk and a computer. The drapes were closed and the sunlight diluted. As I stepped in, thick brown carpeting recorded my footsteps. Scanning the area, I took in a few papers scattered on the desk, a credenza against the wall with a wooden cross hanging above it, and a tan leather chair in the corner. I stopped. Was the carpeting beside the chair and under the window a slightly darker shade of brown? When Peanuts started to whine and pull at his leash, I knew we were onto something. He's no Lassie, but he's got good instincts.

I crossed over to the chair and squatted beside it. Peanuts buried his nose in the darker area, drinking in the scent. Once his lungs were full, he huffed and drew in another snootful. I guess it agreed with him, because he dropped down and began to roll on the stain, writhing on his back like he was enjoying a fresh patch of sweet clover. The area felt stiff like dried paint. I drew my hand away and sniffed the rust-colored residue on my fingers. No mistaking the metallic smell of blood. From what I could see, a good deal of it had been spilled on the carpet. Maybe Kurt Wicklow left involuntarily. When I pulled Peanuts up off the rug, the blood-red powder clung to his coat. I brushed him off. On occasion, dog behavior leaves me a little uneasy.

I drew back one of the drapes and saw blood smeared on

the wall and the windowsill. The room looked out on a wooded area that started about ten feet back from the house. Using my handkerchief again, I raised the window. Peanuts propped his front paws on the sill and stuck his head out the window, sucking in the outside air. No screen. The trail of blood continued over the sill. Ground cover ran along the back of the house. Directly below, I detected drops of red among the green leaves. I considered walking around the back to check it out, but didn't want to add my footprints to what might already be there. I pulled Peanuts back inside and closed the window.

Keeping Peanuts on a short leash, I quickly examined the rest of the room. The papers on the desk turned out to be junk mail. A set of encyclopedias took up much of the bookshelf space. I also found a Bible and several religious and spiritual texts, including Nostrodamus' predictions. When I opened the Bible, I saw it was inscribed to Kurt from Karen. No words of wisdom, just "to Kurt, from Karen," dated a year and a half ago. I wondered if Wicklow had spent an influential weekend at the cabin with Karen and her friends. The cross above the credenza suddenly got more interesting and I started to move around the desk for a better look. When I did, my foot whacked something by the floor. A framed picture was propped against the side of the desk. I crouched down to examine it. Another one of Gina's, it was small and from what I could make out through the broken glass, radiating out like a spider web from the center, it depicted a shop-lined street in a village. Judging from the narrow street and the architecture, the setting was European. Glancing up at the cross, I wondered if the painting had once hung in its place. I stood to get a closer look at the cross, which was simply two pieces of wood nailed together. I lifted it off the hook and turned it over. Carved in crude, block letters down the spine of the cross were the words: "Salvation through Rebirth."

I returned it to the wall and before I left the office obliterated my footprints by dragging my foot over the carpeting along with the nap and picked up a few dog hairs. A brief inspection of the other rooms—two bedrooms, one with a full bath—revealed nothing out of the ordinary. They all had the same blank look as the rest of the house.

As Peanuts and I left, I mulled over my next move. I could have been wrong about the spill in the office, but I'd have bet the money Wicklow owed me that it was blood. Whose blood was another story.

Whether Kurt Wicklow had met with or indulged in foul play, or had simply slaughtered a duck in his den and thrown it out the window, I had to treat it as the first scenario. Admittedly, the signs seemed obvious—almost too obvious—the trail of blood a series of arrows pointing toward the woods. But murder wasn't always subtle, just as murderers weren't always bright. After briefly weighing my options, I decided to find a nice anonymous telephone and make an equally anonymous call to the New Berne police department.

My work for Ellie was finished. True, I'd told her I'd look for Kurt. Said I'd ask around. But, I didn't want to get her (or myself) implicated in whatever occurred here. Let the police figure out what happened to Kurt Wicklow.

Chapter 6

By the time I got back to Foxport the temperature had hit ninety-seven degrees. I began to have serious concerns about the global warming effect.

If I'd had any other news for Ellie, I'd have called her. But, I figured since I had to tell her the only sign of her boyfriend was a dried-up pool of blood, she deserved the news in person. At the same time I wondered who would break the news to Wicklow's wife.

I hoped I'd find Ellie alone, but figured with it being summer and all, odds were that at least one of the kids would be home. I had finally recalled their names.

I'd met them once, not long ago. Foxport's got a class A ball team called the Foxes, and I'd run into them at the opener last spring with Ed. The boy, Aaron, was about ten with tousled hair the color of straw and a way of looking at his dad that made me wish I'd taken the time to have kids. The girl, Diana, was several years older. They called her DeeDee. I expected a DeeDee to be bubbly, vivacious. Possibly to a fault. But DeeDee Carver was a quiet, serious kid and pretty in a somber way. That afternoon at the game, they wound up sitting a few rows in front of me. Whenever I looked over there, DeeDee's face was buried in the pages of a book.

After the split, Ellie and the kids had stayed in the house—a white Cape Cod with a screened-in porch in the older section of Foxport where the homes were modest, but the lawns trimmed, and bushes and small firs framed picture windows. The Carvers' lawn was a little shabby, but then Ellie didn't strike me as the gardening type.

I still had Peanuts with me, so I took him up to the house, figuring he could stay on the porch while I talked to Ellie.

The porch screen door was unlocked, and since I couldn't find anything resembling a doorbell, I went through to the main door. I rang the bell but didn't hear it so I knocked.

Just as I had almost convinced myself that a phone call wasn't all that insensitive, DeeDee answered the door. Her skin was white against the black of her sleeveless shirt and shorts, and her dark—almost black—hair hung long and straight. A tiny gold stud adorned her right nostril. I would have bet dinner she belonged to the drama club and wrote poetry about the absurdity of life.

"Hi, DeeDee," I said, and introduced myself. "Is your mom around?"

"Dee," she said.

"Pardon?"

"My name is Dee."

"Okay. Fine."

"I changed it."

I didn't blame her.

Then she said, "Wait here. I'll get her."

They had the air conditioner on full blast and from my position in the doorway, I felt like I was standing between an oven and a refrigerator, which reminded me of the joke about the guy in similar straits who said, on the average, he was quite comfortable. I wished I could have said the same.

Dee came back a minute later. "She said to wait." Looking down at Peanuts, she added, "Your dog's got to stay on the porch."

"No problem."

"What's his name?"

"Peanuts." I offered no explanation. I doubted she'd heard of Peanuts Lawry.

"Can I pet him?"

"Sure." I stepped aside so she could get down on his level without having to contend with my knees. She tucked her hair behind her ears, bent over and held her hand out to let him sniff, then proceeded to stroke his neck.

"Is he a border collie?"

"Mostly."

Peanuts enjoyed attention, and he seemed to like it most when it came from a female.

"You have a cat too?" she asked without taking her eyes from Peanuts.

"How'd you know?"

"It sheds."

I looked down and saw traces of McGee on my shirt.

"You're pretty observant," I remarked as I picked the hair off. "You got a career with the FBI planned?"

She made a face that implied she thought the humor was lame. "Hardly." She scratched a spot on Peanuts' neck, which he arched so Dee could work the whole area.

"What kind of cat is it?"

I shrugged. "Short hair. White, brown, tan, black." I found another hair and wondered how it got there, since McGee had barely allowed me to touch him. "That way he's got all shades covered."

She almost smiled. "Is it Elaine's cat?" She gave Peanuts one final pat and stood.

"Yeah." I couldn't lie.

"I figured. Dad's allergies." She looked at me as though trying out a new lens. "That's pretty nice of you."

Before I could respond, Ellie appeared in the doorway

wearing a see-through tunic over a bathing suit that was one piece, but cut high on the thighs and low in the front. Her eyes looked puffy and tiny beads of perspiration dotted her upper lip. She carried a tall glass of something in her right hand.

Dee crossed her arms over her chest and regarded her mother with mild disapproval. "You're not using that sunscreen I gave you."

Ellie twisted her mouth and rolled her eyes heavenward. "This skin doesn't burn anymore. It's too tough." Before Dee could protest, Ellie continued, "Now, hon, you keep the dog company out here. This gentleman and I have to talk."

Some nonverbal communication went on between the two of them. I had the feeling that Dee, with her eyebrows arched and her mouth agape, was about to give her mother more advice and Ellie, with her lips in a thin, tight line, was dissuading her of that urge. Finally, Dee sighed and shook her head as she turned toward me. "May I take Peanuts for a walk?"

I handed her the leash. "He shouldn't be any trouble."

We watched the two of them cut across the yard.

"Sometimes it's hard to tell who's the mother," Ellie murmured. Without turning away from her daughter, she asked, "Do you have any kids?"

"No."

"I'm just glad she's getting out of the house. I swear, sometimes it's like living with a vampire."

"A vampire?"

"She worries about skin cancer," she explained. "From May to September I have a child who hardly leaves the house. I don't understand it. When I was her age, the deeper the tan, the better your chance of getting a date with the lifeguard."

"She's got fair skin. She ought to watch the sun."

"I never burn. Of course, she's fairer than I am. Well," she continued, "in the morning Ed's taking her up to his folks. She'll stay with them for a week. It'll do us both some good to be apart for a while." With a shake of her head, she dismissed the topic.

When I followed her into the house, it was like walking into a candle shop. The aroma rushed up my nose, wrapped itself around my brain and squeezed so hard my head went light for a second.

Ellie, putting an entirely different spin on my reaction, smiled and inhaled deeply. I expected her to drop into a dead faint at my feet. Instead, she closed her eyes as she exhaled. "Lavender," she said. "For tranquillity. Isn't it wonderful?"

"Kind of potent," I offered.

"Are you into aromatherapy?"

"No." I preferred the real thing—pizza, char-grilled burgers.

By the time we got to the living room, I'd acclimated to the smell. I wouldn't say I felt tranquil, but the squeeze wasn't on my brain anymore.

The living room was small with a brick fireplace painted white and a braided area rug. An oil painting of a palm-tree-lined beach and bright cabanas hung over the fireplace. Photos cluttered the mantle. A prominent one looked like a high school homecoming court. Four young, pretty girls surrounded a fifth who was seated in a high-backed chair. Their dates stood behind them. One of the attendants looked like a young Ellie.

Behind me, I heard the clink of ice against glass. "High school was the best, wasn't it?"

She wasn't looking for an argument. "Is this you?" I pointed to the one with the short, blond hair and the round face.

"That's me." She spoke with an odd mix of bitterness and

nostalgia. I wondered if she blamed someone for moving her beyond those days.

The tall, broad shouldered kid standing next to the girl in the high-backed chair looked familiar. "Kurt?" I pointed to him.

"Yeah."

"And the homecoming queen?"

"Paula Singleton." She stuck her nose up in the air and pursed her lips. "Rich girl. Had everything. Including Kurt."

I gave Ellie a few seconds to finish the story. When she didn't, I said, "But she's dead now, isn't she?"

Ellie shrugged. "Who could forget that? The whole town went into mourning. You'd think she was a saint or something." She shook her head. "When I go, I'll be lucky to get a paragraph in the *Chronicle*."

"Yeah, well, some of us make more of a splash than others."

She snorted softly. "No kidding."

Without taking her eyes from the picture, she took a sip from her glass and when she lowered it, I caught the piney scent of gin.

"Can I get you something to drink?"

"Ice water, thanks."

"Sure, just a second." She seemed relieved that I'd made it easy. After setting her glass on a low table, she left the room.

The floor creaked as I walked toward the back wall which was taken up by a stereo system, a small wine rack and three large posters. Each poster displayed sandy beaches, blue skies and turquoise waters. I sensed a theme going here. I moved on to a collection of CDs. I would have pegged Ellie a country western fan. Her life kind of reflected some of the basic themes you tend to find there. Sure enough, she had a good-sized collection. I also found meditation CDs that went with all the candles distributed around the room.

"I've found that meditation helps me escape."

I turned and Ellie stood in the arched doorway, extending a glass of ice water toward me. I took it and thanked her.

"To a tropical island?"

She lowered her eyes and smiled shyly. I thought it was the first time I'd seen a completely unaffected display of emotion from her. And when she said, "Where would we be without our dreams?" it kind of touched me.

As she gazed up at the posters, her features softened. "Some day I'm going to live on one of those islands."

"Which one?"

"I'm not sure. Tonga maybe or Bali." She smiled to herself, and for a few seconds she seemed to leave the room. Drifting back, she added, "Someplace where the sand is white and goes on forever. It feels like hot silk between my toes. If any of my family wants to see me, they'll have to come to paradise."

"Better stock up on the sunscreen."

Shrugging, she drew away from the posters. "Dee's such a worrier." She took a pack of cigarettes out of an end table drawer. "She hates that I smoke. Worries. And now she's become one of these health food nuts. Doesn't even eat meat."

"Vegetarian vampire. Adds a new twist to the legend, doesn't it? Carrot juice?"

She smiled politely, and lit her cigarette. Then she moved to stand in front of a large window looking out onto the back yard, and her figure became a silhouette. I couldn't read her face at all. I settled into an overstuffed chair covered with pink and blue flowers and set the water glass on a small table beside it.

"Dee's never had it easy," she said, adding almost as an afterthought, "She wasn't planned, you know."

"I didn't." And I wished that were still the case.

"Anyone who cares to do the math can figure it out." She shrugged. "I knew Ed in high school. We hung around with some of the same people. He dropped out of college and joined the army and then when he got out he finished school in Chicago on the GI bill. Meanwhile I got a nursing degree and started working. It wasn't until he came back to Foxport to join the police department that we started dating." She shook her head and sighed. "I was going back to school at the time. Taking classes when I could. I didn't care much for nursing. Wanted to do something else with my life. Public relations, maybe. Then I got pregnant." She laughed as though making a joke out of it. "So much for plans, right?" Another sigh. "I was almost thirty when we got married. Thought for sure I'd be an old maid."

She moved away from the window and sat on the edge of the couch. After wedging her cigarette in the groove of an ashtray, she wrapped her arms across her chest and said, "I guess I didn't expect to see you so soon."

We'd finally arrived. "Well, I have some news."

She swallowed. "You found him?"

"Not exactly." I told her what I did find.

When I finished, Ellie waited a moment, like she expected more, then when I didn't continue, she looked away. "Oh, God," she breathed.

"I wouldn't jump to conclusions." Actually, any reasonable person would. Then I asked, "Did he have a boat?"

"I . . . Um . . . don't know." Beneath her tan, she had paled a couple shades. "I've never been up there. I don't think he ever mentioned a boat."

She picked up her cigarette and puffed on it a couple times. "Did you call the police?"

"I did. Anonymous."

She managed a tight nod. Then, as though it just occurred to her, she asked, "Are you going to keep looking for him?"

"I would guess the police will be doing that now."

"Oh." She sank back into the couch. "I see." Staring into the fireplace, she murmured, "Would you send me the bill?"

"Sure." I stood, thinking she'd take this as a cue that I was leaving. But she didn't look up. What more could I do? "Ellie, that day you were supposed to have dinner with him, did he say anything about meeting anyone else earlier? Might anyone have been at the house with him?"

"Not that I know of."

I hated to ask the next question, but it had been nagging at me. "Do you know of any reason Kurt might want to disappear?"

She turned to me, wide eyed, and blinked once. "Disappear?"

"Yeah, you know, fake his death. Was there anything he might be running away from?"

From her knotted eyebrows I figured she couldn't fathom what I'd just suggested. But as I searched for another way to word it, her features relaxed and she seemed to drift into herself, tethered to reality only by her gaze which had clamped onto mine. "No," she finally said, pulling away just as I started to feel the tension in my neck muscles. "He wouldn't leave without telling me." She sounded both convinced and terribly sad. "Something's happened to him. Something bad."

Then she dismissed me with a curt, "Thank you," picked up her drink and left the room. A moment later I heard the back door open and close.

When I got outside, there was no sign of Dee and Peanuts, so I leaned up against my car and baked in the sun while I waited. Ellie's reaction to the news puzzled me. While she'd obviously been disturbed by my findings, it had also set her to thinking. Unmitigated grief usually didn't allow much room for rational thought. Let it go, I told myself.

After about five minutes, Dee rounded the corner with Peanuts. They both seemed to be enjoying the outing. Peanuts trotted alongside Dee who bent to pet him every few steps.

"He's really well trained." She handed me his leash and gave him a final pat, which he responded to with a wet tongue.

"He's smart."

"I'm going to get a dog. A Weimaraner."

I nodded. "I can see you with a Weimaraner."

"Yeah," she agreed. "Mom won't let me have one. So, I guess I'll have to wait."

"How's your mom doing?"

Dee gave me an odd look. "Okay, I guess. We'll get by."

"Where's your brother?"

"Oh, he's at some baseball camp." She nodded as though confirming a thought. "It's probably good that he's not around right now. He's always sticking up for Dad. That bothers Mom."

"Does it bother you?"

After a moment she said, "Kind of. I mean, Dad's a good guy and all, but I can see why she's bitter." I waited. Dee crossed her arms over her chest so she hugged herself and looked down at the grass, pushing a twig with the toe of her sandal. "He never had much time for her. But now that he's with Elaine, well, he's got lots of time. It hurts her. I mean, I like Elaine and all. She's real nice. But it's hard on my mom. Real hard."

"Your mom's lucky she's got you."

She glanced up at me, squinting, then shrugged and looked away.

As I drove back through town, I saw the temperature at the bank read 98. Up one degree. Heat rose in waves off the street and the few pedestrians with the fortitude to brave it looked like they were going to melt into the sidewalks, leaving puddles of pink and khaki.

Since I was near the bank, I decided to stop for money. Except for a dollar and some change, my pockets were empty. I pulled up to the cash machine, inserted my card and punched in the magic numbers. All that was fine. But when I tried to withdraw sixty bucks, it told me I didn't have sixty bucks. When it told me how much I could withdraw, I could've sworn I heard it snicker.

Fortunately, the bank was open, so I left Peanuts tied to a sapling near the entrance and marched in there ready to do battle.

I went straight to the bank manager whose desk happened to be a direct shot from the door. The chairs surrounding it were empty and Brenda Wright looked like she needed something to do. She was around fifty with short, dark hair and a pale complexion. She reminded me of Liza Minelli. Her bright red lips parted into a wide smile as she folded her hands on the blotter in front of her and asked how she could help me.

"I deposited a check for twenty-five hundred dollars yesterday. It was written on this bank. Now the cash station tells me I can't withdraw sixty dollars."

Her eyebrows drew together in a show of concern. "Why don't you have a seat and we'll get this straightened out?"

Reluctantly ceding my altitude advantage, I slid into one of the pseudo-leather chairs.

"Do you have your checkbook with you?" she asked.

"I didn't think I'd need it."

"No matter," she said with a little wave of her hand that went a long way in disarming my indignation. "Just show me some identification and we'll get this taken care of."

I dug out my driver's license and sat there watching her key letters and then numbers into her computer. Although, from where I sat, I couldn't read the screen, I could tell from her expression when something bad-smelling turned up. "Hmm." She punched in more numbers. "That check you deposited was written on a closed account."

"What?"

"Yes, let's see." She keyed in more numbers. Concern for her customer had been replaced by curiosity. "Yes, that check was dated the fourteenth—yesterday. The account was closed on the twelfth."

"Who closed it?"

After consulting her screen, she pushed away from her desk. "Wait here, Mr. McCauley." I noted that while she was still smiling, she'd lost that apologetic air that I'd begun to appreciate. On the one hand, all this really annoyed me. On the other, it also made me curious. Gina Wicklow seemed genuine. If she had closed the account, I'd be surprised. If Kurt had closed it, that meant he'd been in Foxport on Tuesday, the same day he was supposed to meet Ellie in Richton for dinner.

Brenda Wright returned with a young man in tow who she introduced as Mr. Lewis. "He's the teller who handled the account closing." Then she clasped her hands in front of her, waiting for us to settle this like gentlemen.

I stood and shook hands with Lewis who was probably in his late-twenties. He had the kind of face you see on the male models in those cologne ads—flinty eyes; narrow, straight nose; generous mouth and a vapid expression. His dark hair was cut short around the sides and long around the crown, and a lock fell over one eye. He wore a somber but busy tie that resembled the Shroud of Turin.

He wet his lips, swallowed and thrust his hands into his pockets. "That account was closed on Tuesday by Mr. Wicklow."

"Kurt Wicklow was in here on Tuesday?"

He made a scratchy attempt at clearing his throat and carefully enunciated each word. "That's what I said."

"You're sure it was Kurt Wicklow?"

"We need an ID to close an account." He finally made eye contact. "I'm sure it was him."

"Did he say why he was closing the account?"

"Even if he did, I'm afraid that would be confidential."

Brenda Wright nodded in agreement. I could tell I'd get no further with either of them, so I transferred some funds from my meager savings account to give me some walking around money.

I collected Peanuts and drove to my office. First thing I did was call Gina Wicklow. The check Gina had given me had Kurt's signature on it, but it was a signature stamp. Maybe she'd be more surprised about the closed account than I was. She wasn't home, so I left a message. As soon as I hung up, I regretted my action. What with a missing husband and that bloodstain, she no doubt had other things occupying her mind. Even if that weren't the case, she'd probably be embarrassed and flustered and I didn't want to bring that on. I considered calling her back and telling her not to worry about it, but figured that would only compound my idiocy.

When I got home, I decided if I didn't do my laundry I wouldn't be fit for public interaction, so I hauled an overflowing basket down to the basement where Louise has her washer and dryer. She's nice enough to let me use it at no cost. I pay for repairs. I was watching my shirts in the dryer when I heard the door at the top of the stairs open and Louise call down, "Are you decent?"

There's a story behind that. I'd been living in the upstairs apartment about a month and was washing clothes at one-thirty in the morning. Since it was so late, and I wanted to start the next day with a clean slate, I took off the clothes I had on and tossed them in. The fact that this effectively trapped me in the basement didn't bother me. When I do laundry, I have to stay with it throughout the dry cycle anyway. I don't iron shirts. I stand by the dryer and wait for that precise moment when the shirts are dry enough but haven't begun to wrinkle. Toward the end, I have to check it every few minutes so I can't go far. Anyway, Louise must have wondered about the noise in her basement at that hour. She came down and found me sitting in a folding chair in front of the dryer, stark naked except for my Reeboks, reading a Ross Thomas novel. It's to her everlasting credit that, instead of locking the door behind her and calling the police, all she said was, "Oh, you're doing your laundry then. Be sure to turn out the lights when you're finished."

To this day, I might wonder if she even noticed my nudity if she didn't preface every visit in the basement with: "Are you decent?" That plus the way she giggles when she says it.

"As decent as I get," I called back up the stairs.

"I suppose that will have to do." She began to make her way down the steps. Lately, she's been taking them slowly. One of her friends broke her hip recently, and now Louise is scared she's next. She instructed me if that ever happens to take her out in a field and shoot her. I don't know what's scarier about getting old—feeling your body's decline or anticipating it.

When she saw me standing over the dryer, she shook her head. "I don't mind ironing your shirts, you know. I rather enjoy ironing."

We'd been through this before. "Thanks, Louise. But this is one of those little challenges life throws at me."

"Yes, well." She seemed distracted and when she started to fold my clean shorts, I didn't stop her. I figured she was working something out in her head. If my underwear could help, then so be it.

"This is about Albert," she finally said.

I hoped he wasn't missing.

"It's also quite awkward, I dare say."

"How's that?"

"Well, he'd be most disturbed if he knew I'd mentioned this to you."

"I won't say a word." At this point, it was useless to plead for Albert's privacy. We'd come this far; she was talking.

"It's a financial matter, actually."

I waited.

"Have you ever invested money in stocks or some such?"

I stopped the dryer and stuck my hand in to feel the shirts. Almost there. "No," I said, shutting the door. "Never had enough to gamble."

"Well, yes, I suppose that's what it is, isn't it?"

I leaned against the dryer and crossed my arms over my chest. "Not exactly. If you know what you're doing, the risk is minimal. If you've got a broker you can—" I stopped, afraid of where this was going.

Louise continued as though she hadn't read me at all. By now, she'd started a second pile of my shorts. "Well, Albert followed the advice of a friend who'd been quite pleased with this young man—a stockbroker, I presume. He recommended some fast growth investments." She stopped folding and gave me a meaningful look. "When you get to be our age, long-term investments aren't what you'd call practical. At any rate, Albert invested a good deal of his savings. That was, oh, I think about eight months ago. Well, Albert showed me some of the stock reports and, while they seem authentic, I suppose with computers the appearance of authenticity is quite a simple matter. Albert had some questions and rang up this man, but he's not returning his calls. Albert's getting quite concerned."

"What about Albert's friend?"

"He's in even worse straits. He's got to get his money out, but can't reach him either."

I asked the obvious question. "What's the broker's name?"

"Kurt Wicklow."

She must have sensed something in my reaction. "What? What is it?"

"I've had some trouble collecting on a bill from him."

"That sounds a bit ominous, doesn't it?"

She didn't know the half.

"His assistant tells me he's out of town," I said.

"That's what Albert's been told as well."

"Maybe he is. I'll look into it though."

"Would you mind?"

I shook my head. "Not at all. In the meantime, I think Albert ought to contact the Securities and Exchange Commission. See if there's any steps he needs to take."

"You don't think Mr. Wicklow has absconded with his investors' money, do you?" It was as though this was the first time the possibility had occurred to her. Louise was not a naive woman. That scared me some.

"It happens."

"Goodness. Albert lives in quite a lovely place a bit up north on the river. But the monthly assessment's so high he's come to depend on his investments. If he were to lose this, why, I'm afraid he'd lose his condominium. He'd have to go live with one of his children." She shuddered. "That would be dreadful for all involved."

After Louise left, my shorts and undershirts were neatly folded but my shirts had started to wrinkle. In light of Albert's problem, I couldn't feel too sorry for myself. While I slipped them onto hangers, I pondered how, in such a short space of time, Kurt Wicklow —dead or alive—had insinuated himself into my life and how rapidly he was establishing so many levels of deceit.

Chapter 7

After dining on a skimpy portion of chicken marsala, I decided the only way to counter a long, fruitless day topped with a mediocre frozen dinner was with a beer or two.

I hadn't planned on taking Peanuts, but he kept getting between me and the door. Relenting, I clipped the leash onto his collar and we walked the mile or so to the Tattersall. I enjoyed the relative cool and he just seemed to enjoy being out of the apartment.

When we got to the door of the pub, I stopped to examine a white S-10 parked in one of the parallel spots in front of the Tattersall. The plates were blue on white with a wavy green line under "Missouri." I couldn't recall the license number I'd recorded. Probably too good to be true.

Although it was Friday night and crowded, I managed to grab a table near the bar. Peanuts stretched out underneath it, ensuring that as much of his body came in contact with the cool, wooden floor as possible. I felt his sigh against my foot. Neither of us really wanted to be home—him because of the cat and me because staring at four bare walls got to me after a while. Maybe instead of a beer, I should invest in some artwork. Yeah. A watercolor. I'd take it in trade.

I scanned the line at the bar, more out of habit than the belief that I could connect any one person to the S-10. But then I saw Brewster Plunkett standing there sucking on a long-necked bottle. Taller than the other members of the line, and wearing a khaki shirt with epaulets, he looked slightly out of place. Sort of like he'd ditched his scout pack. When he saw me, he did a slow double take. I'd noticed that Brewster had a languid way of moving—he wouldn't be rushed.

"How's it going?" he called out over the din.

I shrugged.

He pushed away from the bar, grabbed a basket of popcorn, and headed for my table. I had mixed feelings. This might be my only chance to find out if he had business up in New Berne. But, if I had to listen to any more tales of Eddie Carver before I got an answer, I wasn't sure it was worth the price.

Brewster peered under the table. "Who's that?"

I felt my dog stir. "That's Peanuts."

"Peanuts?" He dropped the basket on the table, then pulled out a chair and sat across from me. "What the hell kinda' name's that?" He spoke with a smile pulling at a corner of his mouth.

"Named after Peanuts Lawry, outfielder for the Cubs back in the forties." I gestured under the table with a nod. "You should see him shag Frisbees." I spent so much time explaining my dog's name, I'd begun to wish I'd named him Fido.

Brewster nodded as though that made sense. His chair scraped against the floor as he turned it sideways. Then he propped one elbow on the table and slumped back into the chair so he could bring his long legs out to the side. Helping himself to a handful of popcorn, he looked around. "Decent place."

"It is."

"You and your friend come here a lot?"

"We're regulars. Dogs are welcome as long as they don't

bite any sober customers."

Nodding his approval, he said, "Back in Cape there's a place called the Sports Tap. Thursday nights between six and eight they got beers for a quarter."

"Yeah, but do they allow dogs?"

"Don't know. A buddy of mine tried to bring his hog in but the owner wouldn't hear of it."

I assumed he referred to a motorcycle and not Babe on a binge. But I didn't know Brewster well enough to be certain. When in doubt, change the subject.

"That your Chevy pickup out front?"

His pale eyebrows drew together in a V. "How'd you know?"

"Saw the Show Me plates."

He picked a popcorn husk out of a back tooth. "Yeah, it's mine."

"How do you like it?"

"It's okay. I'd rather have a Porsche parked out there, but hell, a Porsche isn't too practical in our line of work, is it?"

"You must have a thriving business in Cape Girardeau if the only reason you don't drive a Porsche is because it's too conspicuous." I shook my head in frank admiration. "You're doing a helluva lot better than I am."

"You might consider expanding your line." He wagged a knowing finger at me.

"How do you mean?"

"I'm also in the fugitive retrieval business."

"Bounty hunter?" An image of Josh Randall, sawed-off Remington strapped to his leg, flashed into my head. When I was a kid I thought that Steve McQueen represented all that was right and honorable in this world. Then I learned it didn't hurt to move your lips when you talked.

"Don't knock it. It pays real good."

"So I hear. Not many rules to get in the way."

"That's for damned sure."

"You do all that in a Chevy pickup?"

"I'm quirky. Folks like that about me. They trust me." He smiled again and this time I saw something cold there. "That can be a big mistake."

Leaning back, his chair on its hind legs, he rocked slowly. "Getting so folks don't trust the suits anymore. Who can blame them? I never wear a tie. Never order wine." He held up his bottle. "Always the same brand. Never use a glass. I figure if a person's gonna reject me outright because of that, the hell with 'em." He nodded in agreement, then toasted himself.

I followed suit, and said, "I try to never judge a man harshly just because he's got lousy taste in beer."

He sneered in mock insult. "I've killed for less." Then he chuckled as he settled back into his chair. "I do tend to get a little self-righteous at times. What the hell, we've all got our faults. Right?"

I sure did, but I wasn't about to start confessing them.

"You staying at Ed and Elaine's?" I asked.

He shook his head. "Got a room at the Foxhole. You know, the place by the Dive Inn."

"Ah, yes. The Foxhole." I figured from the way the laugh lines gathered around his eyes, that he knew my history with Ellie. "Ed's telling stories out of school, isn't he?"

He shrugged. "It's a good story." He paused for a brief chuckle. "Especially when you look at it from the other side."

"You been to the Dive Inn?"

"Can't say that I have."

I wasn't even close to believing that Brewster Plunkett had passed on a bar that wasn't fifty feet from his bed. I wondered if he'd been there last night when I'd met with Ellie.

Getting Brewster to talk seemed easy enough. Leading him in the right direction might be a challenge.

"How long have you known Ed?"

"We met at Douglas U. Me and him and Danny lived in the same dorm freshman year." He frowned as he laced his hands behind his head and consulted the ceiling. "Let's see. That was Mitchell Hall. Ed's a good guy."

"Who's Danny?" I recalled the sober way Ed had reacted to Brewster's mention of his name yesterday.

"One of the guys we hung out with," he replied. "He died 'bout eight months ago," and added, "Cancer."

Brewster continued, "I tell you, Eddie can sure use a good woman like Elaine. Lord knows, Ellie never did anything for him." He chuckled. "Good thing their names are almost the same. Easier to cover any slips, if you know what I mean."

I did, but didn't care to pursue it.

Abruptly, Brewster's chair dropped level. Gesturing toward my mug, he said, "You want another?"

"Thanks."

When he went to replenish our drinks, I noticed he was on a first name basis with Sammy, the owner.

When he came back with our beers (mine in a mug), he also brought two shot glasses, setting one in front of me and raising the other in a toast. "Single malt."

"Think I'll take a pass." I hoped Brewster would let it lie.

"Suit yourself." He downed his own and followed with a long pull on the bottle. Then he took mine and repeated the ritual.

When he resumed the conversation, I was a little surprised to find he hadn't lost his train of thought.

"Ellie did nothing for Ed. Nothing. After he got out of the service, he finished college somewhere local. Couple months after he graduates, Ed got a real nice offer from some hotel chain out east. They were acquiring some new hotels, looking for someone to head up security. All set to head out to D.C. when Ellie tells him she's pregnant. Not only that but there's no way she's gonna live in Washington D.C." He mimicked her in an over-the-top whine. " 'Too humid. My hair'll frizz,' she says. So he stuck it out here." He shook his head. "Goddamned shame." Then he stared at the table, looking philosophical. "Ellie Miller got just what she wanted."

"Why did Ed drop out of college?"

"Where'd you hear that?"

"I don't remember."

"Grades, I think." He gave it another moment, shrugged and continued, "Anyway, Ed gets out of the ser- vice, gets his degree, and he's looking around to start his life. There's Ellie. She's an old friend. Familiar."

"Maybe he would have married her anyway."

"Nah. He was sweet on someone else at the time."

"Who?"

"Her name was Terry something. Never met her. Think she's out west now. I was out of the picture then. But, good old Eddie, always gotta do the right thing."

"How do you mean that?"

He paused and his focus seemed to drift off for a few seconds. Then he shrugged and said, "He married her, didn't he?"

"Sounds like you've only heard one side of the story. Ellie might tell it different."

He gave me an odd look. "What've you heard?"

"Nothing," I lied. "It just seems to me you don't give Ellie credit for much at all."

"Maybe not." He pondered that for a moment, then he shook his head. "Nah, you know what Ellie is?" He pointed the bottle's stem at me. "You ever wonder where they dig up those folks you see on those talk shows? The ones that spill their guts along with all those deep, dark secrets?" He didn't wait for my confirmation. "Well," he continued, "that's Ellie. Ed'll be lucky if he doesn't turn on the TV someday and see his ex-wife telling Jerry Springer about Ed's peccadilloes."

"How well do you know Ellie?"

"I thought about moving here after school." He made a sour face. "Too civilized for me."

He hadn't answered my question. "Have you ever met Ellie?"

"Was at the wedding." He took a pull on the beer. "Ellie and me never hit it off."

"I gathered that."

"Ed's too good for her. And she knew it. So did I."

"You're a real expert on the subject of Ed Carver."

"I don't respect many people. Most don't deserve it. I got a lot of respect for Ed." He paused. "I owe him."

"How's that?"

He drained his bottle of beer and raised it above his head like he was trading on the stock floor. Once he caught Sammy's eye, he gestured toward my mug, which I'd barely started. I shook my head and he raised one finger. When he returned his attention to me, he said, "Friends usually owe each other, don't they?"

I wasn't looking for a discussion on friendship and decided since there was no subtle way to bring up Kurt Wicklow, now was a good time to do it. "Saw you up in New Berne this morning."

He gave me a weird look—kind of amused and surprised at the same time. "What gave me away?" He maneuvered so he could rest both arms on the table. Beneath the table, Peanuts groaned as he changed position.

"Well, there's that inconspicuous pick-up with Missouri plates."

"You had business in New Berne?" he asked.

"You were pulling out of the road to Kurt Wicklow's place."

He rubbed his chin, grinning uneasily. "Damn. Maybe I should trade in the truck." His chuckle sounded stiff.

I didn't respond—just sat back and waited for Brewster to keep talking. I can handle long silences better than most.

Finally, he said, "All right. So what if I was up there. Wicklow wasn't home."

"What was your business with him?"

"Looking up an old college buddy. Me and Kurt were on the football team together at Douglas."

I didn't know any of these men back then, but I knew all of them now except Danny. Carver and Brewster I could see together, but Wicklow seemed a different ilk.

"Wicklow was part of the old gang—Carver, you, Danny and Wicklow?"

"Sure," was all Brewster said, eyes narrowing. "You didn't say what your business was."

"Wicklow owes me money."

Brewster frowned. "Long way for a debt collector to drive."

"Not if he's broke."

He nodded, conceding the logic, but not necessarily buying it. "You go in?"

"He wasn't home." Then I asked, "Was he supposed to be?"

He shook his head. "Don't know. Just stopped in. His wife told me he was spending a few days up there."

"Long way to go for a surprise visit."

He smiled, getting into the game. "Not if you really like surprises."

Before I could shoot one back at him, the raw sound of a chair scraping the floor made me look up. I could tell by the way Peanuts reacted—banging against my shin—that the noise had startled him as well.

"Quint, who's your new friend here?" Jeff Barlowe had helped himself to a seat.

Jeff was a good friend, but sometimes his timing left a lot to be desired. I introduced Jeff and Brewster, glaring at Jeff the whole time. He was, of course, oblivious. He never sensed he was unwelcome although, in his line of business, that was frequently the case. I guess that helped make him the *Abel County Chronicle*'s best reporter.

Brewster greeted Jeff like he was someone he'd been waiting his whole life to meet. I figured he was just grateful for the interruption. I stayed for a few minutes as the conversation deteriorated into profundities concerning the weather and then veered off in the direction of television news.

I might have stuck it out and worked at getting rid of Jeff, but I could tell the moment was gone. I figured I'd catch Brewster later. Besides, Peanuts had started whining, which meant, even though he hadn't consumed a couple beers, he still had to relieve himself.

Chapter 8

The next morning I woke feeling tired and uneasy. I don't like sleeping with the air conditioner running. Not only did it make the walls close in on me, but I hated the way the noise drowned out the night sounds. But I wouldn't have gotten any sleep at all without it.

My sleep was shallow at best and when, at 6:20 I felt a small body parading down my back, I gave up. McGee greeted me with a ratchety squeak. Peanuts sat at the door to my bedroom, glaring at both of us.

"It didn't mean anything," I told him as I crossed the hall to the bathroom and splashed cold water on my face.

I fed the livestock and put on a pot of coffee. Then I pulled on a pair of shorts and an old T-shirt. I needed a good run along the river to clear the threads out of my head.

Before I left, I called the office to see if I had a reason to go into work. There was a message from Gina Wicklow asking me to call her ASAP. I cringed, wishing again I hadn't left that message. Her call had come in yesterday afternoon at a quarter to five. I figured she didn't really want me to call her at six-thirty in the morning, so I whistled for Peanuts and we left the cat in search of a square foot of space to claim for his own.

As I crossed the green expanse of yard down to the river, I mentally flipped a coin. When I came to the path, I turned left and headed south toward the Charlemagne Street Bridge, past the park, willows and picnic tables. When I moved to Foxport, I'd been lucky to find a place on the river and even luckier to find a landlady who didn't believe in charging what the market could bear for a one-bedroom apartment with a river view just because she could. Now, we simply deducted my rent from the Jaded Fox profits. If I didn't think about it too hard, it was like living for free.

The river was high this year. It had been a wet spring, and summer had followed suit. A thunderstorm would roll through, drop two or three inches of rain and move on, leaving the air as hot and humid as ever.

In less than a quarter mile I was drenched in sweat, but I focused on the sound my shoes made as they hit the path and tried to key into their rhythm. After I'd gone another quarter mile, Peanuts stopped to herd some ducks. I'd pick him up on the way back. He's a sprinter, not a runner.

I wasn't looking to do anything Herculean this morning. Maybe as far as the bridge and back—a total of two miles. But as I rounded the final bend before the bridge came into view, I noticed some commotion. About a hundred feet of public park, thick with flower beds, separated this section of the path from a small parking lot. A squad car, its lights flashing, was pulling into the lot.

When I looked toward the bridge, I saw a man standing about twenty feet ahead of me, hands on his hips, his back to me. He was dressed for running; I could see the "Bulls 33" on the back of his red and black jersey. On the ground in front of him lay a large, brown bundle. As I slowed my pace, I saw a cop making his way down from the lot to the riverbank.

The man standing by the bundle must have heard me, because he turned and watched me approach. At this point, I was about thirty feet closer than the cop. The man was young, not much more than twenty, with short brown hair and wore a sweat band. As he faced me, he shook his head.

"Thought it was a bag of clothes someone dumped." He spoke as though he was continuing a conversation rather than starting one. "I mean, is that stupid or what? Jeez." He looked down at the object on the ground which was now identifiable as a body.

"Shit, man." He kept shaking his head. "I never seen . . ." He used the bottom of his shirt to wipe his face and rub his eyes.

I had a feeling I knew who he had pulled out of the Fox River. The body's arms were raised over his head like he'd been shot while surrendering. The skin of his right arm was blackened and raw, like he'd been burned. In places, the flesh seemed to be peeling off. His head was turned away from me. He'd been wearing brown pants and a white T-shirt that was pushed up, revealing his pale skin and hairless chest. I walked around so I could see his face and stopped short. Holy shit. I was wrong.

I concentrated on his features—not the part of his forehead that was caved in or the way his eyes stared, but at the pale mustache and the sideburns.

"You know him?"

I shook my head, and at the same time I said, "Yeah, his name's Brewster Plunkett."

I didn't hang around any longer than necessary. In less than five minutes, another squad car arrived and pretty soon we had a crowd. I gave my statement to one of the cops, Barry Hudgins, who I'd met a couple times but, like Brewster Plunkett, I didn't really know. I couldn't tell him much, only that Brewster and I had shared a few beers and that he was a friend of Ed Carver's.

I heard the young guy, whose name was Alex, explain to

the other cop how he thought at first that he'd come upon some discarded clothing. Once he got close enough to see that it was a body, he'd pulled Brewster out. "I guess at first I figured he might be alive. But, no." Then, almost as an afterthought, he added, "You think he hit his head when he fell in?"

The cop said something about an autopsy. I had the feeling that Brewster's death had nothing to do with getting drunk and falling off the Charlemagne Street Bridge. A crowd of gapers had collected on the bridge, filling the narrow pedestrian walk. I left my number with Hudgins and headed back to my apartment, walking rather than running.

It was going on eight when I turned off the path and into the yard. Peanuts lay under a tree, tongue lolling out of his mouth in a pant. Instead of trotting up to me, he stood and waited for me to cross the yard.

I considered calling Ed, then thought better of it. He wouldn't want to hear this news from me. So, I took a shower, shaved and then ate a bowl of corn flakes while I drank my coffee.

It was a little after nine when I returned Gina's call.

"Thank you for calling back." I could hear the strain in her voice. "I'm so sorry about the check. It bounced. And I'm even sorrier that I don't know when I'll be able to pay you."

What could I say? I wasn't supposed to know about Kurt's disappearance and I couldn't tell her it was all right. It wasn't. "What's the problem?"

"Well," her voice got tighter, "it seems my husband is missing." She took a second to clear her throat and control the timbre of her voice. "Police in New Berne called me yesterday. That's where Kurt was. He's got a place up there, you know. They found some blood in one of the rooms. On the carpet. They're running tests on it. There's no sign of Kurt.

His car's there, but none of the neighbors have seen him recently and . . ." Her voice trailed off, then picked up again with a catch in it this time. "And now I find that the bank account I wrote the check on has been closed. I don't know what to think."

"The teller at the bank told me Kurt closed the account on Tuesday. In person."

"He did? Well, I don't understand."

"Look," I started, "why don't you take some time to get yourself together. We can talk later."

"Thank you," she said, then continued as though I hadn't given her an exit line. "It's so strange. I don't know where to start. I'm afraid to look at things, you know." Then she really started to ramble. "I feel like I've been married to this stranger. You think you know someone. It doesn't look like he left much. Just what was in our joint account and that wasn't more than a few hundred dollars. Most strangers treat people better than that. I don't understand." Then she did break down. Through tears, she mumbled apologies and hung up.

I stood there for a minute, the receiver in my hand, feeling about as useless as a penny in Prague. On impulse, I hit the disconnect button and then redial. It rang five times before she answered, sounding pretty much the same.

"Listen," I said, "do you need to talk about this? You want to stop by the office? We could talk."

"That's nice of you. It's just—. Well, I don't feel like going out, you know. I look like I feel."

"That's okay."

"Um," she hesitated.

"What?"

"Do you want to come here? I could make some lunch."

"I don't want to be any trouble."

She managed a small laugh. "Quint, I'm the trouble. Remember?" Then she said, "God knows, I haven't been in the mood to eat. Maybe some company would help."

"You sure?"

"Really. I need to talk about this. I'd appreciate it. Really."

"What time?"

"Noon?"

"See you then."

I told myself that I was just trying to be a friend to someone who needed one, but I knew better.

Chapter 9

I went into the office for about an hour. Mainly, I wanted to get out of the house. The walls were inching in on me.

Brewster's image kept coming, unbidden, to mind. One second he'd be laughing and joking, waving his bottle of beer as he emphasized a point. The next he'd be the color of a fish's belly with his head caved in. I wondered if Brewster had been as surprised by his death as I was.

Two more bills greeted me—compliments of the phone company and American Express. Fortunately, there was also a small check for some surveillance I'd done last month, which just about cancelled them out.

After a half-hour, Louise drifted in from the shop carrying a small shipping box. She often visited on slow days, and left the door open so she could hear the bell if a customer came in. She wore knickers and a vest over a gauzy blouse. I swear, she can pull it off.

"This is one of the carvings I ordered from that couple who were at the festival last month. Their work is quite lovely and doing rather well." She pulled something out of the box. "Here, I think you ought to have this little fellow." She set it on my desk, turning it so it faced me. The shape of the head, the beak and the suggestion of wings gave it definition. Yet, with only those features, it was unmistakably a penguin. I picked it up and found it was heavier than I'd imagined. "What is this?"

"It's some soft mineral found in Africa." She lifted packing straw out of the box. "There's a card here somewhere."

"Never mind." It barely filled my hand and was a pale reddish brown with swirls of white. "Why do I need a penguin?"

"Don't penguins always make a person feel better?"

Startled, I looked up at her, then grudgingly shook my head. It was useless to deny one of Louise's observations. "What gave me away?"

"You've been moping about these days as though you'd lost your best friend." She paused. "That is what this is about, isn't it?"

"Not as much as you think."

She seemed to be waiting for me to continue.

I shook my head.

"Well, then you'd better tell him." She gestured toward the penguin. "Doesn't do a soul a bit of good to hold everything in, you know."

I raised the penguin in the palm of my hand. "All right. This bird will become the receptacle of my every thought, dream, fear, desire. Eventually, it will know so much about me that I'll have to kill it."

Scowling, she gave me a friendly slap on the shoulder. "I should've known better than to appeal to your sensitive, thoughtful side."

"Really, Louise, I appreciate the effort. You're a good friend." I saw a segue and jumped on it.

"Which reminds me. I've learned a few things about this guy who was investing Albert's money."

"What?" From the degree of concern I read in her eyes, she was closer to Albert than I'd suspected. She lowered herself into a chair facing my desk, still clutching the box.

"What I'm hearing isn't good. He's missing. The only sign of him is a bloodstain. No one's seen him." I didn't tell her that he'd cleaned out his own account. If Kurt Wicklow had no qualms about leaving his wife up the creek, I couldn't imagine he'd have reservations about ripping off old men. "I should know more later. I'm going to talk with his wife."

"Gina?"

"You know her?"

"She donated one of her paintings to the Foxport Women's Club to use in a fund-raiser. Does quite a bit of that, I hear. Quite a gifted artist, as well. Pity."

"Did Albert contact the SEC?"

"They recommended a lawyer who deals with this sort of thing. He's meeting with him today. The gent at the SEC said there were ways to recover your money, although if the broker is missing, I suppose that makes it rather difficult."

"Well, if he is missing, my guess is there will be a lot of people looking for him."

A polite ding announced a customer entering the Jaded Fox. "You let me know what you hear," Louise said. As she walked through the storeroom that separated my office from the shop, she tossed a final remark over her shoulder: "Enjoy your bird, now."

Chapter 10

I pulled into Gina Wicklow's driveway a few minutes after twelve. The sprawling, red brick ranch occupied a yard populated with trees, bushes and splashes of flowers. Not a weed in sight, I noted as I walked along the stone path toward the door. I've never cared much for overly manicured landscaping. Perfection makes me leery. As I rang the bell, I noticed a sizable spider web spanning the corner of the porch and part of the overhang. Its occupant—a small specimen with a round, fat body—no doubt anticipated its dinner, which appeared to be a luckless mosquito. One down, twelve billion to go.

Gina greeted me wearing a long, shapeless White Sox T-shirt over a pair of denim shorts, the edges of which were barely visible. Tan and slim, she moved with the slightly pigeon-toed grace of a dancer. Her smile was wide and warm, but behind a pair of purple-framed glasses, her eyes showed the strain.

As I stepped into the large, tiled foyer, I noticed that while it was cooler in the house, there wasn't the abrupt temperature change you get with air conditioning. She shut the door behind me and straightened a small throw rug with the toes of her right foot, the nails of which were painted bright red.

I removed my sunglasses and slipped them into my shirt pocket.

"If it's too warm for you, let me know," she said. "I seldom use the air conditioning. First off, I don't care for it. And then

I'm afraid I take after my father. He was what you might call cheap today, but when I was a kid, he was frugal. I never left a room without turning off the lights. If he were alive today, he'd have no such thing as air conditioning. 'A person's supposed to sweat. It's God's air conditioning.' Kurt's the opposite. The temperature creeps toward eighty and it goes on." She stopped short and shook her head. "I'm babbling again."

"It's all right. Makes my end of the conversation easier to carry."

"You're way too nice." She smiled and the corners of her eyes crinkled.

We turned left onto carpeting and I followed her down the hall and into the kitchen, passing a formal living room on one side and a dining room on the other. The kitchen was large and comfortable with stools tucked under the counter and a fireplace against the outer wall.

As I walked behind Gina, I noticed how her short hair revealed a long, slender neck. Right now she rubbed it as though trying to disperse the tension.

"Iced tea?" she asked.

"Sounds good."

Ice clattered into two glasses as she filled them from a dispenser on the freezer. Then she took a pitcher out of the refrigerator and filled the glasses. Wedges of lemon spilled into the tea as she poured.

"Sugar?"

"No thanks."

"I've got a sweet tooth." She poured a heaping teaspoon into one glass, stirring as she handed me the other.

"Let's go out on the sun porch," she suggested.

That sounded like a hot idea to me, but I followed her. We passed through a family room. A wide-screen television dominated one wall and the room's furniture surrounded it like leather supplicants. I recalled Kurt's former profession.

"I take it Kurt likes his sports events life-sized."

"Oh," she glanced at the TV. "I confess I'm as bad as he is. Maybe worse. I can't think of a sporting event I won't watch."

"Curling?"

"Sorry. Thanks to cable we get the national curling competition." She smiled as she spoke, but I didn't know her well enough to be certain she was joking.

The sun hadn't hit the porch side of the house yet and it was fairly comfortable. An overhead fan spun slowly. As I settled into a green, wrought iron chair with striped cushions, I noticed an easel and a wooden table at the other end of the porch. Below the windows along that wall were shelves of paint supplies.

"This is your workshop?"

She had curled her legs up beneath her and set her iced tea on a wrought iron table with a glass top. "In all but the worst weather. I love it out here."

"Who wouldn't?"

"I can see my garden, my trees. And then there's my little animal friends." She laughed, reddening slightly.

"Sounds like a Disney setting," I offered.

"It really is. I feed the chipmunks, birds, rabbits. Once they find a good thing, they won't leave you alone, you know. Those squirrels practically mug you."

She took a sip of tea and held onto the dripping glass. "Where do you live?"

"In an apartment above a house. It's on the Fox."

"That's nice."

"You know, I don't think I've lived on the ground floor since I left home. Even then, my bedroom was on the second floor."

"So, you've never had a garden?" From the tone of her voice, I might have said I'd never had a bike.

"Not to speak of."

"That's too bad."

I shrugged. "You get by."

Her laugh was brittle and she shook her head. "Don't I sound like one who's lived the life of the privileged? Sorry."

"No need to apologize."

As she returned her glass to the table, her features tightened and she pushed her fingers through her cropped hair. The condensation she transferred from the glass left her hair sticking up a little. "I think my days as a member of the privileged class are over." I heard no remorse or bitterness. When her eyes focused on me again, she said, "I'm sitting here in this magnificent house, knowing the next time they try to deduct the mortgage from our checking account, the money's not going to be there. Already I feel like I'm living in someone else's property. I recognize all the furniture, the artwork, but I can't let myself feel anything for it anymore."

"What was the account he cleaned out?"

"That was the business expense account. He'd sometimes use it for emergencies."

"How much money was in it?"

"Between eight and ten thousand." She paused. "Not a whole lot of money, but enough to give me a month or two to figure out what the hell I'm doing."

"What about money from your painting?"

"That's in our joint account. Sales haven't exactly been brisk."

"Do you have any family who can help you out?"

From the way her chin dimpled as it tightened, and her eyes watered, I gathered that wasn't an option. "You know," her voice was a raspy whisper, "the worst part is I don't know whether to be cursing the bastard or mourning my spouse."

"I think you've got a right to be angry no matter what happens." What I couldn't figure out was why someone who wanted to disappear would clean out his business account. Seemed like a red flag. Wicklow struck me as being a little too smart for that. Maybe Ellie had been right. He really was dead.

I heard a cracking sound coming from the garden. When I looked, a female cardinal was picking at sunflower seeds in a feeder suspended from a tree near the window. She'd cock her head, then poke at a seed.

"If he did leave, then how could he . . . I don't understand how he could do such a thing."

I turned back to Gina who watched me like she really expected an answer. All I had were more questions. "What about stocks? CDs?"

"We didn't have any CDs. Only stocks. That was Kurt's expertise, though I can't find any papers on them. They're probably gone as well." She shook her head. "I hate to keep saying this, but I just don't get it."

Neither of us spoke for a minute. She seemed deep in thought. I broke the silence. "When's the last time you saw Kurt?"

"A week ago Friday, before he went up to the lake."

"He left on Friday?"

She nodded.

"Did he call you while he was up there?"

"No, but that wasn't unusual."

I recalled it had rained last weekend and we'd enjoyed a couple days respite from the heat. When the sun came out on Monday the heat hit again like it had barely broken stride. If Wicklow liked his air conditioning as much as Gina said he did, then he would have had it on since Monday. If he'd been there. "Did Kurt often go up to the lake on his own?"

"Most of the time. I've only been up there once this summer myself." With a shrug as though it didn't matter, she added, "It's his place, not mine."

She sat back, resting her forearms on the chairs' arms. "My idea of a vacation retreat is not some place where thousands of other people retreat to as well. I like seclusion. Kurt likes to have people around who will listen to him."

"How long have you been married?"

"Almost four years. We met in Paris where I was studying watercolor painting and paying rent by working in a bistro." Smiling as though it were a good memory, she continued, "Kurt has a way of coming on to a woman that's damned near impossible to resist. He's not only physically imposing, he's intense, single-minded. I didn't have a chance." As she paused, her expression sobered and she cocked her head, a gesture that reminded me of the cardinal outside. "A woman, a piece of property, a business opportunity," she waved her glass in front of her, "it's all the same to Kurt. Throw enough money at it, and it's yours."

She unwrapped her legs and pushed herself up from the chair. "I promised to feed you, so let me get lunch started. That way you don't have to listen to my trials on an empty stomach."

She tossed a loaf of Italian bread into one of the ovens and then removed several plastic containers from the refrigerator. Declining my offer to help, she proceeded to create our lunch, placing generous portions of a vinegar-and-oil based pasta salad on top of large lettuce leaves. Then she scooped fresh raspberries into small bowls. It was a far cry from my usual smoked turkey and I welcomed the change.

While she worked, we talked of the weather, the wet spring. She arranged our plates on a large tray, added a plate of butter pats, each shaped like a tiny sheep, the bread, wine glasses and a bottle of California Chardonnay. She did let me carry it out to the porch.

The salad was good, with chunks of tuna and salami, Greek olives and peppers. Contrary to her earlier threat, she didn't bring up her situation while we ate. We talked about Chicago sports teams and then she asked me about my family.

"I'm the youngest of five brothers—hence the name. After me, Molly came along. Surprisingly well adjusted for one who was spoiled senseless by her brothers."

She chewed thoughtfully for a minute, swallowed and said, "Really? You don't impress me as coming from a large family. You seem like a very private person. People from large families don't usually have that option."

"I had to work at it."

"How many are still in the area?"

"Not a one." I took my glass of wine and leaned back in the chair. "My parents retired to Scottsdale. Roger—he's the oldest—is near Seattle. Michael is in Louisville, Ryan in Sacramento, Kevin in Dallas, and Molly is in Nova Scotia."

"What do they all do?"

I ticked off my siblings' occupations on one hand. "Claims adjuster, economics professor, career navy, carpenter, and mother-slash-freelance journalist." Before she could ask, I said, "I have eight nieces and four nephews ranging in ages from thirty-two to thirteen."

"That's quite a spread."

"Last time I saw my oldest nephew—Liam's an independent film producer in New York—he fixed me up with his girlfriend's sister." I shook my head. "Seemed strange."

"I'll bet you're their favorite uncle."

"They don't see me much so I'm a novelty." I paused.

"Actually, one of the many things in my life that I've regretted is not making more of an effort to get to know them. They're good people." I set the glass of wine on the table. The stuff was making me maudlin. "Back to you," I said. "Have you been to Kurt's office?"

A drop of wine had spilled on the table, and she wiped it up with her fingers and blotted them on the hem of her T-shirt. Then she poured the rest of the wine into my glass. "After the bank called, I went there."

"You got past Karen?"

"She wasn't there."

"What did you find?"

"A lot. Let me show you." After untangling her legs, she excused herself and left the room.

The cardinal had returned and I watched her peck at seeds until she lifted off from the feeder.

A few minutes later when Gina returned, she carried a pile of papers which she handed to me and pulled her chair around the table next to mine. "Every one of these letters is from a client of Kurt's, instructing him to withdraw their money from the investments he'd made. All dated within the last month. Most within the last two weeks. Some certified. Letter after letter. Some of these people are mad as hell. Apparently Kurt wasn't returning his calls."

Just a quick glance at the letters confirmed her statement. Kurt had some angry clients, not all of whom were above using colorful language to emphasize their point. In all, there were at least twenty letters. Add Albert and his friend to the lot, and that made twenty-two.

"What do you think?"

I shook my head. "I'm not a financial expert."

"He had a good reputation, which he earned. He made some nice profits for a lot of people."

I wondered if it might be a ponzi scheme. Pay off the earlier investors with the later ones and get the hell out of town before it catches up with you.

I tried to find a less negative scenario. "Maybe Kurt just made a few unwise investments on behalf of his clients."

She shook her head. "Kurt was a smart investor. He knew his business. When we were first married, we'd go to Europe two or three times a year. We'd spend some time together and then he'd leave me in Paris to bum around with my old friends while he'd go off and talk international investing."

"You never went to any of these meetings with him?"

"No." As she lowered her gaze, her smile turned a little sheepish. "I'm not proud of this." Lifting her hand in a defensive gesture, she added, "And, I assure you, I am self reliant . . ."

"But?" I prompted.

"When it comes to finance, I am ignorant. I don't think it's because I'm not smart enough or anything. I really don't. It's just that I find it profoundly dull. I realize that says more about me than it does about finance. I mean, I know that for many people, it's fascinating. But, I just can't see it. In the middle of a discussion on—" she waved her hand as though trying to snag an example from midair, "triple witching hour—I can feel my eyes and my brain just sort of glazing over. No matter how hard I try, I cannot stay connected."

I nodded. "That happens with me during that little speech the flight attendant gives. I don't know—something about oxygen and the nearest exit. I have this fear that we're going to be plummeting into the Atlantic and I'll be trying to remember what the hell it was she said about how my seat made a handy flotation device."

She smiled.

"Sorry," I said. "Getting back to Kurt—the smart investor."

It seemed to take her a few seconds to find her place, but then she said, "Kurt was one of those jocks who turned out to be worth more off the field than on it."

I didn't say anything.

"Oh, Lord." She leaned back in the chair. "Am I financially responsible for all this? I mean, if he stole money from all these people, of course that's not right. They should get restitution. But, I haven't got any money."

"You need to see a lawyer. I can't advise you on that." I wished I could. I wished I could tell her she wasn't responsible if her husband had run off with his clients' money. That's what we both were wondering. But all I could do was offer her my lawyer's name.

"God, I'd never have believed he hated me enough to do this."

"Okay," I said. "Let's assume he's alive. He stole his clients' money and then staged a disappearance so everyone would think he's dead. He had to do something with all that money. Did you find records of any other bank accounts? Out of state? Overseas?"

She shook her head. "Kurt isn't stupid. He'd have covered his tracks. I know him. At least I thought I did."

"If he is dead, then he was probably killed by someone who knew his plan—possibly was in on it with him—or someone who found out he'd embezzled their life savings. Any ideas?"

"The line forms at the right." She waved her hand over the pile of letters.

"Had he been acting strange lately? I know that's an obvious question, but it's one of those things you sometimes don't notice until after the fact."

She crossed one leg over the other. "Things between us had been strained for a while." Staring into her folded hands, she continued, "More than anything, anything in the world, Kurt wanted a child. I knew that was important when I married him, I just didn't think it was a requirement. As it turned out, it was." She looked up at me. "We'd been trying since we married. It just wasn't happening. I even had tests, which didn't show any problems. Kurt never had any tests, but he said he knew for a fact that it wasn't his problem."

"How'd he know that?"

"Male ego." She paused. "The doctor told me I was too uptight about it. He said I should just relax. Jerk." She snorted her disdain. "How was I supposed to relax? I felt like one of Henry the Eighth's wives. Deliver or else." She drew her finger across her throat and managed a grim smile. "Once he decided it wasn't going to happen, he started distancing himself from me. He got involved in this weird church group. He's always been religious, and sometimes tried out these alternative religions, but he never stuck with any of them for long. This one was different."

"How's that?"

"Well, for one thing, he stayed with it. And then he built this regimen into his life. He's always been physically fit, but he became obsessive. Working out a couple hours a day at the gym. He stopped eating meat, even fish. It got so it was hard to cook for him. I'm not saying there's anything wrong with being health conscious, but it came on so sudden and I know it was because of the church."

"This church—what was it called?"

"The Church of Everlasting Salvation."

"It wasn't an offshoot of some established religion?"

She shook her head. "It wouldn't have been. Kurt had already given those a try."

"A try? What was he looking for?"

"I wish I knew." From the way she spoke—thoughtful, almost reflective—I gathered she'd asked herself that before.

"Did you ever go to this church with him?"

"A few times. When Kurt first started going, he pushed me to come with him. I really tried to be interested. But the people were clannish. Not at all open to any belief but their own. I just didn't get it. I stopped going." She seemed to hesitate.

"What?"

"That was when he really started to distance himself. In the morning, before he'd talk to me or even kiss me, he'd drop down on his knees and pray for twenty minutes or so." She shook her head as though she were trying to understand. "Religion isn't supposed to make you turn away from the people you love, is it? As things got worse, I really tried to meet him halfway, you know. I offered to go back to church with him. He wouldn't let me. He didn't want me there anymore."

"Did he say why?"

She blinked a couple times. "He never said, but I had the feeling he didn't think I was worthy."

Abruptly, she stood and walked over to the screened windows. Beyond her, in the yard, a sparrow drank from the birdbath. I wouldn't have known Gina was crying; she made no sound. But as she bowed her head her shoulders moved up and down in the uneven rhythm of sobs. I set my glass on the table and went over to her.

She used her thumb to swipe at the tears running down her cheeks, then shook her head and waved me away. "I'm sorry," she said. "I don't mind that he's gone. I just didn't think this was how he'd do it."

I put my hand on her shoulder and after a couple seconds, she slumped into me. I held her while she cried, careful not to cross the line between friendly support and an embrace—one arm as opposed to two. Her head fit under my chin and I could feel her ragged breathing. I also noticed that her hair smelled like clover and her arm was slightly damp.

After a minute or so, she drew back slightly. "God, I'm all out of tears." I really thought that was going to be it. Even though my majority wanted more, my head was on tight enough to nix that notion. But then she tilted her chin up, looking into my eyes for strength or something I could give her. I kissed her forehead, thinking that would defuse the moment.

"I'm sorry . . ." I began, not sure how to finish.

"Don't be." Closing her fists on my collar, she pulled my mouth down to meet hers.

She was small-boned and seemed to meld into my embrace. I wasn't sure where the line was, but I was definitely crossing it.

Then she was unbuttoning my shirt. Her hands felt like a small, edgy animal on my chest.

"Gina," I said, "I don't know if this is a good idea."

"Oh God," she gasped, drawing away. She covered her mouth with her hands. "What am I doing? I'm sorry."

"Don't be."

"I don't know . . . Jesus. What's wrong with me? It just seemed . . ."

"You're upset. Look, I'd better go."

"Yes. Yes. I guess so."

Just as she put her hand on my arm, the doorbell rang—a three-note chime that echoed through the house.

"Shit," she said. "Who the hell is that?" She used the edge of her shirt to wipe her face, then raked her fingers through her hair, pushing it back. Though her hair looked less ruffled, it drew attention to her flushed face and reddened eyes.

"Do I look presentable?"

"Incredibly," I said.

That got a small smile out of her. "I hope to God this is someone I can tell to get lost."

The bell rang again and she said, "Maybe I won't answer it."

"I think you'd better."

"You're right. Wait here."

Where was I going? Good question. I decided the interruption was probably a godsend. Although the situation had been defused, I couldn't deny the fact that this woman woke up parts of me I'd been anesthetizing for a while.

I couldn't hear what was going on, so I didn't realize the police had arrived until I saw the guy in a blue uniform Gina led out to the porch. He was average height with a bit of a gut and a ruddy complexion, made ruddier by the thick, red hair surrounding it. A rather prominent chin seemed to lead him into the room.

"Quint, this is Officer Hinkley with the New Berne police. This is Quint McCauley. He's a . . . friend."

When we shook hands, Hinkley gave me the once over—his gaze lingering as it dropped below my neck. When he looked up at me again, I saw a flicker of something—suspicion?—as he narrowed his eyes. "Quint McCauley is it?"

"That's right."

That was when I realized I'd forgotten about the two buttons Gina's deft little fingers had unfastened. Rather than tending to them, I figured maybe if I ignored them, this guy might think it was a personal preference.

"Officer Hinkley was just telling me it looks as though that blood in the cottage was Kurt's blood type. They're doing more tests." She slipped the fingers of her right hand under her glasses and rubbed her eye.

"How much blood was there?" I asked Hinkley.

"Looks like he lost at least a couple pints," Hinkley said, then pointed his jaw at me. "You know Mr. Wicklow?"

"Did some work for him."

"What kind of work?"

"Surveillance. I'm a private detective."

"What kind of surveillance?"

"It involved a personal injury lawsuit."

Not sure whether my presence would be a help or a hindrance, I decided to let Gina decide. I turned to her. "You want me to stay?"

She shook her head. "That's all right. You've been a help already. Thanks so much."

"I'll find my way out," I said. I've always thought that phrase made the act of negotiating the interior of a house sound like you were hacking your way out of the jungle, but it was a convenient phrase for one in a hurry to get the hell out of a place.

"I'll call you," Gina said as I left the room.

I had the feeling from the look Hinkley gave me, that he'd be in touch as well.

Chapter 11

"Ed's really upset," Elaine said as she leaned on a glass display case, arms folded and head bowed. Summer weekends were usually busy for Foxport's merchants, but this summer's heat had taken its toll, thinning out the tourist population. Who wanted to dash from shop to shop in the blistering heat when there were climate-controlled malls to satisfy those urges? At Elaine's urging, Louise had gone home. Elaine, on the other hand, was trying to avoid going home. Not only did she miss her cat, but her remaining roommate was being less communicative than usual.

"I can't talk to him. He, you know, closes himself off. Won't let me near—emotionally." She hooked a lock of hair behind her ear. The afternoon sun caught her in a patch of light, sprinkling gold in the red of her hair. The spark of color was in sharp contrast to her face which looked drawn and pale.

"And that surprises you?"

Frowning, she gave it a moment. "No." She looked up at me. "But it disappoints me. I thought we'd made some progress."

"This is a tough test," I offered. "He might need some time to work it out on his own." When she didn't respond, I added, "Sounds like he and Brewster were pretty good friends."

"That's the thing. He hadn't seen him in years. Never

even mentioned him to me."

"But, he is an old friend."

"I guess." She shrugged.

From the way she clasped her hands under her chin and leveled her gaze at me, I knew she was about to ask another favor. "I wondered if you could talk to him."

"Me?" I couldn't have been more shocked if she suggested I negotiate an Arab/Israeli settlement. "You think I can make him feel better?"

"No," she said quickly. "But I do think he may talk to you about it. There's more to this than losing a friend. Something else is bothering him." She paused. "The night before last, Ed and Brewster were up late talking. They weren't laughing either. Serious tones. I think Ed was either angry or upset. Maybe both. When he came to bed I asked him what was going on. He said it was nothing; they were just reminiscing about college." She shook her head, rejecting his response. "I never went to college, so I'm no authority, but don't you think two guys talking about the good old days should be laughing some?"

I tried to picture Ed and Brewster having a serious exchange regarding the courses they flunked and the women they scored with. "You may be right. But no one can force him to talk."

"I know. But, Ed's old fashioned in some ways. He tries to protect me."

"He should know you better." I'd always admired Elaine's strength and I felt sorry for Ed if he hadn't recognized it.

Acknowledging the compliment with a wan smile, she pulled her hair over one shoulder and gathered it in her hand. "I know you two don't see eye to eye on a lot of things, but he does respect you, you know."

I was reminded of Brewster's words last night about his respect for Ed. Wasn't that nice? We all respected each other so goddamned much and now one of us was dead. "I can't promise anything."

"I know. Thanks."

"When did he hear about Brewster's death?"

"Late this morning when he came back from taking Dee to stay with his folks up in Crystal Lake." She paused. "He came home depressed. Sometimes it's hard for him to be with the kids. I mean, he loves the time he's got with them, but it's hard for him to leave them. Even with his folks." She wiped at a smudge on the glass case, making it worse. "You know, that surprised me about Ed. I think it surprised him, too. Those kids mean everything to him. Just about. Maybe it's got to do with losing so much. What you've got left becomes precious."

While searching for something profound to say regarding Ed, I must have looked as perplexed as I felt because Elaine patted my hand. "That's all right. You don't have to say anything."

"Thank you."

Then she gave me kind of an odd look and said, "I heard you had a few beers with Brewster last night."

"Ran into him up at the Tattersall. Who told you?"

"Jeff was in earlier. Wanted to know if there was any way I could get him a quote from Ed."

"Did you ask him if he thought the temperature might drop below freezing in the next twenty-four hours?" As deserving as Jeff Barlowe might be of respect, Ed wasn't going to cut him any. He rated reporters right up there with ambulance-chasing lawyers.

"I said something to that effect."

"Actually, I left Jeff with Brewster. Did he say how long Brewster stayed?"

"Until around ten. Brewster said he was going back to the Foxhole."

She opened the back of the glass case and rearranged a necklace chain. "Jeff said that Brewster seemed to be feeling no pain when he left."

I thought she was going somewhere with this but I wasn't used to evasive tactics from Elaine. Finally, she closed and locked the case and, looking up at me, said, "You know, he was funny. Entertaining. Easy going. Seemed like the nicest guy in the world. But, sometimes it was like he'd forget himself and he'd get this really cold look in his eyes."

I'd noticed that too, but had written it off to the early stages of intoxication. Trying to keep a room in focus can raise hell with your sense of humor.

"I don't know," she continued, "my opinion of him may be influenced by his occupation."

"I assume you mean the bounty hunter part."

"Isn't that something?"

"Was he here on business?"

She waved her hands in a "Who knows?" gesture. "Said he was taking some time off. Don't know if I believe him." She paused. "I know Ed is under a lot of stress right now. He's been looking for a job and he's got some possibilities but nothing definite." She hesitated, then continued as though giving voice to a dire thought for the first time. "I wonder if Brewster was trying to talk Ed into going into business with him."

"Ed Carver as a bounty hunter? No way." I shook my head. "Ed's Mr. Law and Order. He needs rules. Those guys don't have any. No. I can't see it."

"You're right," she sighed, obviously relieved. "I guess it's a moot point anyway. He's just so closed off right now. There's this big wall and I just can't get past it."

"And you think I can?"

"It's worth a try, isn't it?"

My visit with Ed Carver went just about as well as I expected it would. He greeted me at the door with a scowl and a hearty, "What do you want?"

"Just wanted to say I'm sorry to hear about Brewster." I paused, stumbling. "Actually, I was at the scene. So I didn't exactly hear about it."

His eyebrows drew together in a question. "You were there?"

I nodded. "I was out running. Another guy found his body, but I happened along right after that."

After a second, he asked, "Did it look like he hit his head on something? Fell in?"

He sounded almost hopeful; I hated to ruin it. "I don't know. It looked more like he'd been hit with something." Carver lowered his gaze to the floor. "I guess an autopsy will have to verify that." Then I added, "But, even if he did hit his head, how'd he manage to get himself burned?"

Carver's head shot up so fast, I thought he'd give himself whiplash. "Burned?"

I nodded, slowly. "That's what it looked like. I noticed it on one arm. The skin was charred, peeling."

His eyes narrowed as he looked past me, as though reading something over my shoulder.

"Why?" I asked.

After a long moment, he said, "Nothing. Just weird." Rubbing the back of his neck, he turned away and walked into the living room. I closed the door behind me and followed him.

While he stared out the window, hands in his pockets, I didn't think he was even aware of my presence. I waited. Initially, Elaine's idea of my talking to Ed had seemed ludicrous.

I couldn't understand her reasoning. But the more I thought about it, the more I realized it was probably an effort on her part to get us to develop some rapport. Probably a lost cause, but Elaine tended to be an optimist and sometimes they deserved extra effort.

When he finally spoke, I wasn't sure he was addressing me or the space between us. "Hard to believe it happens so fast. One second you're there, being yourself, going about the business of living, the next—bang—you're gone. Empty."

Ed wasn't prone to the philosophical. I was beginning to understand Elaine's concern.

"Elaine said you were bothered about something."

As he turned toward me, I saw his anger bubbling to the surface. "She told you to come?"

"No." I had to cover for her. "I was wondering if you could tell me why Brewster went up to New Berne to see Kurt Wicklow."

He stared at me without answering.

"I saw him pull out of the road to Wicklow's place."

"What were you doing up there?"

"Wicklow owed me money," I told him. "Why was Brewster there?"

Carver shook his head. "I don't know."

I don't believe you, I thought. But I didn't challenge him because that was when I noticed the fifth of Dewar's and an empty glass on the coffee table. Next to it was a folded newspaper which had a circle around what appeared to be a classified ad. I assumed it had something to do with Carver's job search. That kind of pressure on top of everything else can make booze an attractive option. The thing was, Carver didn't drink. I'd never seen him imbibe so much as a beer. He wasn't vocal about it. In fact, he kept the stuff. But his drink of preference was definitely coffee. And while I hadn't smelled any liquor on his breath, he'd surely been thinking about it.

"Any luck with the job search?"

He glanced at the paper on the table for a second before answering. "Nah. Nothing."

"Brewster told me he was a bounty hunter."

"Brewster was crazy that way."

"Not something you're thinking about going into?" I tried to keep my delivery light.

"Are you kidding? I might as well go into your line of work." He almost laughed. "Yeah, right."

I was more relieved than insulted.

"Well," I said, feeling awkward, like there was something I still needed to say but couldn't think of it, "I'd better go."

"Good idea."

The way his stubbornness showed when his jaw hardened reminded me of what I wanted to say. "You know, I'm the last person who thought I'd be giving advice where Elaine's concerned. And I don't guess you're real open to it. But just let me say this. Don't underestimate her. She's a strong person. Real strong. And if you don't let her be that for you, then not only are you missing out, but you're liable to lose her to someone who will let her be strong."

I left before he had a chance to tell me to go to hell.

Frustrated, I drove around for a while. I got to thinking I should tell both the New Berne and the Foxport cops that I saw Brewster leaving Wicklow's place yesterday. Of course, that begged the question: "What the hell took you so long?"

But I had a few questions of my own. Brewster didn't like Ellie Carver. He spent part of our talk last night saying as much. I wondered what Ellie's opinion of Brewster was. From past experience, I knew a good way to get people to open up was to tell them what someone else had said about them. Ellie might be interested to learn that Brewster had tried to visit Wicklow. Then I'd go to the cops. I'd waited this long; an hour more wouldn't make much difference.

It was almost four-thirty when I got to Ellie's house. I didn't know what hours she worked at the hospital, and was relieved to see her Skyhawk parked in the drive. I did wonder who owned the Grand Prix parked behind it.

As I walked up to the porch, a tall, gangly woman dressed in a white tunic and pants peered at me through the screen. If she wasn't a nurse, she was a wannabe. She looked uncertain as she clung to the strap of a black purse which hung from her shoulder. I opened the porch door and she backed up a foot.

I stopped. "You a friend of Ellie's?"

"I work with her." She glanced at her watch, an oversized model I could almost read from where I stood. "She was supposed to be at work an hour and a half ago. We called a couple times. Got a little worried."

"Sure." I introduced myself. "I'm a friend of the family."

She nodded, expectant. Then, "Oh. I'm Linda O'Brian." Her smile deepened the lines around her mouth. She had a round face and large eyes. Her gray-framed glasses were tinted.

"Did you check out in back?" I asked.

"No. I just got here." She glanced over her shoulder at the closed door.

"I'll look back there," I offered. "Maybe she fell asleep or something."

"Good idea." Some of the tenseness left her shoulders.

I had the feeling she was relieved to get rid of me for a minute or two so she could decide whether she had to worry about me or not.

The yard was shaggy with grass and weeds. A half-hearted

attempt at a small garden had died beneath the summer's brutal heat. A lounge chair was spread open in the middle of the yard and a glass sat on a yellow plastic table beside it. The glass was half empty (or half full, depending on your take on life), warm, and smelled like watered-down gin. A curl of lime floated on the surface like a dead guppy.

The back door was locked, and I wondered what made Ellie forget about her drink. That seemed out of character. I knocked and waited. Of course, Ellie might have walked to a neighbor's, but with her being late for work, that didn't make much sense. Unless there'd been an emergency. I knocked again, and called her name. No response. Curtains prevented me from seeing inside.

When I returned to the front porch, Linda was still there, apparently reconciled to my presence. I told her what I'd found.

She pressed her face up to the glass pane on the front door, cupping her hands on either side to block the glare. "I can't see anything." She sounded frustrated. "I just wonder if she's had an accident. She's never late for work."

The front door had four small windowpanes creating one large rectangle; once broken, you had easy access to the lock—the kind of door that cops tell you to avoid. Shame on you, Ed.

Linda seemed to be waiting for my call on the situation.

"Ellie?" I pounded on the door.

"Should we call the police?"

I put my ear to the door. "Did you hear something?" I whispered, drawing back.

She leaned into the door, giving me a quizzical look. "No."

"I thought I heard someone moaning."

"No," she said slowly, then as she looked up at me, I saw

the light go on. "Wait a minute. Maybe I do. Yes, I think I do."

"Me too."

I found a serviceable rock in the front yard under the bushes—about three inches in diameter—and wrapped it in my handkerchief. Linda stood back as I swung the parcel against the lower right pane. It made a tinkling sound as it shattered. I picked the shards out of the frame, carefully reached in and unlocked the door.

The house felt cool as we stood in the small foyer, our eyes adjusting to the dim light. "Ellie?" Nothing. Linda called her name with the same result. We moved down the narrow hall toward the living room. A sweet, floral smell hung in the air, but didn't overpower. The light in the powder room was on and the door partially shut. Linda pushed it open and peered in, looking around. Then she shook her head and we kept walking in the direction of the living room. When I passed under the arch, I saw Ellie. She lay sprawled across the braided rug, her head resting on the hearth. I moved around her and saw a small pool of blood had collected beneath her forehead. Her open eyes stared into the palm of her right hand as though reading something written there.

"Oh, my God." In what seemed an instinctive reaction, Linda tossed her purse from her shoulder, dropped to her knees beside Ellie and checked for a pulse, first at her wrist and then at her throat. Then she allowed herself to go slack. "Oh, God, Ellie," she murmured, her head bowed, hand to her mouth.

Ellie wore the tunic and bathing suit I'd seen her in the day before. I glanced around the room and saw a suitcase, open on the couch, which appeared to be filled with folded clothing.

Looking somewhat dazed and distracted, Linda reached

for a framed photo that lay next to Ellie. It was the homecoming picture, its frame cracked and glass shattered.

"Don't touch that," I said.

She looked up, confused at first, then said, "Oh, God. Of course." She jerked her hand back as though it had been shocked.

I went out to my car and dialed 911 from my cell phone. This time I'd leave my name.

Chapter 12

Although Lieutenant Abigail MacKenna held no personal grudge against me the way Carver had, she wasn't any more inclined to cut me slack. And right now she was real curious about my behavior of late.

"Tell me," she crossed her arms over her chest as she leaned back in the chair, "why didn't you give the New Berne police your name?"

I'd never met MacKenna before. She had a pretty good reputation, having battled her way up through the ranks. I knew that Carver thought a lot of her. She was probably in her mid-thirties with shoulder-length brown hair and a sharp, angular face. Her eyes really threw me. They were narrow and the irises a pale shade of green. The effect was unsettling.

We were sitting in the "soft" interrogation room—the one with the comfortable chairs, the pale yellow walls and the coffee machine—and I had just explained the work I'd done for Ellie.

"I wanted to remain anonymous out of respect for my client's privacy."

"I see. But now that she's dead you don't feel you need to respect her privacy anymore?"

"Well, I'd like to help you find whoever did this to her." I paused. "If something was done to her."

"She told you that she and Wicklow were having an affair."

I nodded. "That's what she said."

"But you didn't offer to help in his disappearance."

"I called it in. Didn't make much difference who I was."

"You found blood in one of the rooms at the house, but you didn't think it worth mentioning to the police that you saw someone leaving the area?"

"Well, for one thing, the blood was dry. It had been there a while. And at the time I didn't know who the truck belonged to." I explained my meeting Brewster Plunkett at the Tattersall, how I saw his license plate and put two and two together.

"We'll see what the New Berne police have to say." She consulted a note pad. "A Deputy Hinkley is on his way."

I couldn't wait.

"Have you two met?"

"We have." I shifted in my chair. "At Gina Wicklow's house."

Her eyebrows pulled together, darkening her features. "Kurt Wicklow's wife?"

"That's right." While it seemed pointless to deny, it also seemed pretty obvious to me that for a guy who had done nothing wrong, I was in pretty deep. "A, um, check she'd given me for some work I'd done for her husband had bounced."

"And that required a house call on your part?"

"Well," I hesitated, "the check was for twenty-five hundred dollars."

"I see," she said, though it was clear to both of us that she didn't. "Do you always make house calls to collect your debts?"

"I sometimes do." I figured the less said, the better. She'd get an earful from Hinkley.

Resting her arms on the table, she said, "So, when you went up to New Berne, did you break into Wicklow's house as well as Ellie Carver's place?"

I'd have been deaf to miss the sarcasm. "His door was open." Linda O'Brian, bless her, had been adamant in backing up my story—we'd heard a moan from inside and breaking in seemed our only option. "I am a nurse," she'd told the first officer on the scene, "I thought someone was hurt." Who could argue? When MacKenna wondered what had caused the noise, since it hadn't been Ellie, Linda suggested the wind. I'd never have gotten away with it, but Linda, being a member of a respected profession not to mention one of Foxport's busiest volunteers, pulled it off.

At this point, the cause of Ellie Carver's death was under investigation. It had not been ruled a murder or an accident. They'd have to perform an autopsy and blood tests. People who have consumed too much gin have been known to misstep.

To me, the fact that she'd left her drink outside, suggested she'd been interrupted, but I wasn't asked for my opinion, and I didn't offer it. The locked back door seemed puzzling as well. Maybe it was always kept locked.

MacKenna leaned against the table separating us, resting her arms on its surface. Her eyes narrowed so it looked like she was squinting. But I could still see shards of green through the slits. "Here's the situation. I've got two, possibly three victims within twenty-four hours. One murder and the other a possible—we'll treat it as a homicide until we know better. And then one of Foxport's leading citizens is missing."

I waited.

"I only accept coincidences when all other possibilities have been exhausted. And even then I don't like them." She placed one hand on the table, spreading out her long, narrow fingers. "Now, I've got Brewster Plunkett here." She put her other hand down next to it. "And Ellie Carver here." Another pause. "And Kurt Wicklow somewhere in the middle. I'm looking for connections." She clasped her hands together and smiled at me. "And you connect to all three."

"I've told you everything I know."

"I'm sure you have." From the withering look she nailed me with, I guessed that she was not being sincere.

When I left the interrogation room, Elaine was sitting on a couch pushed up against a wall of a narrow hallway near the concourse. She stood when she saw me.

"Where's Ed?" I asked.

She nodded toward another hall which contained the "hard" interrogation room—the one with the cement walls, the table screwed to the floor and the chairs attached to the table. There was no coffee machine.

While searching for some words of encouragement, I heard a voice behind me. "You must be Elaine Kluszewski."

Elaine started, then looked over my shoulder.

I'd already recognized MacKenna's voice by the time I heard her introduce herself to Elaine.

"Ed's mentioned you," she said to Elaine, smiling as she shook her hand.

Elaine returned the smile, though it looked strained. "He's mentioned you too."

"You two know each other?" She glanced at me.

"Yeah," Elaine said. "We go back a long way."

MacKenna made a "go figure" gesture which involved a small shrug and a twist of her mouth.

Just then a uniformed cop poked his head around the corner. "Lieutenant?"

MacKenna excused herself and after a few words with the cop, followed him down the hall.

"I can't believe this is happening," Elaine said, dropping

down onto the couch. I sat next to her. "First Brewster and now Ellie." She looked up at me. "What were you doing at her house?"

"I'd done some work for her."

From the tight little lines around her mouth, I thought she was about to ask for the entire story. But she shook her head as though making an effort to dismiss it for now. "You know what I think?" she said. "I think she got drunk and fell."

"That's possible."

"Did it look like she'd been, you know, assaulted?"

I shook my head. "I couldn't tell."

Nodding as though that confirmed it for her. "That's probably it then. She drank a lot, you know." Her eyes begged me to agree with her.

"I know." Then I said, "We'll just have to wait for the test results."

"I think she fell." I know what wishful thinking sounds like when I hear it.

"How's Ed handling all this?"

"He called me at the shop. I don't know. I guess he's okay. It's getting so it's hard to tell anymore." She unzipped her nylon purse and started digging through it.

"How are you doing?"

"Me? I'm fine. You know me. Always fine." She pulled out a tin of aspirin, stared at it for a moment, then dropped it back into her purse and zipped it up.

"There's something else, isn't there?"

"In less than ten hours Ed's friend has been murdered and his ex-wife . . . almost ex-wife . . . has died. Maybe killed. Probably an accident though," she added. "Do I need something else to be upset?"

"I guess not." I didn't believe her. Elaine's strength is most apparent in the face of other people's misfortunes. She holds them together. It's like she disconnects herself emotionally from the situation so she's got all her strength to offer. She may fall apart later, but seldom at the time.

I stayed with Elaine while the cops talked to Ed for almost two hours. At one point I suggested I run out and get us a couple burgers, but she said she couldn't eat. I could, but figured I'd wait. Now and then I'd sneak a glance at Elaine. She seemed pale and there were dark smudges under her eyes I didn't remember seeing earlier that day.

When he finally emerged from the narrow hall, Ed looked drained. If he was bothered by my sitting with Elaine, he didn't show it. She stood and he smiled. That's when I figured things were bad. With Ed Carver, a smile is either a sign that he is deliriously happy or a cover for a bad situation.

"It's okay." He wrapped his arms around her and she pressed into him, burying her face in his shoul- der.

He thanked me for staying with her and then walked her out of the building, leaving me standing there.

"McCauley?"

I turned and saw Abigail MacKenna. I figured she must have been in on Ed's interview. Now she seemed mildly curious as she stood there watching me, arms folded across her chest, chin cocked to one side. I wondered how long I'd been staring at the space Ed and Elaine had occupied. When I didn't answer, she took a step closer. "Are you all right?"

I shook my head, trying to activate my brain. "Yeah," I mumbled. "Just forgot where I was for a second."

"Well, Officer Hinkley is here." She smiled. "I'd be happy to help you find your way to him."

"Thanks."

It was almost ten thirty when I pulled into the long driveway leading to Louise's house and my apartment. I had called

Louise from the police station, explained the situation and asked her to let Peanuts out. He'd never have lasted.

I'd stopped at MacDonald's and bought a burger and fries. I didn't have much in the house to eat and didn't feel like talking to anyone other than the kid on the other end of the box.

Damn. Someone was parked in my spot next to Louise's car. Usually when Louise had company, he parked behind her so we weren't playing musical cars all night. But then, as I pulled in and my car's headlights shed some light on the scene, I saw someone sitting on the driver's side of the convertible, a Ferrari. I turned off my car and climbed out, taking my bag of food and drink with me.

The three-quarter moon was hazy as its light hit the face turned up toward me.

"I'm in your space, aren't I?" Gina said.

"That's okay." Definitely okay.

"Hop in." She reached across the seat and opened the passenger door.

When I hesitated, she said, "You're not going to eat standing up, are you?"

"Nice car," I said. "Spider?"

"Yes."

I admired it as I came around to the passenger side. "What's one of these things like to drive?"

She flicked her nails against the keys hanging in the ignition. "Want to take it for a spin?"

"Better not," I said.

"Then climb in and help me enjoy it before it's repossessed." Then she added, "Though, to be honest, I won't miss it all that much."

I settled into the leather seat. "You're not the sports car type?" I asked, placing my Coke on the floor.

"I'm not the car type," she said. "I don't really like to drive and this thing is so noisy I can barely hear myself think." Then she added with a smile, "Though I do like the looks I get."

"I can imagine."

She shifted in the seat, drawing one leg up under her so she faced me. "You've had a long day, haven't you?"

Her pale T-shirt seemed to glow under the moon's light. A long chain dangled between her breasts.

"How did you know?" I unwrapped the hamburger and took a bite.

"Word travels. Actually, Officer Hinkley—you know, the one from New Berne—he called me."

I nodded, still chewing, and offered her the box of fries. She pulled one out but didn't eat it. I washed the bite down with a swallow of Coke and said, "What did he tell you?"

"He told me you'd been up to New Berne. In fact, you're the one who made that anonymous phone call."

Might have known that little deception would come back to bite me on the ass any number of times. "Guilty."

She shook her head. "I'm not doing any accusing. I just want to understand."

When I hesitated, she said, "Look, I'm not surprised to learn that Kurt wasn't the faithful type. It doesn't even bother me all that much. Any semblance of a marriage has been absent for a long time. I just want to know what was going on."

"I'm not sure how much I can tell you. I really don't know that much. Yes, Ellie Carver asked me to see if Kurt was up at the place by the lake. She was supposed to see him a couple nights earlier but he never showed. I went up there, found the room with the blood and called the police. That's all I know."

She stared out the window toward the house for a minute.

Finally, she ate the french fry and said, "What about that man whose body they found in the river this morning?"

"Brewster Plunkett. He was the guy I saw drive out of the road to Kurt's place. He said you told him where to find Kurt."

She shook her head. "Never talked to him."

"I'm not surprised. I don't know what his business with Kurt was. Claimed they were old college buddies." Then I said, "Though they did go to school together, they didn't seem the type to stay in touch."

"Why do you say that?"

"Brewster was a little rough around the edges."

She took another fry. "Were you close to Ellie Carver?"

"Not really. We had some history together."

She leaned back into the leather seat and wrapped her hand around the gearshift. "I'm sorry," she said.

"Why?"

"I'm prying."

Instead of agreeing with her, I listened to the night sounds—the chirping crickets and the cars driving by on 35—and let her work out where this conversation was going.

Finally, she said, "I talked to a lawyer. It doesn't look promising." She snorted softly. "All I want are some answers. Why? I mean, what did I ever do to Kurt? If he stole from his investors, he did that because he's greedy. But he used to love me." She turned toward me. "Would you do this to someone you used to love? Leave her without a way to pay next month's bills?" Then she shook her head and looked away. "Sorry. You wouldn't do this. Period. Most people wouldn't."

"What did the lawyer tell you?"

"I may have to file for bankruptcy. Start over. I can do it. It's strange. In Paris I lived in a nasty little flat, sometimes ate only one meal a day and that was at the place where I worked. I painted, I had my friends, I was happy. Then along comes Kurt who offers me—pushes on me—all this security, all this stability. Up until then I never thought I needed it. Now I don't know if I can live like I used to. I don't know. He took my independence."

"Maybe he just threw some dirt over it."

I tossed my half-eaten food in the bag; how could I eat a Happy Meal while this woman was bleeding all over her car? "I guess after a certain age you start to think about security, stability. Bare walls and frozen din- ners just don't cut it any-more. It's got nothing to do with losing your independence. It's about finding something."

"What?"

"Permanence—or something like it. Mortality's staring you in the face and you start to sweat."

She regarded me for a moment. "Have you found it yet?"

"I wouldn't know where to start." Then I said, "You've got your painting."

"That's right. I do."

"And you can forget that money Kurt owed me." Easy for me to say. I wasn't going to see it anyway; might as well make myself look like a good guy.

She reached over and squeezed my hand. "You're a nice man, Quint McCauley."

"I'm a prince."

"Were you ever married?"

"Once. Years ago."

"What happened?"

"She wanted more."

"I'll bet she's kicking herself now."

"Well, if she is, she's doing it in the Kenilworth mansion she shares with her corporate lawyer husband and two kids."

I paused. "Tennis courts."

Her mouth twisted into a wry smile. "You've been keeping track of her?"

"Not intentionally. Well-meaning friends and family feel the need to keep me informed."

"That's tough."

"Could be worse."

Our eyes locked and she said, "Could I have a sip?"

"Sure." I handed her my Coke.

She looked into the lidless cup, the ice mostly melted.

"Straws are for sissies," I said.

Smiling, she took a drink then held onto the cup as she stared up at the sky. Her skin seemed translucent. I studied her profile: her mouth, sharp chin and small, bent nose.

"You've got a great nose." It slipped out.

She turned toward me, eyebrows raised. "My hawk nose?"

"More like a kestrel."

She laughed. "I like that." Settling back against the door, she drew her legs up from under the steering wheel. Her feet were bare. She stretched out her legs, tucking her feet under my thigh, and wiggled her toes. "When I was sixteen, my mother offered to pay to have it straightened."

"What stopped you?"

One side of her mouth curved up. "I knew it bothered her more than it did me. What more could a sixteen-year-old ask?"

"I'm glad you didn't have it straightened."

"Me too." She took another drink and handed me the cup.

"I've been sitting here a while," she said. "May I use your bathroom?"

"Sure."

Unless I'd seriously misread the signals here, this was not

a simple request for a way station. I looked up into the night sky and saw a cloud bearing down on the moon. “You’d better put the top up. It’s supposed to rain tonight.”

“Good idea,” she said.

Chapter 13

The storm hit in the early hours of the morning. As a flash of lightning illuminated the room, I drank in the sight of Gina straddling me, her back arched and her small breasts raised toward the ceiling.

The air conditioning was off and the window beside my bed open. Occasionally, a gust of windswept rain cooled our sweat-drenched bodies.

Two thunderstorms passed through Foxport that night and we answered each of them.

It was about seven-thirty when I untangled myself from Gina and left her asleep under the sheet. After a glass of orange juice, I went for a short run with Peanuts. The only signs that there had been a break in the heat were the branches on the ground, attesting to the severity of last night's storms.

The prospect of another day of unremitting heat wasn't intolerable. Things seemed possible now.

When we got back to the apartment, Gina was standing in the kitchen peeling a coffee filter off the stack. She wore the Evergreen State College T-shirt a nephew had given me. Her legs looked tan and lean. Peanuts trotted up to her, skirting McGee who lay in the middle of the living room floor, his legs folded beneath him so he resembled a muff with a head.

"You're a sweet-faced creature, aren't you?" She knelt to greet Peanuts. He let her pet him before moving on to his water dish.

I had picked up one of the two *Chicago Tribune*s from Louise's doorstep and now I tossed it on the kitchen counter next to the disassembled coffeepot.

"Coffee and a fat newspaper on a Sunday morning. It doesn't get much better." I watched her dump a few scoops into the filter, waiting for our first morning-after-the-night-before eye contact. I didn't want to read any regret there. She looked up at me and smiled. Relieved and a little elated, I kissed her. Her response seemed reserved, but I might have been expecting too much. The fact that I was dripping with sweat probably figured in there.

Drawing away, she said, "I was trying to put together something to eat. But your refrigerator is a little on the Spartan side." Then she added, "Unless, of course, we want frozen dinners for brunch."

Determined not to lose my stride, I confronted the contents of the refrigerator. Behind me, I could hear her fitting the filter into the coffee maker.

"How long have those cartons of Chinese food been in there?" she asked.

I shook my head. "Can't remember. Scared to look."

"Here's something."

I turned and she was pulling a box out of a cupboard next to the stove.

"Pancake mix." She checked the ingredients on the back of the box. "I saw an egg in there. Is it as old as the leftovers?"

"Let's pretend it's not." I took it out and handed it to her along with the milk and butter.

She'd found a bowl and a measuring cup and was already mixing it up. Didn't look like my expertise was required.

"Guess I'll take a quick shower."

"Good idea." She cracked the egg over the batter.

By the time I'd showered, shaved and thrown on a pair of

old jeans and a T-shirt, Gina had breakfast ready.

I had to clear all the clutter off the small kitchen table, which I never use for the purpose of eating, preferring the coffee table in the living room and the company of the television to my own.

Once we'd settled into eating and I had congratulated Gina on her success, she set her fork down, wiped her mouth with a paper towel and said, "Thank you for last night."

That was kind of like thanking the guy who was drowning for letting you pull him out of rapids. I had the feeling last night was Gina's way of lashing out at Kurt, but refused to let that spoil the moment.

She dabbed her finger on the pat of butter melting on the remains of a pancake and licked it. "Mm. Sweet butter."

"I use it only on Sundays."

"What else do you do only on Sundays?"

"The crossword puzzle."

"What else?"

"Want to stick around and find out?"

"I don't know." She studied me over the edge of her coffee mug. When she set it on the table, she kept both hands wrapped around it. "Maybe that's not such a good idea."

I wanted her to give me one reason why it wasn't. At the same time at least a dozen crowded into my head on their own. Dead or alive, Kurt was at the top of the list. I nodded.

"When did Officer Hinkley talk to you?" she asked.

"Yesterday. After the Foxport police were done with me, New Berne got its chance."

"Did he tell you they found a bullet in one of Kurt's bookshelves?"

"No. Hinkley wasn't offering much information, just looking for it." Then I asked, "Do they have a gun to go with it?"

She shook her head. "It's the same caliber Kurt used in his gun, but they haven't found that yet."

"Anything else?"

"They also found his pen in the ground cover under the window." She paused. "It was one I gave him."

"Did he tell you about the Bible in Kurt's office. It was inscribed from Karen."

Gina's eyes narrowed and she looked away from me, focusing at something over my right shoulder. I waited a moment, but she didn't respond.

"The other day you mentioned Kurt suddenly getting into this new religion. Was that Karen's church?"

Slowly turning back to me, she said, "It was."

"That check you gave me. It had a signature stamp on it, didn't it?"

"So?"

"Karen's authorized to use it."

Sipping her coffee, she seemed to be working something out in her head. Finally, she set the mug down and said, "You don't think she took the money out of the account, do you?"

"Why not? Especially if she's got reason to believe Kurt isn't coming back."

"You think she killed him?"

"Not necessarily. But she might be an accomplice."

"Did you tell Hinkley about her?"

"I mentioned the Bible." I paused. "But maybe someone should tell him they were close."

Then she leaned forward and perched her chin on her fist. "What did Hinkley ask you?"

"Among other things, my shoe size."

She nodded as though that made sense. "They found a partial print outside Kurt's office window."

"So he said."

"What about the Foxport police? What did they ask?"

"After grilling me on finding Ellie's body, they asked where I was late yesterday morning, early afternoon."

She nodded, as though she'd anticipated that. "You told them we were together?"

McGee meowed and rubbed up against the side of Gina's chair. She reached down to pet him and he arched his back under her hand.

"We're not their prime suspects, Gina."

"Maybe not you, but I'd make a great suspect." The cat hopped up on her lap and began kneading the soft flesh of her stomach. She continued to stroke him as he settled into a ball on her lap, looked at me and yawned, then closed his eyes and dropped his chin to his paws. "My husband is missing, possibly the victim of a violent crime and his lover is dead. I'm the wife. I have an alibi for only part of that time and last night I slept with him." She looked at me and I saw grim defiance in her eyes, as though she were daring me to find a flaw in her logic.

Maybe I'm either naive or vain—probably some of both—but until that moment, I had not considered that Gina might be using me. Then it was just a small leap to the possibility that I could be implicated right along with her. In a flash I recalled the movie "Body Heat," and the line Kathleen Turner used on William Hurt: "You're not too bright. I like that in a man." I swallowed and tried to divert.

"They're not even sure Ellie was murdered," I said. "You've got enough to handle with Kurt missing. Don't go looking for complications."

As soon as the words were out, I knew I'd made a mistake. I should have told her I knew she didn't kill anyone. Wasn't capable of it. The very idea was so far out of the realm of my thinking that I couldn't even grasp the concept. But I hadn't said any of that. In other words, I blew it.

She kept stroking McGee, but her eyes didn't waver. "You're wondering about me now, aren't you?"

"It's not that." I wasn't sure what I was going to say; at that point I didn't know what I thought. But I was spared a response when the phone rang. McGee leaped off Gina's lap and fled from the room. As I walked into the kitchen to answer it, I hoped it wasn't a wrong number.

"Quint."

I couldn't place the female voice. "Who's this?"

"Elaine."

It sure as hell didn't sound like her. "What's wrong?"

"They've just arrested Ed for Ellie's murder."

Be careful what you hope for.

The flowers Ed had given Elaine had wilted, but the water in the vase looked fresh as though someone was willing them back from the dead.

Elaine sat, cross-legged, on the couch, huddled into its corner, a box of tissue beside her knee. She looked pale and still wore the green cotton robe she'd thrown on when the police came for Ed. I'd made her some coffee, but she didn't seem interested in drinking it.

I had too much energy to sit but tried not to seem antsy as I paced the living room.

"I called Cal Maitlin, but he wasn't home." She glanced at the grandfather clock in the dining room. "He's supposed to be home by one. His wife said she'd have him call me." It was just twelve-thirty.

"He's a good lawyer. And a good man," I added.

"I know." She shook her head as though she couldn't believe this was happening.

"What have they got on him?"

"Well," she made an effort to focus, "they've just about ruled out the slipping and falling theory. Apparently there were only traces of alcohol in her blood. Ed's prints are on that picture frame they found beside her. There's a contusion to her jaw. She'd been hit. And then a neighbor saw him leaving her house around the time of her death." She looked up at me, suddenly hopeful. "That's all circumstantial, isn't it?"

Exceedingly. "Was he there?"

"He was, but he just went there to sign the divorce papers. She said they were with her lawyer."

"What did he do then?"

"He left. He stayed for only a minute or two."

Long enough. "Was he angry?"

"Well, sure. Ellie had been dragging her feet. Ever since I moved in." She shook her head. "I hate to speak ill of the dead, but she could be a real bitch. You know what else I think it was? I think Ellie was waiting for Ed to get a job so she could get more out of him in the settlement." She scowled. "God knows he was giving her enough in child support. But, no, Ellie figured she had more coming to her."

"Is there anything else?"

"Yes." She swallowed and took a deep breath. "They found a suitcase in her closet. It was filled with almost a hundred thousand dollars. Mostly in twenties."

"Damn," I breathed.

She looked at me sharply. "Ed doesn't know anything about it."

"I'm not saying he does, but . . . never mind." Then, I couldn't help myself. "Well, she didn't earn it licking envelopes in her spare time. He's got no idea how she came by it?"

"None."

"What does he say?"

"What can he say? He doesn't know."

"Does he at least say he didn't do it?"

She looked at me as though I'd just asked a stupid question. "Well, of course."

"What about motive? Other than the hundred thousand."

"Whoever killed her didn't take it. Probably didn't even know about it."

Neither of us spoke for a minute. I was thinking about ways one might come into that much money and then try to keep it a secret. None of them were legal. I didn't know what Elaine was thinking about until she said, "Have you got a cigarette?"

Elaine rarely smokes. "You don't want a cigarette."

"I want a cigarette."

When she speaks through gritted teeth, I know she's serious.

"They're in the car."

"Never mind."

"I'll get you one."

"No," she shook her head, determined. "I don't need one. You're right."

Back to Ed. "If I try to help, is Ed going to cooperate?"

"I doubt it." Then she said, "I just need a little time to convince him." She paused, rubbing her face with her open hands. "I don't know what's wrong, Quint." Her voice was muffled as she spoke into her hands. "Ed's been acting strange for a couple months. I thought, you know, he was having second thoughts about us. But he swears he's not. Moving in together was his idea."

"Define strange."

She breathed a deep sigh as she dropped her hands to her lap and looked up at me. "Preoccupied sometimes. Like his mind is a thousand miles away."

"It could be the divorce."

"That's what I thought." She sounded hopeful but not convinced. "And then I wondered if it had something to do with his friend dying."

"Danny?"

"Yeah. I don't know. Ed saw him a couple times a year. It wasn't like they were really close or anything. I think they used to be. But Ed would help him out. This guy didn't have much in the way of a life. He never married or held down a job for long. Lived with his mother. She called Ed and asked him to come down when Danny was near the end. He got there the morning after Danny died and stayed for the funeral. Helped Danny's mother go through his things."

"Where was this?"

"Douglas. Same town where they went to college." Then she said, "Sad. I think Ed felt sorry for him. Well, I thought Danny's death might have left him depressed. Vulnerable. Mortal."

"Did it?"

"He wouldn't talk about that either. Hell of a communication system we've got." She dropped her head into her hands again and sat there, slumped over. "Shit," she said, her voice so soft I could barely hear her.

I sat next to her on the couch. "There's something else, isn't there?"

"I have to tell someone." The words came out as a protracted whimper.

I waited. When she turned to me, her eyes glistened with tears. I couldn't imagine what she was going to tell me.

"I'm pregnant."

At first I thought I'd heard wrong. But she nodded like she knew that's what I'd be thinking. "Pregnant," she repeated.

I felt like I'd been kicked in the gut. "Are you sure?"

She nodded.

"Have you seen a doctor yet?"

"No. I took one of those pregnancy tests." She yanked a tissue out of the box and wiped her nose. "Twice."

"Sometimes they're wrong." I had the feeling that wasn't going to be much comfort.

"It's not wrong. I feel different." She took a deep breath and swallowed hard. "I missed a month. That happens sometimes. But then I was late this month. I tried to tell myself it was just—I don't know—all the things that have been going on. You know, moving in with Ed when he's acting so strange and all. But then I started getting sick in the morning." She forced a dry chuckle. "In the morning. I wish it was just mornings."

"Does Ed know?"

"I haven't told anyone yet. Except you now." She pressed her lips together for a few seconds. "Great timing, huh?" With a shake of her head, she added, "One time I forget the damned thing and zap, I'm pregnant."

"Do you want a baby?"

Locking her eyes onto mine, she said, "I do." She paused. "Ed and I want kids. Two maybe. We've talked about it." She pulled at the ties to her robe, wrapping them around the knuckles of one hand. "The timing isn't the greatest, but it'll be okay." Then she said, "I don't want Ed to know yet."

I nodded. "What can I do?"

She looked at me for a moment before saying, "You can find out who killed her."

"What if it turns out to be Ed?"

"It won't."

Before I could respond, the phone rang. We both checked the clock. "Please let it be Cal," Elaine muttered as she picked up the portable phone and punched a button. I could tell from her side of the conversation that it was Cal Maitlin.

While they talked, I helped myself to a beer. I tried to concentrate on Ed's problem, but Elaine's news kept interfering. For a while there, when things had been going well between Elaine and me, I assumed one day we'd marry and have children. One of the reasons that idea appealed to me was that I knew Elaine would make a great mother. I still believed she would, only now Ed Carver would be the father. Our relationship had settled comfortably into friendship; she'd moved on to someone else. Someday I would do the same. So, why was my throat so tight I could barely get down a swallow of beer?

I heard Elaine say, "Thanks Cal," and then break off the connection.

"He'll meet me at the jail in an hour." She didn't move, just sat there with the phone in her lap, staring past me. I tried to imagine how she felt right now but knew my emotions didn't go nearly as deep as hers.

"Have you eaten anything today?"

She shook her head, then shrugged. "Well, yeah, if you count the toast I threw up."

"I think my sister told me she lived on crackers for a while. Crackers and ginger ale."

Nodding slowly as though trying the idea on for size, she said, "I thought about crackers. All we've got are wheat thins." She curled her lip and stuck her tongue out. "Stomach says no way."

"What about saltines?"

She made a wobbly gesture with her hand. "Stomach says maybe."

Relieved to have something useful to do, I said, "I'll go get some. You get ready."

Chapter 14

Elaine thought it would be best, and I agreed, if she and Cal approached Ed without me in tow. She seemed confident she could talk him into accepting my services, but also thought it would be easier for him if I weren't there to thank.

I tried to think who, other than Ed, might want Ellie dead. If Wicklow were alive, he'd be one possibility. Their relationship might not have been as idyllic as Ellie described. Then there was Gina. I wasn't ready to entertain that possibility. Not yet.

When I'm staring at a blank wall, I look for the facts. Ellie Carver worked at Foxport Memorial and drank at the Dive Inn. She claimed to be Kurt Wicklow's lover. That was all I knew about her. I'd see what more I could learn from her co-workers and fellow barflies.

I let Peanuts out when I got home and turned on the water faucet for the cat.

Gina was gone. Even though we'd parted on reasonable terms, I figured she was still a little angry with me for thinking—albeit briefly—that she might have killed someone.

She'd left her pendant on the nightstand. I picked it up and examined the gold star and the silver slice of a moon.

When I walked back into the kitchen, I saw the note beside the coffee machine.

Dear Quint,

You were exactly what I needed. Thank you. But I think we need to let things cool for a while. Maybe later.

She'd signed her name without a closing. I started to crumple it up, then tossed it on the counter. What did I expect? It was never a good idea to place your salvation in the hands of anyone besides yourself. Especially someone who never signed on in the first place. Grateful for other matters that needed my attention, I reached for the phone book.

When I punched in Linda O'Brian's number, a little girl answered, "O'Brian residence." When I asked for her mother, she said, "One moment please."

When she came on the line, Linda said she was going to work in a couple hours but agreed to meet me on her dinner break and introduce me to a couple of the other nurses who worked with Ellie. When I told her Ed had been arrested for the murder, she was silent for a few seconds, then said, "You know, I guess that doesn't surprise me."

"What do you mean?"

"Well, I only met him a couple times, but he was so—I don't know—grim. You know? He never said much, never smiled much. Not that he was mean or anything—just grim."

I knew what she meant. Ed really did make an ideal murder suspect.

It was going on three-thirty and I knew the Dive Inn would be open for business. I'd spent a number of Sunday afternoons there, trying to convince myself that it beat the hell out of family obligations.

In the middle of the day, the Dive Inn was even more depressing than at night. Walking from the hot, sunny day into the dark, beery, smoky atmosphere was like a scene out of a bleak futuristic movie. The combination of sparsely occupied tables, CCR's "Bad Moon on the Rise" echoing off the dark walls, and the harsh brightness of the neon beer signs made me think there was nothing but scorched landscape on the other side of the door. When I looked at the faces at the tables, I saw that most of them were around my age. For the first time I realized the Dive Inn was a hangout for baby boomers who had missed out on the fruits of the eighties. Not a Mercedes in the lot.

I recognized the bartender from the nights I used to spend there, and though I couldn't recall his name, I knew he owned the place. He was around sixty and thick around the middle with heavy bags under his eyes. Two televisions vied with each other, one at either end of the bar. On one set, the Cubs played the Marlins. At the other end, a movie played to an audience of one: the bartender, who leaned with one arm on the bar's edge as he watched space ships glide by on the screen. I had to watch for only a few seconds before I recognized "2001: A Space Odyssey." As soon as I did, the bartender's name came to me.

"Hal," I said, settling onto one of the barstools.

Shaking his head, he pulled himself away from the movie and, turning toward me, yanked a cigarette from a notched ashtray. It looked like a miniature in his beefy hands. "Never could make a goddamned bit of sense out a' that movie," he muttered in a gravely voice. Then he shrugged as though it didn't matter anyway and took a drag off his cigarette, hooking his forefinger over the top, and when he exhaled, he squinted one eye as the smoke rose in front of him. Once it dissipated, he continued to squint. I figured it was permanent. A smile came to him and he wagged his finger at me. "I know you."

Before I could tell him my name, he said, "McCauley."

"Good memory."

He tapped the side of his head. "Gotta use the brain cells for something." He reached for a bottle of Scotch.

"You are good," I conceded. "But I think I'll have a beer."

He nodded as though that was no problem. "Fewer folks ordering the hard stuff these days. Don't mind that, but now everyone—especially the ladies—comes in and orders these fancy wines. Finally started carrying Merlot; now they're asking for Pinot Grigio." He curled his upper lip.

When he set the beer in front of me, I reached for my wallet. He waved me off. "First one's a welcome home drink."

I thanked him, feeling a little guilty because I didn't plan on making the Dive Inn my home again.

"How's business?"

He glanced over his shoulder, saw the station had gone to a commercial and then turned back to me. "Not bad."

"I was in the other night. You've got a new bartender."

"Yeah, that's Mick."

"How long has he been here?" I wondered how long he and Ellie had been friends.

"Stopped in 'bout a month ago looking for work. Darcy had left a couple weeks before. Timing is everything, isn't it?"

"You bet." I drank some of the beer.

He smashed out his cigarette and immediately went for another. When he found the pack empty he crumpled it up and tossed it behind the bar. I pushed mine toward him. He grunted his thanks and knocked one out of the pack. I don't think he noticed the brand.

While I'd come there intending to talk to Mick about Ellie, it occurred to me that Hal was probably the man to see.

"A shame about Ellie Carver, wasn't it?"

Hal slammed his hand on the bar. "Damn, I couldn't believe that. I knew Ed was an SOB, but never figured him for a killer." With a weary shake of his head, he leaned against the bar. "Ellie had a lot of friends here." He paused. "A shame. She was a sweet kid. Misguided, but sweet."

"Misguided?"

"You know, I gotta wonder why folks bother to get married anymore. I never did. Never sorry either." He squinted his eye at me again. "You ever married?"

"Divorced."

"See what I mean," he said as though I proved his point.

"What about Ellie? How was she misguided?"

He hesitated, then shrugged. "Doesn't seem right talking about her. You know?"

"Yeah, I do. I just want to make sure they've arrested the right guy."

"Had to be Carver. It's always the husband." He snorted his disgust. "Even when the jury lets him off like they did O.J. Guilty as sin."

"What about Dr. Sam Sheppard?"

"Who?"

"The guy they based 'The Fugitive' on."

"Oh. Yeah." He took a few seconds to digest that, then one corner of his mouth curved up in a smile. "You think the one-armed man did it?"

"Could be."

He nodded as though that actually made sense. "Well, Ellie'd take up with different guys. Some married, some not. Don't know what she was trying to prove except maybe that she still had it."

"Was there one she came in with more than the others?"

He thrust out his lower lip as he thought for a moment. "Nah, don't recall any of 'em lasting more than a time or two." He finally lit the cigarette with a butane lighter. From the way he settled his forearms on the bar, I figured I was in for a story. But then, a plump, middle-aged woman who didn't quite fit into her shorts and T-shirt came up to the bar and pushed two empty beer glasses toward him. He kept talking as he refilled them. "Ellie'd been coming in here for years, you know. I think she felt safe here. We watch out for our regulars." He glanced at the woman. "Ain't that right, Judy?"

"Sure is, hon." She'd been watching me. "You here about Ellie?"

"I knew her."

She pushed a strand of blond hair behind her ear. Even though it was cool in here, her face seemed damp. Or oily. Her T-shirt had a skeleton of a panting dog on it. The line below the creature read, "In dog years I'm dead."

"Did either of you ever see her with a big guy? Six four. Two thirty or forty. Real dark hair. Expensive dresser."

Judy barely had to think about it. "Not that I remember." Then she added, "And I'd remember someone who looked like that."

Hal snorted. "Expensive dresser. That fits. Ellie was always looking for something better, you know."

"Like she was gonna find it here." Judy paid for the beers. "If Prince Charming ever walked through that door, this place would get hit by lightning." With that, she tossed Hal a wink and took the beers back to a table she was sharing with a painfully thin, nervous- looking man wearing the same T-shirt. It worked better on him.

"I don't know," Hal said thoughtfully. "Depends on how realistic you are. Ellie—Judy's right about her. Living in a fairy tale. Guess she wasn't so different than the rest of the regulars. They ain't coming up here to discuss philosophy."

I sure hadn't gotten into any fistfights over Sartre. "When's the last time you saw Ellie?"

He thought for a few seconds, rubbing the thick pad of his thumb along his lower lip. "She stopped in Friday after work.

Didn't stay but for one drink. Tried to use the pay phone but it's out of order. I let her use the one in my office."

"Do you know who she was calling?"

He shook his head. "Pity. She liked people. Folks liked her." His shoulders jerked in a spasm of silent laughter and he coughed a couple times. "Except for her old man, I guess."

The hospital cafeteria smelled of antiseptic and pizza—interesting mix. Reminded me of the time I smuggled a Home Run Inn pizza past the nurses' station to a friend waiting the results on a biopsy. We caught hell from Nurse Ratched but neither of us cared. Turned out to be his last pizza.

Linda talked a little about Ellie as we made our way through the food line, pushing our trays along the chrome runners. "Ellie got along with everyone pretty well. Though she didn't have any real close friends that I know of. She'd visit with us at dinner, but when she was done for the day, that was that. I think. You'll have to ask Wilma. She's single. Sometimes a group goes out after work to unwind a little." She selected a taco salad. I went with a grilled chicken sandwich.

I paid for our meals, then followed Linda as she threaded her way through the round tables. A short pile, blue speckled carpet dulled the sounds. It was almost six but not crowded. We passed one table occupied by a couple who looked shell-shocked, each staring off into space. Hospitals depress me.

Two nurses were sitting at the table we approached. A wall of windows just beyond them overlooked a large pond that must have been a convention site for the area's Canada geese. A couple hundred of them surrounded the water. One of the nurses waved at Linda as we neared the table. She was heavy set with short, gray hair and a pasty complexion, which contrasted sharply with the warm brown tones of the other woman. Linda introduced the first woman as Martha and the other as Wilma.

"Ladies," she said, "this is Quint McCauley." She transferred the contents of her tray to the table and deposited the tray on the table next to us, which was vacant. I followed suit. "I've warned them about you. You break into houses and I tag along." She smiled when she said it, though. Earlier, when I'd thanked her for backing up my story to the police, she'd merely shrugged and said, "I figured something was wrong. Didn't make sense to wait, did it?"

As I settled into a chair next to Martha, I tried not to invade anyone's space. Elaine once told me if you want to know something about a woman, get together with her friends, sit back, pretend you're not there, and listen. I told Elaine that was probably a sexist thing to say (she never fails to point out the times I cross the line) and she said, no, it was just human.

"Terrible thing." Martha shook her head. A pencil jutted out through her hair from behind her ear. She dipped her meat loaf into the mashed potatoes and gravy and shoved the whole mess into her mouth. "Such a nice girl," she said, before she finished chewing.

Wilma regarded me with intelligent eyes behind glasses with thin, dark frames. "Linda says you're working for Ed Carver."

"Sort of."

Sighing, she shook her head. "He's one hard-ass, isn't he?"

I had to smile. "He's been called worse."

"You don't think he did it?" She forked a chunk of tuna nestled in a large, green salad.

I considered my response. "He claims he didn't. The Ed Carver I know is as good as his word."

Wilma eyed me suspiciously. "You know, I'll bet if George Washington did something worse than chop down a cherry tree, he'd have lied too."

"Wilma," Martha scolded. "You're always expecting the worst from people." She snapped open a can of Diet Coke and poured it into a tall glass. No ice.

"I just don't like being disappointed."

"Still," Martha sniffed, though her disapproval seemed mostly for show.

"He's not a violent man," I said. Although Ed and I had exchanged blows, it had been a mutual effort. "I think it'd be safe to call him unemotional."

"Look out." Wilma pounced on my remark. "Those cool, controlled ones can surprise you and go ballistic just like that." She snapped her fingers.

"Did Ellie every appear to be physically abused?"

"No," Wilma admitted. "But I've seen women in the ER who claim this is the first time their husband has laid a hand to them. A lot of them are lying, but every now and then I can tell we've got a first timer. They're the ones who look so damned bewildered."

"I never met Ed," Martha started, then paused and cocked her head as though someone were whispering in her ear. "Wasn't there some talk about why he was thrown off the police force?" As she spoke she waved her hand, missing the glass by only an inch or two. I wished I'd sat next to Wilma.

"That happened, in part, because he was taking too much time off to try and save his marriage. And then he wouldn't play their political games." I realized, to my own surprise, that defending Ed Carver came without much effort.

"I heard about that," Linda agreed. "I also remember Ellie going on vacation with Ed around that time. Didn't he get called back because of some crisis?"

I nodded. "He didn't get back fast enough."

Then I asked, "Do any of you know if she was seeing someone?"

"She never mentioned anyone to me," Martha said. "Not that I'd expect her to."

Wilma shook her head. "I don't think so. You know how women kind of glow when they first get involved with someone they really like. Well, I never saw Ellie glow."

"What was she like?"

"Nice enough," Wilma said, picking at her salad. "I kind of felt sorry for her. She seemed lonely. I think she probably drank more than she should. And with those puffy eyes and loose skin, it looked like she was aging hard."

"Wilma," Martha said, "show some respect." She took a swallow of Coke and set it near the table's edge. "The poor girl's dead. Can't defend herself."

Wilma shrugged. "I'm not saying anything that wasn't true, am I Linda?"

"She's not." Linda sounded a little regretful.

"Well, I think—" Martha started, but never finished. She swung her hand to emphasize whatever point she was getting at and hit the glass of Coke square on. It toppled off the table, bounced on the carpet, spilling most of its contents on the rug and the rest splashed on the leg of my chinos.

"Oh, my God, I'm so sorry." Martha grabbed her napkin and Wilma's, bent over and started wiping my pants. I envisioned gravy mixing with the soda.

"It's okay. No problem." I waved her off. "It'll come out in the wash."

"I am sorry." She pushed herself away from the table and took off in the direction of the kitchen.

Linda shook her head in a tolerant way. "Happens at least once a week. She's got her own sponge in the back."

I looked down at the spill which was less than half the size of the one I'd seen in Kurt Wicklow's study. Martha hadn't drunk much of the Coke, so this was slightly less than twelve ounces. I filed that away.

"Did she seem upset by the divorce?" I asked.

Wilma swallowed a bite of green pepper. "Not at first. She got to talking about moving somewhere warm. South Seas, I think. I had the feeling she was planning to make a big break from Ed."

"Did she say when?"

"No. I guess I figured it'd be after the kids were out of the house. But, who knows?"

Linda nodded in agreement. "I think maybe that's why I'd be surprised to hear she was seeing anyone. She wanted to go somewhere, but she never said she wanted to go there with someone special."

"Right," Wilma said, then added, "Although I've gotta tell you, she got her nose out of joint when Ed started dating that woman he's living with now. 'Ed's bimbo,' she'd called her."

Hearing the word "bimbo" applied to Elaine seemed grossly inappropriate. "Did she do anything more than make comments?"

"Not that I know of, though I think that's why she was taking her sweet time about signing the divorce papers."

"She said as much?"

"Yeah. I guess she had a nasty streak. Said something about giving him some time to stew."

"Will she be missed?"

Without hesitating, Wilma said, "Ellie was a good nurse. But she wasn't much of a mixer, you know. Kept to herself. Sometimes a bunch of us go out after work for a drink. Every now and then she'd come, but usually she wouldn't. Someone said they saw her up at that little dump east of town."

"I don't want you to get the impression her work here won't be missed," Linda said. "She was a hard worker. Real patient with the volunteers. Last year she organized a blood drive."

"A donor drive?" I asked.

She nodded.

I glanced at the spill on the carpet. "How much blood can you take from a person at one time?"

Linda glanced at Wilma as though wondering if she knew what this had to do with Ellie.

"A pint."

Hinkley had said the blood in Wicklow's office amounted to at least two pints. Thirty-two ounces.

"Say I'm having an operation and I know ahead of time. I can donate my own blood to myself, right?"

"Sure," Wilma said. "Believe me. A lot of people—when they have the luxury of knowing ahead of time that they'll be needing surgery—a lot of people are doing that."

I thought for a minute. "Could you store it in your own refrigerator?"

"I suppose. As long as you didn't get it mixed up with the beef au jus," Linda deadpanned.

Wilma chuckled. "Gives new meaning to blood sausage."

These nurses had a warped sense of humor. I liked that about them.

It was a few minutes after seven when I left the hospital. I figured it would take me about an hour and a half to get up to Richton. Beaumont's, the restaurant where Ellie was supposed to meet Wicklow, stayed open until nine on Sundays. I wasn't in the mood for a three-hour drive, but so far the only person who claimed there was something going on between Ellie and Kurt was Ellie. Maybe someone at Beaumont's would remember.

Beaumont's turned out to be a classier restaurant than I had figured from the outside—it was a big, rustic building with a rope railing leading up to the door. Although most of the evening crowd had cleared out, the remaining diners occupied candlelit tables covered in white and the clink of silverware seemed muffled and restrained.

The host, a white-haired man with painfully rigid posture and an expression to match, regarded my casual attire right down to my Coke-stained cuffs with obvious disdain. Then he swallowed hard and said, "Will there be anyone dining with you?"

"No. I mean I'm not here for dinner."

Giddy with relief, he almost smiled.

I showed him Kurt Wicklow's photo and asked if he'd seen him, probably on a Tuesday night.

He barely glanced at it as he informed me that he didn't work on Tuesdays. Then he added, "I doubt that the wait staff can help you either. We respect our patrons' privacy."

"Even the ones who turn up missing?"

I guess he didn't think that was worth a response.

"Where's the bar?" I asked, pocketing the photo.

He arched a knowing eyebrow and directed me down some stairs to the left.

I figured if Ellie met Kurt here, the odds were good that they didn't arrive at the same time. Where else would Ellie wait but in the bar?

The big room had a pleasant atmosphere, with a long, smooth, dark wood bar and tables for four surrounding a dance floor. A small stage backed against a wall and a photograph of "The Mike Kelly Trio" informed me that they played Fridays and Saturdays. All three of them had smiles that looked just about as phony as their hairpieces.

Only a few tables and a couple stools at the bar were taken. I ordered a Sam Adams from the tall, slender red-haired woman tending bar and slid onto one of the stools. She wore a starched white shirt with a black bow tie. Her hair had a lacquered look to it and her eyebrows were drawn in a state of perpetual surprise. But, she had a nice, slightly crooked smile and knew how to pour a beer. The black and white tag pinned to her blouse read "Mitsy."

When she set the stein down in front of me, I took the photo of Wicklow out of my pocket. "Have you ever seen him in here before?"

Mitsy held the photo at arm's length, squinting at it. After a moment, she looked at me. "Why are you asking?"

"A woman was supposed to meet him here the other night—last Tuesday—and he didn't show up. She asked me to try to find him."

She continued to scrutinize me. "She asked you or she hired you?"

"Hired me." I paused. "And now she's been killed."

Mitsy drew back, eyes wide. "Ellie's dead? When?"

"Yesterday."

"My God." She set the photo on the bar. "The poor kid. What happened?"

I told her about Ellie's murder and Wicklow's disappearance and asked again if Ellie was here on Tuesday.

"She was."

"You're sure it was Tuesday."

"It was always Tuesday."

"Did he ever show up?" I tapped Wicklow's smiling face.

"No. No, he didn't." She picked up his photo again and seemed to be scouring his features. Then she gave me an odd look. "They don't think he did it, do they?"

"Right now they think it was her estranged husband."

She nodded as though that figured and handed me the photo.

"And, like I said, Kurt's still missing." Then I asked, "Do you remember the last time you saw him?"

She tapped a red nail on the bar as she thought. "Let's see, it would have been last month. The last time he met Ellie."

"They met here on a regular basis?"

When she didn't respond, I figured she was trying to decide if I was on the level. I took one of my cards out and handed it to her. She studied it for a few seconds.

"If Ellie's dead, then who are you working for?"

"I'm not convinced her estranged husband killed her."

"Well, I'd bet it wasn't Kurt."

"Why?"

"They seemed to get along real well. I don't know exactly what their relationship was, but whatever it was, it's been going on since I've been here, which is almost three years now."

"How often did they meet?"

"Second Tuesday of the month."

"What do you mean you don't know what their relationship was?"

Mitsy cocked her head to one side as she considered her response. Finally she said, "I'm not sure it was romantic. They didn't seem like lovers sneaking out on their spouses, you know."

I shook my head. "What do you think it was?"

"They were friends. I could see that. She'd show him photos of kids. But there wasn't any, you know, passion there. I have to admit I used to wonder about them myself."

"Did they come down for a drink after dinner?"

"Sometimes. Sometimes Ellie would come down by herself. Stay for a drink and then leave."

An older guy with a long neck and large ears came up to the bar and Mitsy went to fill his order. I watched as she scooped ice into a glass and selected a bottle of Early Times from the row behind the bar.

If Ellie had such a good friend in Kurt Wicklow, why did she tell me they were lovers? Wishful thinking? Or maybe there was more to their monthly meetings than she cared to explain. She called him her lover so I wouldn't ask questions.

Mitsy rang up the drink and handed the man his change. He collected his bills and coins, leaving a quarter on the bar. Mitsy drilled him with a withering look, which he returned with a pleasant smile and then took his drink to a table. She slid the coin off the bar and dropped it into a jar. It landed with a hollow clink.

"Did Kurt and Ellie ever leave together?" I asked.

"He usually left first."

"Did he kiss her good-bye, or anything?"

"Maybe a peck on the cheek."

I returned Kurt's photo to my wallet and pocketed it. "What did Ellie drink?" I wanted to make sure we were talking about the same person.

"Gin and tonic." She emitted a soft chuckle. "Kurt used to drink Scotch. Single malt. I'd keep a bottle of Glenfiddich for him. Then everyone got to liking the stuff."

"What replaced Scotch?"

She gave me an odd look. "He went from single malt to club soda. No weaning himself with beer or wine."

"Do you think he had a drinking problem?"

"I think it was a health thing with him."

"How long has he been off the Scotch?"

"Hard to say." She frowned and little lines appeared between her eyebrows. "Year. Year and a half."

I nodded, making a mental note to check with Gina on the

timing of Kurt's religious transformation.

The bartender filled a glass with ice and poured a Coke for herself. "That's so sad about Ellie. Nice kid." She chuckled. "Kid. She was close to my age. Still, there was something little girlish about her."

"What did she talk about?"

"Lately she'd been talking about her divorce a lot. She was pretty bitter. I guess her ex—almost ex—had a girlfriend. That really bothered her, I could tell. As sweet as she was, to hear her talk about her ex, she had to have a vindictive streak." She shook her head. "I guess he did too."

Chapter 15

Ed had his bond hearing on Monday morning at nine-thirty. State called for a million dollars. The judge agreed with Cal Maitlin's assertion that Ed wasn't likely to flee and set bond at two hundred and fifty grand. With some financial assistance from Louise Orwell, Ed came up with ten percent and was out.

I met up with him back at his apartment. He didn't look bad for having spent a night in jail.

"I'm only cooperating with you to make Elaine feel better," he growled.

What a prince.

"I can't believe what all this is doing to her. She looks pale, she hardly eats."

Think about it, Ed. "Where is she now?"

"She went to pick up some groceries."

I hoped no one stuck a chili sample under her nose.

He had removed his sports jacket, yanked his tie down a few inches and unbuttoned his collar. He handed me a mug of coffee. It was already pushing 90 degrees outside, but I accepted the hot liquid without protest. Ed walked over to the picture window and stood with his back to me as he looked out into the courtyard where trees shaded a circle of white benches surrounding a small fountain. A stone fish leaped from its center, water spouting from its gaping mouth.

"How are your kids doing?"

He glanced over his shoulder at me. "Okay, I guess.

They're with my folks in Crystal Lake."

I waited a minute, sipping the strong coffee. Ed continued to stare out into the courtyard; his only movement involved lifting the mug to his mouth. I cleared my throat. "What did you and Ellie talk about?"

"What difference does it make?"

During a brutal winter several years ago, I endured a brief stint driving people to O'Hare airport from Chicago's far-west suburbs. I felt the same way about that job as I did this situation. You shouldn't have to work so hard to get somewhere you don't really want to be.

"Why did you go to her place?"

When he didn't answer, I said, "Look, Ed. Neither of us likes this. Let's face it. We're both here for Elaine. Now, I'm not going to be the one to tell her I didn't try."

Finally, he said, "I wanted Ellie to sign the divorce papers."

"Did she?"

"She said they were at her lawyer's office and she'd take care of them on Monday." He paused. "Today."

"Why was she dragging her feet?"

He turned to me, irritated. "Look, I don't know for sure, but I think she was really bent out of shape about Elaine. Bad enough when we were dating. Once she moved in, well, Ellie didn't like seeing me happy."

"What time were you there?"

"About ten, ten-thirty."

"She was sunbathing?"

"Not yet. I mean she was dressed for it. But she was inside when I got there. I figured she was planning on it."

"But she left her drink outside."

He shrugged. "Might have been last night's drink. She was forgetful that way."

"I guess that would explain why the door was locked."

He didn't offer an argument.

I sat down in the large chair and balanced the coffee mug on its arm. "Was Ellie surprised to see you?"

He frowned and shrugged as he turned back toward me. "Not really." Then he said, "Well, maybe a little. I don't know. She was never real thrilled to see me." He set his coffee on the windowsill and removed his tie.

"Why didn't you call her first?"

"I figured if the papers were there, I'd see that she signed them right then. Whenever I call her, she puts me off." He folded his tie in half and then quarters and placed it on the coffee table.

"Notice anything strange? Out of place?"

"No."

"Did you see the suitcase?"

"I don't remember seeing a suitcase."

"What about the hundred thousand?"

He closed his eyes and shook his head as though a severe headache had struck without warning. "I don't know anything about that money." From the way he spat out every word, I had the feeling he was tired of telling this story.

"No idea how she came by it?"

"No."

"Did you know Ellie was seeing Kurt Wicklow?"

His look implied I needed my brain adjusted. "Wicklow? No way."

"I'm not sure what their relationship was, but they'd been meeting at a restaurant up in Richton the second Tuesday of the month for at least three years."

Shaking his head in disbelief, he looked down at the floor. "Well, I guess that was her business."

"She said they'd dated some in high school."

"Ellie dated about ninety percent of the guys in high school." He seemed more resigned than bitter about that statistic.

Recovering his mug of coffee, he sat on the couch. "How'd you know all this?" he asked after taking a drink.

"The bartender at the restaurant. Beaumont's."

"They'd been meeting for three years?" He'd passed quickly from disbelief to contemplative. Three years ago he might have believed he still had a decent marriage.

"At least." I told him what I'd learned at Beaumont's. "When he didn't show up last Tuesday, Ellie got worried. She hired me to go up to New Berne and look for him."

"You hard up for work?"

I ignored the baited question and asked, "Do you know about Wicklow's current investment problems?"

"I've heard some things."

"I've got a theory. Hear me out."

He sat back into the cushion, taking his coffee with him.

"If Kurt Wicklow embezzled his clients' money, he needed to disappear," I began. "If everyone thought he was dead, all the better. Nobody looks for a dead man. As far as I know, all they found of Kurt Wicklow was his blood. And they do believe it is his blood. It's his type and they're doing DNA tests for further proof. Ellie was a nurse. She knew how to draw blood and how to store it. What if she drew enough to make it look like he'd suffered a fatal wound? But, what if Kurt's plans didn't include Ellie? And if he left town without her, he knew she wasn't going to keep quiet about her part in the deception. He had to keep her from talking. He's got the perfect alibi—he's dead."

As Ed listened, he leaned forward, his elbows on his knees and his hands clenching the mug. Finally, he nodded. Once.

"It's possible." He drank some coffee and set it on the low table.

"He'd probably have some hard-to-trace accounts where he's been putting this money all along."

Rubbing his upper lip with his forefinger, he pondered that for a minute. "Say he is alive. You got any theories on where he might be?"

"No. Do you?"

"No."

"You and Wicklow were pals in college, weren't you?"

"That was a long time ago."

"You, Wicklow, Brewster and Danny used to hang around together. Right?"

"So?"

"So, Danny's dead. Brewster's dead. Wicklow's missing."

"Your point?"

"You know damned well what my point is." I gave him a couple seconds. When he didn't respond, I blundered on. "Why did you drop out of college in the middle of a semester?" I was guessing at that last part.

He waved his hand as though batting at a gnat. "You know how kids that age get. Restless. Didn't see any point in school. Thought I already knew everything."

"Couldn't wait to get drafted."

He ignored that remark.

"Brewster was up in New Berne the same time I was. I saw his truck. When I asked him about it, he didn't deny it. But he didn't say why he was there either. You have any ideas?"

Instead of answering, Ed got up and took his mug into the kitchen. I couldn't see him, but I heard him pour coffee. He said, "Brewster didn't talk about his work. I don't know what his business was with Wicklow."

I disliked talking to a disembodied voice, but I sure as hell wasn't going to chase him. "So, this old friend of yours who happens to be a bounty hunter, stops by on his way to—what? A convention?"

"Look, I said I didn't know." He appeared in the arched entry to the kitchen.

I stood. "I don't believe you."

"I don't give a damn whether you believe me or not."

We were facing each other off when Elaine came through the door, carrying a small bag of groceries. She looked from Ed to me and back again. "Are you two working this out?"

Neither of us responded. Elaine dropped the groceries and her purse on the dining room table. The bag tipped and a small carton of yogurt tumbled out. She caught it as it rolled off the table and threw it back toward the bag. It missed and rolled off the other side, breaking open as it hit the floor, but she didn't notice. The smudges under her eyes made her look haunted. She must have done a quick read on the situation because the fatigue in her eyes gave way to anger. She turned to Ed. "Look," she said, her words controlled and deliberate, "Maybe you don't think you need help, but everyone else knows you do. I sure as hell don't want to spend the next twenty years visiting you in Joliet. Would it kill you to cooperate with someone who's trying to help you?"

"I don't need his help," Ed said, then turned and walked out of the room and down the hall. Moments later a door slammed.

Elaine confronted me. "What the hell happened?"

"This isn't going to work," I said.

She took a step closer so she had to tilt her head up to look me in the eye. "Yeah, well, I guess it won't if you don't want it to work." Her mouth settled into a thin line and I could see the muscles in her jaw tighten. Made me wonder what she was holding back.

"I can't help him if he doesn't want my help."

"Can't you put yourself in his place for one minute?"

Not without squirming. "I try. And the only reason I can think of that he doesn't want any help is—" I stopped.

"Is what?" She crossed her arms over her chest. "Why doesn't he want any help?"

"Because maybe he did it."

She drew back and stared at me blankly for a second, started to form a word and then stopped.

I swallowed. "Maybe he did kill Ellie."

She slapped me. Hard. It didn't hurt so much as burn.

I saw a flicker of astonishment in her eyes, but then she blinked and it was gone. "Get out." She barely whispered the words.

"Elaine, you have to consider the possibility." I could still feel her hand's imprint.

Stepping back, she crossed her arms over her chest again. "The hell I do! Now get the hell out of here!"

I moved closer; she took another step back. I wanted to touch her, hold her, but she shook her head, furious. "You just can't stand to see anyone happy, can you, Quint? The happier everyone else is, the more you realize what a miserable, lonely person you are. Well, this is my chance and I'm not going to let you or anyone take it away from me." She backed up to the door and pulled it open. "Get out."

"Elaine—"

"Out!"

I could think of nothing to say that she wanted to hear, so I walked past her and out the door. She slammed it behind me.

I needed to cool off. For a change, it wasn't the humidity that had me hot. I should have known this would happen. I did know. I guess I figured if Ed was halfway cooperative, then we could all ride it out. Wishful thinking.

My car found its way to the Tattersall without any direction from me. I paid for a Sam Adams and took it to a table in the corner. I had almost convinced myself to take a vacation. Go someplace cool. Alaska. But, no matter how teed off I was at Elaine, no matter how much of my ire she deserved, the bottom line was the same: she needed my help. It didn't matter how ambivalent I felt about Carver; I didn't want to see Elaine having their kid while he was in jail. I wasn't doing this for Carver; I was doing it for Elaine. And so, as I worked my way through the beer, I went from deciding to tell the two of them to go to hell to opting to proceed as though our fight hadn't happened. Once everyone cooled off, we could talk. But, if I waited until that happened, I'd be losing valuable time. I fished a quarter out of my pocket and called the *Abel County Chronicle*.

I hadn't lived in Foxport long enough to know the history of the major players in this scenario, but I knew that, as a reporter, Jeff Barlowe did, and his knowledge could be purchased for the price of a beer and a sandwich.

Once I told him there was a lunch in it for him, it took him all of fifteen minutes to get to the Tattersall. He ordered a corned beef on rye and I had my usual smoked turkey.

Small and wiry with John Lennon glasses and hair down to his shoulders, Jeff would have been better served by the sixties than I was. He was born about ten years too late to get much out of them, but he made the most of his firebrand spirit by routing out corruption and injustice in the suburbs. He's active in a weekly newspaper association and has several news reporting awards to his credit.

When our sandwiches came, he eyed my smoked turkey as he spread spicy mustard on his corned beef. "When did you start eating that stuff?"

"Trying to be healthy," I said around a mouthful.

He frowned. "Yeah, but that's smoked."

"So?" I said, the bite frozen in my mouth in case I had to spit it out.

"Carcinogens, man. From the smoke."

"Shut up, Jeff." I finished chewing and swallowed.

He shrugged it off.

"What can you tell me about Kurt Wicklow?" I asked.

"I know that nobody in this town wants to believe what it's starting to look like. That he ripped off his clients, many of whom were his friends. If it turns out that's what happened, Foxport will desert its golden boy faster than you can say 'tight end.' "

I nodded. "I know all the football hero stuff, but what else can you tell me about him? He's this town's favorite son, but would he get a unanimous vote?"

"No." Jeff picked a strand of corned beef from his sandwich and popped it in his mouth. "He's got a ton of friends. Well, you met the guy. He's hard not to like. Liked to donate big bucks to charities. Always made a big production out of it."

"He appreciated media coverage?"

"Yeah, he did." He shrugged. "Still, he was real generous."

He swallowed some beer and continued. "But, if you're looking for a slightly different view, you might try talking to Kurt's former mother-in-law, Kathryn Stapleton. She lives over on Second Avenue, across from Iroquois Park. One of those big old houses. Her family goes back in Foxport's history about as far as anyone's."

"What will she tell me?"

"Maybe nothing. Maybe she's put it past her, but I doubt it. That kind of thing you don't get past."

"What kind of thing?"

"You know that Kurt's first wife, Paula, died, don't you?"

"Some kind of hiking accident."

"That's the story." He continued without prompting. "I'd just started working on the paper. When Paula died, the whole town took it hard. She'd been real popular. Prominent family. Homecoming queen. She and Kurt were the Ken and Barbie of Foxport. There was never any suspicion about her death. I forget where they were. Out west somewhere. Or southern Illinois. Wherever. She stepped on a loose piece of stone and it went out from under her. Sent her falling about a hundred feet. Died instantly. Kurt was devastated. Anyway, we were doing an article on Paula. A tribute kind of thing. I went to talk to Kathryn."

He paused and looked past me like he was trying to recreate the meeting. "She never came right out and said it, but she strongly implied that Kurt killed Paula."

"What did she say?"

"Well, for starters, she thought about hiring a detective. Asked me if I knew of any. That was before you got here, so I told her no. Told her to try the yellow pages. When I pressed it—you know, trying to figure out why she'd need a detective—she said her daughter hated heights. Couldn't imagine what she was doing hiking someplace where a fall could kill her."

"Did you think she had a point?"

Jeff frowned. "I'm not sure. Mrs. Stapleton has kind of an eccentric personality. She might have dreamed the whole theory up. But, maybe not."

"Did she hire anyone?"

He shook his head. "No. I guess she figured it would always come down to her story versus Kurt's."

"What about Paula's father?"

"He'd been dead a couple years at the time."

"Did Kurt inherit some money when Paula died?"

"You bet. The Stapletons are old money."

"Was there another woman?"

"No rumors, nothing like that."

"It was a while before he remarried, wasn't it?"

"I forget how long, but it was a while. He went off to Europe for a few weeks, wound up staying six months and brought Gina home with him."

"Was Wicklow always in investments?"

"No. You know those ex-jocks. One opportunity after another. He got interested in the market after Paula died and he had all this money to invest. Took some courses." He shrugged. "Turns out he was a natural. As his own investments grew, his friends started asking his advice. They became his first clients. Eventually, as his reputation grew, his client list did the same."

"Until now."

"Yeah. From what I'm hearing, they're starting to think Wicklow just up and split with his investors' money. Or, he did something with the money, then got himself killed. Either way, it looks like he planned to leave for parts unknown."

"Have you heard anything about him making bad, possibly illegal decisions with his investors' money?"

Jeff shook his head. "Not so far."

"Let's say he had to disappear. Was it something he'd planned for a long time or did he have a sudden need to make himself scarce?"

"I'm assuming you're musing aloud. If I knew that, do you think I'd be sitting here having lunch with you? I'd be back at my desk writing a story." He leaned forward, elbows on the table. "Maybe he just wanted to start over, you know. Clean slate, lots of money. Who hasn't dreamed of pulling that off?"

I had to concede his point. There was something powerfully seductive about erasing one's past.

"Anyway," Jeff continued, "let's say he disappeared. Why? Aside from the clean slate theory."

I was fishing here. "Maybe it's got something to do with his first wife's death. He was afraid they'd prove that he did kill her."

"I don't know how."

"Think I'll go talk to Mrs. Stapleton."

Jeff emitted a dry chuckle. "Good luck."

"What do you mean?"

"Last time I saw Mrs. Stapleton, she was walking down Main Street, window shopping and carrying on an animated conversation with a parrot on her shoulder." He shook his head. "I remember she was wearing this dark blue suit and she looked so dignified. Except, of course, for the talking with the parrot part. But then when I looked back at her, I saw that the parrot had crapped on the back of her suit." He crumpled his napkin and tossed it in the basket. "Sort of ruined the effect, you know."

Chapter 16

I called Kathryn Stapleton and wound up communicating with her through the maid. No matter. She said Mrs. Stapleton would see me at four o'clock.

With a couple hours to kill, I decided to check out Kurt Wicklow's new church. Maybe it had nothing to do with Ellie's murder, but something about his newly discovered spirituality combined with the timing of his disappearance and Ellie's murder nagged at me.

The Church of Everlasting Salvation was a small, neat building made of red brick and trimmed in white with a white steeple. It might have been lifted from a New England post card and set on the top of this hill in the sparsely populated southwest corner of Abel county. A small sign set into the lawn welcomed all. Reverend Ronald Christopher had officiated at yesterday's service which addressed the issue of "Bartering One's Soul."

On a Monday afternoon, I wasn't sure I'd find anyone there. However, as I pulled into the gravel lot I saw three cars near the building. I parked beside a late model Camry.

The church appeared to be one large room with no vestibule. It was cool and dark. About twenty rows of pews, separated by a center aisle, faced a small altar area dominated by a podium. I didn't see an organ anywhere or room for a choir. To the right of the altar was a single door. Behind the altar, a stained-glass window depicted a cross on a mountainside illuminated by an orange sun. In the foreground, a herd of sheep stared out across the room with blank but oddly human eyes. One of them stood behind the others so that only its eyes were visible, peering over the back of another. I felt like it was watching me. Creepy.

"May I help you?"

I started, took a second to collect myself, and turned toward the voice. I had to look down to see the small, solid man with a thick head of curly white hair, which contrasted with the deep tan of his skin. At first I thought the voice hadn't come from this guy. That kind of depth and resonance couldn't possibly belong to a guy barely five feet tall.

Smiling slightly, possibly at my reaction, he repeated the question. The voice continued to amaze me. If he wasn't the minister, he should be.

"Um, yeah." I tried to sound nervous, which turned out to be pretty easy. "My name's Roger Kafka. I'm looking for Reverend Ronald Christopher."

He stood for a moment, pale blue eyes taking me in, hands on his hips, and then said, "You've found him." He extended his hand and I shook it, noting his powerful grip. The reverend may have been small, but it was hard to miss the broad shoulders and thick neck.

"Well," I shifted and looked down at the floor, "I've heard some about your church. I was, ah, going to come yesterday." I shrugged. "I guess I felt kind of funny coming to a service, you know, just like that. Wanted to introduce myself first. Kurt Wicklow said you were a decent guy."

His eyebrows inched up. "Kurt?"

"Yeah. Kurt Wicklow. You—you know him, don't you?"

"Of course."

"Nice guy," I said. "We belong to the same chess club."

After a few seconds of scrutiny, he said, "I didn't know

Brother Kurt played chess."

"Better than I do. He's rated around 1500."

Finally, he flicked his hand toward the door by the altar. "Why don't we go in my office?" Then he added, "And, please, call me Reverend Ron."

"Sure thing." I followed him into a narrow hall with three doors. He stopped at the first, opened it and waved me in, patting me on the shoulder as I passed him. I heard muffled voices through the wall. The small, stuffy office had a window overlooking the wooded area behind the church. Two brown vinyl chairs faced a desk which took up a good part of the room. I sank down into one of the chairs. It was lower than I'd estimated and threw me off balance for a second. Christopher settled himself into the chair behind the desk, which was larger and higher than the vinyl ones. Between my low chair and his high one, Reverend Ron wound up looking down on me. Neat trick. He folded his hands on the papers in front of him and smiled.

"What has Kurt told you about us?"

It felt close in here. I wiped my hands on the legs of my pants. "Well, he said you were good, decent people."

He nodded. "I like to think so."

"And that if I wanted some kind of, you know, direction in my spiritual life, this was a good place to look." I paused. "He seemed real satisfied too. Always had good things to say."

"Such as?"

"Well, that he felt like this was a family to him." I was walking a thin line. I had to make this both specific and innocuous. "He said you people understood him and his needs."

Christopher turned his hand over as though reading something on his palm. "When did you last see Kurt?" Although the question sounded casual, I caught an edge to his voice.

"Oh, let's see," I glanced at my watch. "It would've been the first Thursday in August. Haven't been to a meeting since then." Roger Kafka wouldn't know that Wicklow was missing.

Christopher nodded. He also seemed to relax a little. "Brother Kurt is one of our most compelling disciples." Lifting his hands in an expansive gesture, he asked, "What can I tell you about us, Mr. Kafka?"

"Roger," I said.

He smiled and nodded.

"Well, Reverend Christopher—"

"Reverend Ron," he corrected me.

"Well, Reverend Ron, I guess I—well for starters, what are you about?" I quickly added, "Kurt talked about salvation through rebirth, but he never got specific."

He nodded vaguely, his pale eyebrows drawn together in a vee. "Tell me, Roger. What is it you do for a living?"

"Physicist. Over at Fermi," I added, jerking my head in the general direction of the nuclear accelerator lab east of town. I hoped he didn't ask me how to split an atom.

"Impressive," he said.

I shrugged.

"May I ask where you went to school?"

"I got my Ph.D. at the University of Chicago." I shrugged as though it were nothing and glanced around the room. A painting on the wall next to me caught my eye. First, because it looked like Gina's style and then because of its subject. "What building is that?"

Christopher followed my gaze and smiled as though I'd complimented his favorite kid. "That is the kingdom where we shall go to prepare for the millennium and wait out Armageddon when it comes."

"Um, aren't you a little late?"

He smiled. I had so much to learn. "The year 2000 was an estimate. No one can know the precise year. Until it's upon us, that is. We believe we still have another five years."

"That's good," I said. "And where is this, um, kingdom?"

Sighing his regrets, he said, "I can't reveal that. I'm sure you understand. If we reveal its location to anyone but our members, well, it's not going to be much of a sanctuary, is it?" He nodded at the wall. "That is a painting of it."

I stood and walked over to get a better look. The painting hung above three Reverend Ron photographs. In one, he shook hands with Jimmy Carter. The middle one appeared to be an army photo. In it, he and another guy stood in front of an ambulance. They both wore medic armbands. In the third, Reverend Ron posed with George Bush. All three photos were dwarfed by the painting—in size and subject. Massive white building. Fountains, swimming pool. Tennis courts.

"If you've got this waiting for you, what are you doing here?"

"Well, it's not quite finished yet. That is what it will look like."

"How many are in the congregation?"

"Two hundred and eighty-six."

As large as the main building was, I didn't think it could hold that many sheep. "How is everyone going to fit?"

"There will be additional accommodations."

"How are you paying for this?"

He smiled. "Our members are both generous and, in many ways, of a like mind."

"Kurt Wicklow's wife painted that, didn't she?"

He blinked. "Why, yes. She did."

"Is she one of your congregation?"

Instead of answering, he said, "Why don't you sit, Roger. Tell me a little about yourself. Just what is it about our church that intrigues you? A church is so much more than a physical object."

I returned to the chair, this time prepared for the drop. The atmosphere in the room had gone from close to warm. Sweat accumulated on my upper lip and the back of my neck.

Reverend Ron continued, "I'm a bit confused by your questions. One doesn't join a church for its accom- modations. One joins a church because it fills a part of his soul that is empty and in pain. What is your reason?"

I nodded. "Okay. I'll tell you my reason, and you tell me if you're what I'm looking for."

"I'm listening."

And I'm almost out of bullshit, I thought. But I took a deep breath and plunged ahead. "As a scientist, I've always been an atheist. That's not uncommon. Among scientists. I believed . . . and I still believe there's an answer to every aspect of the physical world. We don't have all the answers yet, but they're out there. There is a universal building block and we will find it. Some scientists believe we already have. The smallest particle that cannot be split."

Christopher nodded as I talked, his eyes fixed on me. I didn't know if it was the closeness of the room or the hard thinking I was doing, but I didn't believe I could draw away. I kept going.

"It was that particle that made me think. Where did it come from?" I paused and got a nod from Reverend Ron. "And then, well, I look at all this, the way it all fits." I laced my fingers together. "And I can't keep telling myself it's all an accident. It had to be a design. An intricate, incredible design. A miracle. And the only explanation is a creator." I dropped my hands to my lap and added, "Now, I know I'm not the first scientist to reach this conclusion. But I do know that I can't reject it anymore." I'd have to remember to thank

Louise for leaving those copies of "Discover" magazine down by the clothes dryer.

The reverend nodded, smiling slightly. The lines around his eyes deepened. "You have seen the glimmer of light and now you thirst for more."

"That's right." A drop of sweat slid down my neck. "As a scientist, I can see the end. I know it's coming. It can't hold together much longer."

Reverend Ron got up from his chair and came around the desk. He sat on its edge, hands folded in his lap. He didn't seem at all affected by the heat. "Please, continue."

"Well, not much to tell, really. I guess I'm looking for a church that can accommodate someone like me. I haven't been a bad person, but there are parts of my past I'm not proud of, and I'd like to believe God won't reject me because of them."

"Roger," he began, "God is about forgiveness. There is no sin so terrible that he cannot forgive. He made us. He made us imperfect. Some of us have more imperfections than others." He looked up at the ceiling like he was searching for an example. It was the first time he'd broken off eye contact, and I had to repress the sigh of relief. But, then he was back. "Does God not love the blind man? The crippled child?"

I nodded, though I thought the comparison lacked something.

"These are merely other forms of imperfection. The point is that He can forgive all our pasts as long as we pledge ourselves to His future. And show our sincerity." He paused. "We believe in salvation through rebirth."

I frowned as I stroked my chin with my thumb. "This doesn't involve suicide, does it?"

Smiling, he nodded his understanding. "Of course not. It's a fairly common religious tenet. In order to be saved, one must first die. Symbolically. Undergo a rebirth. Death of self allows cleansing. One must be cleansed prior to being reborn."

I nodded as though trying it out in my head. "I like that."

"It is exciting." He leaned toward me. No more than six inches separated us. "Roger, are you prepared to confess your sin? Begin the road to rebirth?"

I noticed he said 'sin.' Singular. Must be looking for a big one.

"The world could be yours, Roger. There is no limit to what you can attain." His eyes locked onto mine and I felt their pull again. "You see, that sin is what eats at you. What devours your soul. Once you are free of it, there is nothing you can't achieve."

I pretended to give it some thought. "Do I have to tell anyone other than you?"

"You tell whom you choose to tell." He emphasized the point with a nod.

"Tell me," he backed off a few inches. "Do you have family?"

I shrugged and looked away. "I'm kind of the black sheep of the family."

"I find that hard to believe."

"Well," I pushed my hand through my hair, mopping the moisture on my forehead, "you'd have to know my family." I shook my head in a way I hoped Reverend Ron would interpret as frustration. I was actually trying to shake up the creative juices. "You see, it's a weird situation. I was my grandfather's favorite. He had a lot of money. Petroleum. He left it all to me and, well, my two sisters didn't take too well to that. I don't blame them, but what could I do? It's what he wanted."

Reverend Ron nodded his sympathy.

"So, I've sort of been an outcast for a while. My sisters have families, married well. They're doing fine. But we've had absolutely no contact in, let's see," I squinted up at the ceiling, "it's been five years since my mother died. I have my colleagues, but," I shrugged, "it gets lonely."

"Of course."

"I've tried other churches in the area. They're all kind of, I don't know, bland. Trying to be everything to everyone so as not to offend anyone."

Reverend Ron had been nodding as I spoke. Now he said, "I know exactly what you mean."

I sighed my relief and returned the nod. At the same time I heard movement behind me and as I turned, a guy walking past the open door stopped, looked in, saw me, and then hurried on. I'd only gotten a glimpse of him, but he triggered a memory. Still, I couldn't place him.

"Brother Randall," Reverend Ron called after him, "did you need something?"

No response except a door clicking shut. He shrugged and continued. "You see, Roger, your confession must be totally voluntary. No one can wring it from you. It is actually the first step in your rebirth." His phone rang and he kept talking as he reached behind him to pick it up. "A most important step—. Yes," he said into the phone and held up one finger, indicating I should wait. "Yes, Brother Randall." Slowly he focused on me and I started to worry. "Roger Kafka," he said and I knew I was in trouble. Brother Randall did most of the talking. Finally, Christopher said, "I see. Yes, thank you." He hung up and crossed his arms over his chest.

I tried to appear relaxed, but it was hard.

"Quint McCauley," he said.

"Busted," I replied.

"I think you'd better leave."

"Does this mean I lose my place in line for salvation?"

He stood and gave his presence a second to fill the room. "I don't know what your agenda is and, frankly, I don't care. But, before you mock us, you should give some thought to judgment day. The end is coming. Let there be no doubt. What are you doing to prepare?"

I pushed myself up from the chair and, making a point of looking down at him, I said, "I'm not putting my money on some whacked-out religion that believes God is a commodities broker."

He graced me with a thin smile.

I closed the door behind me and tried the next office. Locked. Damn. I really wanted a better look at that guy.

The air outside wasn't much hotter than it had been in Christopher's office, but the tension had sure eased. I didn't doubt that Reverend Ron delivered a powerful, convincing sermon. People like that scared me.

When I got out to the parking lot, I copied down the plate numbers. Maybe a last name for Brother Randall would be enough.

Kathryn Stapleton lived in the old, wealthy section of Foxport, which was distinguished by large homes set way back from the road on deeply wooded lots. The Stapleton home was tan brick with ivy climbing up the walls and thick white pillars on either side of the door supporting an overhang.

The maid, a young woman with thick, black hair, a wide smile and a slight limp, ushered me into a room I guess you'd call a parlor. A couch and two chairs surrounded a coffee table situated in front of a fireplace. Above the fireplace was a painting of a young woman astride a white horse. Rather than one of those frozen, posed portraits, this one implied movement. The wind whipped through the woman's long, blond hair as she controlled the horse which seemed on the verge of taking off. Literally. All the animal needed was wings and the woman some kind of flowing gown and the painting could have been a scene from mythology.

I studied it for a minute, figuring this was probably Paula Stapleton. She had the kind of strong, intelligent features that tended to improve with maturity. If this was Paula, she never had the chance.

As I lowered myself into one of two green brocade chairs, a voice behind me said, "And now for something completely different." I stopped.

The voice came from the corner by a window with heavy drapes partly opened. The sun coming in the window created such a glare that I couldn't see anything at first.

"And now for something completely different," it said again.

I saw no shape or movement, but the voice had definitely come from that corner. As I moved out of the sun's glare, colors jumped out at me—a cascade of bright red, green, and yellow with deep blue for accent. I don't know birds, but I felt pretty secure in calling this one a parrot, although it seemed on the small side. It wasn't in a cage, but sidled back and forth on a wooden perch. As I walked up to it, it started bobbing its head like it was keeping time to a lively number in its head.

"So you're a Monty Python fan." For some reason it didn't seem odd to make conversation.

"Monty loves Monty." It began to mimic the rousing theme song and did a remarkably good job carrying the tune and marching in place.

"You'll have to excuse Monty. He's a fan of British comedy."

I assumed the small, dignified woman approaching me was Kathryn Stapleton.

"So am I." Then I added, "And I guess there's no excuse for it."

"I'm Kathryn Stapleton." She smiled and held out her hand to me, wrist arched, fingers drooping.

"Quint McCauley," I responded. I'm not sure I've ever kissed the back of a woman's hand, but it seemed the thing to do. I had to bow slightly to manage it and Mrs. Stapleton acknowledged the gesture with a gracious nod and a curtsy.

Then she came up alongside me, her attention fixed on the parrot. She barely came up to my shoulder and had a small, birdlike frame, contrasting with the image of her daughter above the fireplace. Paula must have taken after her father. Mrs. Stapleton's hair was a pale shade of red and sculpted in soft curls. Bending slightly, she leaned toward Monty who obliged by hopping onto her shoulder. After accepting a soft peck on her cheek from the bird, she looked up at me with the clearest, bluest eyes I'd ever seen. "Shall we sit?"

We walked over to the arrangement by the fireplace. I settled into the brocade chair I'd been aiming for earlier, and Mrs. Stapleton sat on the end of the couch closest to me.

I pulled at my tie, loosening it a half inch. I'm not used to ties and sports jackets, especially in the summer, but when calling on someone of Mrs. Stapleton's age and station, it seemed the only way to go. She wore a pair of tan slacks which hung on her and I could see the line of her collarbone beneath the fabric of her red blouse. A double string of pearls seemed to weigh down her neck and accentuate her rounded shoulders. She took her time giving me the once over. I was starting to wonder if I shouldn't have gone with a suit instead of a sports jacket when she asked, "Do you believe Kurt Wicklow is dead?"

"I think there's a chance he's faking it. He's got a lot of angry clients. Whether he lost their money or kept it for himself, either way he's got good reason to disappear. At the same time, for every angry client you've got a motive for murder. Then again, it's possible that someone unrelated to Kurt's business wanted him dead." I hesitated. "I'm also wondering if he didn't set all this up to escape some part of his past that's come back at him."

She nodded and didn't speak for a minute. Monty appeared to be, alternately, cooing into her ear and rubbing against her cheek. At one point she nodded as though acknowledging something he said. Finally, she leaned toward me, placing her elbows on her knees. Monty compensated by backing up so he stood on the rounded part of her shoulder. Her voice was almost a whisper as she said, "Do you think he killed my daughter?"

I had expected the question. "Well, I don't think I can give you any answers regarding Paula's—"

Her eyes widened and she sat up, bringing her forefinger up to her lips. At the same time, Monty threw back his head and wailed, "PAAAUUU-LAAA. Where's PAAAUUU-LAAA?" It made my scalp crawl. Mrs. Stapleton put her hand up to the bird who proceeded to rub its head into her palm.

"Please," she said, "don't use her name around Monty."

"Sorry."

"You couldn't know," she said, softening. "Monty belonged to her." Twisting her neck so she faced the parrot, she added, "Whoever said animals don't experience emotions never spent ten minutes with this fellow."

Whoever said people weren't getting weirder by the day, never spent ten minutes with this woman.

She turned toward me so abruptly, I wondered if I'd spoken the thought. "You must think me demented."

"I'm sorry. I didn't mean—"

"Don't apologize. I know that people believe I obsess about Monty. I suppose I do. The fact is, he's the only creature who feels her loss anywhere near as much as I do."

The two of them watched me with—I swear—similar expressions. Chin and beak up, eyes alert—like they were waiting for me to challenge the statement.

"I've got a dog," I offered. "Sometimes I think he's all I've got."

She nodded as though she appreciated the effort.

I shifted slightly. "Mrs. Stapleton, what did Monty think of Kurt Wicklow?"

"Kathryn," she corrected me, but smiled like she was pleased that I'd asked that question. "Monty despised him."

"Why?"

She glanced at the bird, then put her hand in front of his beak as though shielding him. She leaned closer and whispered, "He abused my daughter."

"You know that for a fact?"

"Of course I do. I was her mother." She sat back in the couch and Monty positioned himself right by her ear.

When she didn't elaborate, I lowered my voice and said, "Did you see signs of abuse? Emotional or physical?"

She stared at me with this blank expression, and I thought she had decided not to answer. But then she leaned toward me again, her hands clasped in anticipation. "Did you know," as she paused, her eyes turned mischievous, "that my daughter was homecoming queen?"

"Uh, yes. Yes I did."

She smiled and nodded like she wanted me to continue.

"You must have been very proud."

"Oh, yes." She turned her face up toward the painting and

drew in a deep breath as though inhaling a bouquet of roses. "She was so lovely."

I tried to give her a way back to the present. "Kurt Wicklow was homecoming king, wasn't he?"

"Why, yes. He was quite handsome."

"A football player."

"Yes," she said, slowly. "My daughter always used to say that he didn't know his own strength."

"Did he ever hit her?"

She cocked her head as if I'd said something she didn't quite catch.

"Bruises? Did you ever see any bruises?" I repeated.

The light went out of her eyes and the lines around her mouth deepened. "Bruises to the soul are invisible." As she squeezed her fists together, the skin went taut over sharp knucklebones and she focused on me. "My daughter was a strong, confident woman." The rancor in her voice surprised me. "She could have gone to any college, but she followed him to Douglas. A perfectly good school, I'll grant you, but no Cornell. He convinced her that Cornell would be too difficult." She snorted. "My daughter could have been anything she wanted to be—a doctor, a physicist—but Kurt needed her in his shadow. If she were to outshine him, he wouldn't have been able to bear it."

I nodded my sympathy and sure as hell wasn't going to argue, but it seemed to me that people who wound up in other people's shadows did so because they liked the shade. At the same time I understood it was pointless to try to press the abuse issue. If Kathryn had ever known Kurt to strike Paula, she couldn't tell herself about it, much less me.

Monty had hopped off her shoulder and was sidling his way along the arm of the couch, heading in my direction. I hoped he didn't mistake me for Kurt. In a flutter of red and green, the parrot launched himself from the arm of the couch to the arm of the chair. He made it.

As I braced for a beak attack, Kathryn said, "He likes you." She sounded surprised.

"You think?"

"Of course. But he doesn't usually like men. I suspect they remind him of Kurt. Let him up on your shoulder. Perhaps he'll tell you secrets."

Monty hopped on my forefinger and I transferred him to my shoulder, hoping he didn't receive nature's call any time soon.

His feathers tickled my ear and I thought I felt a puff of warm breath on my neck.

"Where did your daughter die?"

I thought I'd lost her again as she settled back into the couch and closed her eyes for a minute. But when she opened them again, they seemed lucid, as though another person had taken over. "She and Kurt were hiking in southern Illinois. Giant City." She leaned toward me, taking me into her confidence. "That in itself wasn't unusual. My daughter was quite athletic. She enjoyed hiking. What she didn't enjoy was heights. They terrified her. I don't see how she would have allowed herself close enough to a precipice like that." She shook her head in disbelief. "A hundred feet."

"Why didn't you pursue your suspicions?"

She sighed. "What could I prove? It was just my daughter and Kurt that day."

"Why would he have killed her? Was there another woman?"

"I wouldn't have put it past him."

She probably wouldn't have put the Lindbergh kidnapping past him either. I tried to steer her toward specifics.

"What about Pa—" I caught the parrot's eye and quickly

shifted the gears in my mouth, "—your daughter's inheritance?"

"That would have been a contributing factor," she conceded. "But, you know, I believe the main reason was because my daughter couldn't have children. And Kurt wanted them—a son in particular—very badly."

This was sounding familiar.

Kathryn continued, "They tried for years and then my daughter finally had tests done. As it turned out, her—" she hesitated, "reproductive system was not quite right."

"Was Kurt ever tested?"

"Oh, heavens no." She raised her hands in mock alarm. "That would have been an affront to his manliness. To even suggest that he couldn't reproduce. Oh, my no."

"What about adoption?"

"That was what my daughter wanted, but Kurt wouldn't hear of it." She shook her head. "So sad."

Brightening, she said, "Would you care to stay for dinner?"

The abrupt change in topic threw me for a second.

Monty had shifted his footing so that he stood on the edge of my shoulder, facing me. Both he and Kathryn seemed to be awaiting my response. "No, thank you," I mumbled. "I guess I'd better be going."

"Oh," she seemed disappointed but barely paused before continuing. "Well, do call again. We'd both love to see you."

I smiled as I pushed myself up from the chair. Monty stayed on my shoulder. Kathryn stood, looking up at the two of us.

"He really likes you." Apparently this amazed her.

"Well, I think he's fine too."

Kathryn took my wrist in her hand. "Would you like to adopt a parrot?" It was an urgent whisper.

I wasn't hearing this. "You're giving him away?" I transferred him from my shoulder to Kathryn's.

"Lord, no." She kissed his beak. "I wouldn't dream of it. But Monty's only eighteen. He's probably going to outlive me."

"How long do they live?"

"Up to seventy years."

"Monty may outlive us both."

"Please, think about it." She patted my hand. "I can't die at peace until I know he has a good home."

I said I would. Not that I didn't wish Monty well, but I hoped he and Kathryn went together. I needed a parrot about as bad as I needed a cat.

Despite Kathryn's habit of wandering, I didn't think she had said anything I couldn't believe. She'd probably exaggerated Kurt's faults some, but the part about Kurt wanting a son coincided with Gina's experience. If he wanted a son and Paula's money, she'd have to die. Maybe he didn't push her. Maybe he just didn't grab for her arm as she went over.

As I walked out to my car, I reminded myself that this hypothesis, no matter how inspired, didn't do Ed Carver any good. No one had called either Wicklow or Carver physically abusive. Whoever struck Ellie probably did so out of anger. You didn't murder someone by hitting her and hoping she landed hard. It occurred to me that, while my insight into Kurt Wicklow was interesting, it might have nothing to do with Ellie's murder.

My dubious methods reminded me of the stale joke about the guy who stopped to help a woman crawling around on her hands and knees under a street light as she groped the pavement. When he asked her, she said she'd lost her contact lens. As he got down on his knees to help her look, he said, "You're sure this is where you dropped it." And she said, "Oh, no. I lost it in the middle of the street. But the light is better here."

Chapter 17

I tried calling Gina when I got back to my office. No answer. Since I was in the area, I decided to drop by the art gallery where her work was on display.

As I walked the block and a half to the gallery, the heat rose in waves off the pavement and shimmered on the asphalt. I passed a woman walking a poodle. The animal's head drooped and its tongue lolled out the side of its mouth. You know it's hot when hyper-kinetic creatures such as poodles and small children start moving as slowly as the rest of us.

A small bell chimed as I walked into the Campbell Street Gallery. For a moment I just stood there, enjoying the cool, feeling the sweat on my neck start to evaporate. Someday scientists are going to discover that abrupt changes in temperature trigger some lethal affliction. I hope I'm dead before then.

I noticed a table set back in the alcove created by a small bay window. Centered on this table were a pitcher of lemonade and a stack of paper cups. A fan of napkins and a plate of cookies—gingersnaps from the look of them—completed the image. It was the kind of gesture you tended to find in Foxport—the merchants wanted you to feel more like a guest than a customer.

No one came running to assist me so I drifted from room to room, examining the offerings of our local artisans. Most were paintings, but there was some pottery and a couple sculptures that appeared to be made of old bicycle parts. Go figure.

I'd come to one of Gina's paintings. I recognized her style before I saw her signature. In it, a small waterfall tumbled into a river. The way the light played on the water and the rocks gave the painting an unearthly quality.

The wooden floor creaked with the presence of another person. "Lovely, isn't it?"

"It's nice," I agreed, noting the price tag in the high three-figure range.

The woman who had spoken was around forty with bright red hair and wore a colorful, tent-like dress that almost touched the floor. A pair of glasses hung from a chain around her neck, resting on her rather substantial bosom. She was large in both height and girth and with a robe and a horned helmet would have made a terrific Valkyrie.

"I'm Retha Burt." I detected a slight drawl as she smiled and held out her hand.

When we shook, I was surprised by her delicate grip. I introduced myself and she nodded as though that was of great interest to her.

Pointing a stout finger at me, she said, "You own the Jaded Fox with Louise Orwell."

"That's right."

"Louise has told us about you."

"Us?"

"Foxport Women in Business."

Louise belonged to several civic groups. I wondered what she'd told them about me.

"Louise is one of my favorite people," she said.

"Mine too."

She watched me with this expectant expression. Finally, without my encouragement, she said, "We'd really love to have you as a speaker."

That sucked the air right out of me. "A speaker?"

"Oh, yes. We're all curious about the business of being a private detective." Her brows crowded together. "Hasn't Louise mentioned it?"

"She probably has. Slipped my mind."

"You should think about it. You might be able to pick up some business." Even though we seemed to be alone in the shop, she leaned toward me and lowered her voice as she said, "I'm telling you there's a couple women who should hire a detective to keep track of wandering spouses. If you know what I mean."

"I think I do."

Then she laughed—a full, boisterous sound and oddly contagious. Retha Bert didn't so much occupy a room as encompass it. Her gestures alternated between expansive and fluttery, depending on whether her reading glasses were involved.

"Gina Montague spoke at one of our meetings."

"About her painting?"

"Yes." She nodded. "She's local, you know."

"Yeah," I said, "I know her."

"Lovely woman. Quite talented. Her paintings sell well."

Her expression sobered and she clasped her hands together. "Just terrible what she's going through now."

I nodded and turned to examine another of Gina's watercolors, in which a cabin could barely be seen through a glade of trees edging a lake. A motorboat was tied to a small, white pier. I had one of those déjà vu things; all of a sudden my brain showed me a clip of grainy film from forty years ago. A lake. A boat. The cottage. Family vacation or something.

"Is this Michigan?" I asked.

"I don't think so." She slipped her glasses on and bent

down for a closer look. "I believe she told me these are all set in northern Wisconsin." She straightened and allowed the glasses to drop to her chest. "Why don't you ask her yourself? Gina should be in this evening around seven." She consulted her watch. Its hands revolved around the Mona Lisa's face. Came out of her nose, in fact. "We're having a number of local artists in for a reception. Cheese and crackers. A little wine."

"Gina said she'd be here?"

"I spoke with her less than an hour ago." She sighed. "Such a difficult time for her, but she sounded determined."

That made sense. As hard as it might be for Gina to appear in public right now, she probably couldn't afford to miss a chance to sell a painting.

I thanked Retha and said I'd be back. On my way out I stopped to look at a watercolor in which the late afternoon sun cast a red hue over the Fox River. A heron balanced on one leg, its reflection mirrored in the water. Behind it was the Charlemagne Street Bridge. You could barely make out the bronze foxes on the parapets. Its price tag was in the low three figures.

Sensing that Retha wasn't far away, I asked, "Why the price difference between this guy's stuff and Gina's?" They were about the same size, so it wasn't a square foot thing.

"Gary Niebuhr is a young artist. This is the first time I've carried him. He's just making a name for himself."

"Who sets the price?"

"We do. That's our business." She paused. "Sometimes we'll consult with the artist."

As she stood right behind me, I got a strong whiff of perfume. "Art is an investment," she continued. "In four years, Mr. Niebuhr might very well be asking as much as Gina is. He's quite talented." I noticed an earnestness in her tone that hadn't been there when she talked about Gina. Maybe she thought I could actually afford this one. "This would be an excellent investment for you."

Until she said that, I hadn't considered buying the painting. Once said, it still seemed pretty absurd. The walls in my apartment had always been bare. I kind of liked them that way. "I'll think about it." I didn't want to offend anyone.

She raised a red eyebrow. "He who hesitates . . ."

I told her I'd take my chances and walked out into the heat.

I had decided that Karen Lassiter was as likely as anyone to be privy to Wicklow's extracurricular activities. Maybe she'd also know how Ellie Carver figured into them. I doubted she'd be forthcoming with me, but I figured it was worth a shot. While I was looking for trouble, I thought I might also ask her about that empty business account.

I knew she lived in a suburb near Foxport. It took just a couple minutes using one of my database CDs to track her down to a town a little ways east, where the rent wasn't as high and the views weren't as good.

Her apartment was in one of two identical tan brick buildings, each about ten stories high. Although it was a security building, the door was propped open with a folded up *Sun Times*. As I walked in, on my right were three rows of mailboxes, most boxes dented if not mangled, and on my left a pair of elevators, one of which had an "Out of Order" sign taped to its door. After checking the black, peeling labels under each mailbox for Lassiter, I took the surviving elevator up to the seventh floor. The doors opened onto a long, dim hallway. Several of the overhead lights had burned out and the carpet had a dank, moldy smell. The first apartment on the right was 701.

As I started down the hall, I saw a woman come out of an apartment toward the other end and cross the hall to the adjacent apartment where she rapped on the door. I thought it might be Karen, but she was in a shadow and I couldn't be sure. I slowed my pace.

The woman spoke to the metal door. "It's Karen. I've got that dish I borrowed." I was close enough to see that she clutched an object to her chest. After a few seconds, during which she put her ear to the door, she said, "Karen Lassiter. From across the hall." Fortunately, she faced away from me as she did this. A moment later I heard the clink of a chain and the door opened a few inches. "Sorry I kept it so long." Karen held out the dish. A hand emerged from the doorway, took the dish and then disappeared. The door clicked shut and the chain engaged. Karen scowled as she turned back toward her apartment. Then she saw me and the scowl deteriorated.

She moved quickly, covering the distance to her open door faster than I could. I thought I'd lost her, but instead of going in, she yanked the door shut and turned toward me, standing defiant with one hand on the doorknob and the other planted on her hip.

"I hope you've got your key," I said.

Her demeanor slipped as she cast a nervous look down at the soiled, rust-colored carpet, then at the door.

"You know," she said, speaking louder than necessary for me to hear, "there's a reason people live in security buildings."

"Someone should tell that to the person who jams the newspaper in the door."

"What do you want?"

"Just had a few questions."

"I was on my way out." She shifted her weight to the other

hip and adjusted her hold on the doorknob. "In case it hadn't occurred to you, I'm looking for a job."

I noted her attire—white T-shirt tucked into a pair of cut-offs. Well, mostly tucked in. No shoes. She wore make up, but her hair needed a comb.

"It'll just take a minute."

"I haven't got a minute."

"I guess I could come back. I'll tell the guys checking out Kurt's files that you helped put together those stock reports."

"Look," Karen's shoulders sagged as she shook her head, "I don't know anything about Kurt's problems. I'm sorry about the money he owes you, but I can't do anything about it. I worked for him. Period. I put reports on the computer, but I just used the figures he gave me. It wasn't my job to check them out."

"But you didn't just work for him. You were also his spiritual adviser."

She stepped toward me. "You have some nerve bothering and poking around my church. It's a church. A sanctuary. Did you think we had Kurt hidden behind the altar?"

"You called it a sanctuary. I didn't."

She got right in my face and planted her fists on her hips. "This is all a big joke to you, isn't it? You wouldn't know where to look for God. You wouldn't have a clue."

I planted my feet and looked right down into her angry, brown eyes. "Maybe not. But I wouldn't start my search on the tennis courts of some estate built with the money of people who think they can buy their way into heaven."

"You have no idea—"

"Spare me the lecture, Karen. Instead, why don't you tell me about your boss's very old and dear friend."

She stopped. "Who?"

"Ellie Carver."

She seemed genuinely surprised. And confused. "You think they were having an affair?"

"I didn't say that. I know they were good friends."

"Kurt never mentioned Ellie Carver."

"You know who all his friends are?"

"Well, no. I mean," she sputtered, "Kurt took a lot of personal calls at the office. I never heard him talk to an Ellie." She paused. "Who is she, anyway?"

"That's past tense. Ellie was murdered."

She opened her mouth, then snapped it shut.

I said, "You and Kurt must be pretty close if you're that sure he never talked to Ellie." During the course of our debate, I heard a couple doors opening. No one had left their apartment, but we were attracting some attention.

With a glance up and down the hall, Karen lowered her voice and said, "I know Kurt's faith. It wouldn't allow what you're suggesting. It just wouldn't."

"What do you think I'm suggesting? That Kurt was an adulterer? Or a murderer?"

"Leave." She spoke through clenched teeth.

"Did you know that Wicklow's business account was closed? Cleaned out?"

"Mrs. Wicklow has that right."

"She didn't do it."

As she hesitated, her glare faltered. "You think I did?"

"You had the signature stamp."

"Get out of this building."

"I'm on my way." Then, I added, "Thanks for the information. You've been real helpful."

I turned and walked down the hall, feeling Karen's eyes drilling a hole in my back the whole way. As the elevator doors closed on me, I heard her knock on her own apartment door.

I pulled out of the lot, drove around the block and parked along the street behind a green Taurus where I had a good view of Karen's building. Whoever let her back into her own apartment was someone she didn't want me to see. Probably wishful thinking on my part, but I had to wonder if it might be Mr. Wicklow himself. I figured I could invest some time in the possibility.

I sat sweating in the car, binoculars on the passenger seat. As bad as that had gone, I had come away with some answers. If Wicklow and Ellie had any kind of relationship, Karen didn't know about it. I also didn't think she'd taken the money out of the account.

Forty-five minutes later, Karen emerged from the building with a man who, even from a distance, I could tell wasn't Kurt Wicklow. Not big enough. I adjusted the focus on the binoculars. Damn. Well, if it wasn't Brother Randall. The squealer. He wore a jersey that let the world know the hours spent at the health club weren't wasted. Damn if they weren't a healthy-looking flock. And where in the hell had I seen him before the glimpse I got in the church? They exchanged a few words on their way to the parking lot. The whole time he couldn't keep his hands off her. When he kissed her good-bye, it wasn't the kind of kiss you expect to see in public except maybe on a college campus. There was a lot of groping involved, much of it centering around the other's posterior, a little humping, and one long, final look before they separated and moved on to their respective cars. Hers, the Cavalier. He got into a white Tercel and pulled away from the curb.

As I followed him into Foxport, I tried to place him, recalling where I'd been the past few days. It felt like a recent memory, but I was drawing blanks. As we drove past the bank on Main Street, I checked the temperature. Eighty-nine degrees at seven forty-five the lighted numbers flashed above the

"Cash Station" sign. Then it clicked. The teller—Lewis—the one who had personally closed out Kurt Wicklow's account. That's where I'd seen Brother Randall.

I followed him to a blue ranch house with masonry bordering a large window and a privacy fence surrounding the back yard. As he pulled into the driveway and the garage door rose to ingest him, I decided that Randall Lewis either lived with his parents or he did really well for himself as a bank teller. I considered paying him a visit, but I was already late for the gallery reception.

I didn't get back to Campbell Street Gallery until almost eight. I was afraid I'd missed Gina, but that wasn't the case.

"She isn't here yet." Retha didn't seem overly concerned. The gallery was busy, with women in sleeveless dresses and men in sports shirts. You could spot the artists—they stood beside their works like protective parents. "I called her house, but there was no answer," she said, shrugging. "Something must have come up. Can't say I'm surprised, but I wish she'd called." With a sigh, she added, "Gina is a dear, but she's not the most dependable. Even by artists' standards." She didn't elaborate.

I drove to Gina's house. No one answered the door; it was locked. The window to the attached garage didn't provide much of a view, and I couldn't see in well enough to tell whether her Spider was there or not. I drove home thinking I was overreacting. Gina had no reason to inform me of her plans. Her note said as much. Her absence at the gallery seemed odd, but apparently she wasn't the most reliable person in the world.

I wanted to talk to Elaine but knew that more time had to pass before either of us was ready to face the other. I wondered what she'd say if I were to tell her about Gina. By sheer coincidence, my vehicular wandering brought me to Elaine and Ed's neighborhood. As I was about to turn onto their street, I saw a couple walking together. It took me a second to realize it was Elaine and Ed. They were less than a block away, heading back toward the apartment building in the dusk. He had his arm around her shoulders and hers was around his waist. She sort of leaned into him as they walked. I kept going straight.

Back at my apartment, I let Peanuts out and checked my phone for messages. Nothing. I called Gina again. The sound of her voice on the answering machine sent me reeling back to last night. That was when I finally admitted I'd taken a serious turn for her. Probably too serious.

I felt too restless to watch TV, too distracted to go to a movie. Conversation didn't appeal to me, so the Tattersall was out. I got in the car and started driving. Bad idea. Driving made me think. I thought about Elaine, Gina, and Louise's friend, Albert, as I roamed Foxport. When I looked up and saw the Dive Inn's green neon sign, I barely hesitated before pulling into the lot. And they say you can't go home again.

Chapter 18

A foot in my mouth woke me. A cat's foot. I'd been dreaming someone held a pillow over my face and was suffocating me. Soaked in sweat, my limbs moved only with the greatest effort, and when I tried to draw in a lungful of air, I couldn't. I opened my eyes to the dark. In a faraway place, a dog whined. Right next to my ear a cat mewed. I fought nausea as I tried to breath, gagging at the effort. A smell overwhelmed me. In the back of my brain, something connected. Gas. I groped for the window, found the ledge and tried to pull myself up, but my hands kept slipping and couldn't find a hold. I rolled on my side, coughing and gagging. My shoulder hit the wall and I managed to get my arm on the window ledge and pull myself up. Shut. What the hell? I pounded on the pane thinking I couldn't take the time to open it, then realized I didn't have the strength to break it. I fumbled with the latch. The dark grew darker; images in my brain faded. With a grunt, I pushed the window up and slammed my fist into the screen. It held. But a whiff of moist, clean air motivated me and I tried again. The screen gave and tumbled to the lawn. I stuck my head out the window and sucked in the fresh air. McGee perched on the sill, gathered himself, then jumped for it. I breathed deeply a couple times, then pulled in another breath and held it. At the same time, I felt the nausea rising from my gut.

When I got in the hall, the whining had stopped. I flipped on the hall light and saw Peanuts lying half in and half out of the bathroom. Gathering him in my arms, I ran for the door. I managed to get us both down the stairs and place him on the ground before I vomited up dinner and countless Scotches.

As I knelt on the ground, trying to spit the taste out of my mouth, and at the same time fill my lungs with clean air, I realized I was naked. Just as this occurred to me, a first floor light went on and a moment later I heard Louise's door open. "Who's there?"

Fortunately, I was out of the light's range. "It's me." And then, because even I didn't recognize my voice, I added, "Quint. And I'm not decent."

She stepped out on the porch. "What the devil is going on?"

"Gas," I managed.

"Gas?"

"Fumes."

"Good lord, are you all right?" She started down the steps.

"I think so." I still felt sick and my head pounded, but I didn't know whether that was from the gas or all the Scotch I'd consumed. Whether I could stand was another matter. I didn't know if I had the strength to try.

Peanuts' nose against my bare ass motivated me. "I'm going up for just a second." I pushed myself up off the ground and patted his ruff. He licked my hand.

"Are you sure you should? Perhaps I should call the fire department. I wonder if the gas company has a twenty-four hour line." She was closing in on me.

"No. Don't." I started up the stairs. "I have to check something."

I took another deep breath and entered the apartment, feeling my way into the kitchen. The combination of moonlight streaming in through the living room window and the hall light helped me see. I didn't need the gas company to find the problem. The oven door hung open and all the burner knobs were turned on high. Gas hissed into the room. I shut everything off, and had time to grab a pair of shorts off the bedroom floor before my lungs forced me outside. Louise stood at the bottom of the steps, looking up, her hands clasped in front of her. A little self conscious, I stepped into my shorts, telling myself that she'd undoubtedly seen her share of naked men.

"Did you see anyone around here tonight?" I asked.

"No. Why?"

"Someone put out the pilot light and turned on the gas."

Her hand fluttered to her mouth. "Good lord. It was intentional?"

"Sure looks that way."

Next time through, I opened all the windows, grabbed a T-shirt and joined Louise at the bottom of the steps.

"Shouldn't we call the police?"

"For what?" I pulled the shirt over my head. "I didn't see anything. Hear anything."

"Well, couldn't they get fingerprints?"

"I doubt it." Maybe they could; I just didn't want anyone else crawling around my apartment. I shoved my fingers through my hair and realized my hands were shaking. God, I was tired. Tired and more sober than I deserved to be. "What time is it?"

"Just past two-thirty." She took my arm. "Come on, now. I'll make up the sofa bed in my guest room."

"Don't bother. The couch will do fine."

We checked all the rooms on the first floor. No gas smell. Fortunately, she slept with the air on so none of the windows had been open.

After fussing over me for a while, Louise finally left me in her living room with a pillow and a light blanket.

As I lay on the couch, staring into the dark, I couldn't turn off my brain. On the floor next to me, Peanuts sighed. I reached down and rubbed his neck. I assumed McGee would find his way home when he got thirsty. "Little bastard saved our asses." Peanuts sighed again.

When I closed my eyes, memories of the night came back to me in odd snatches, although much of it was still a Scotch-soaked blur. I remembered Gina gave me a ride home, but I didn't remember why she had been up at the Dive Inn. She helped me get into bed. And then she'd kissed me and said good night. I didn't want to think about what she'd done then.

At first I thought it was the jackhammer in my head, but then I realized the noise wasn't in sync with the relentless throbbing. Peanuts started barking. I opened one eye and focused on my watch. Seven-thirty. I sat up and my brain overloaded. Where the hell was I? Then I remembered the gas and recognized the furniture in Louise's living room. That solved, I turned my attention to the pounding. Peanuts stood between me and the door, clearly wondering why I wasn't doing something to stop the racket.

I couldn't imagine how the day could get worse until I opened the door and saw my favorite representative of Foxport's finest—patrolman Otto Henninger. He looked disgustingly cool and rested. He also looked a little surprised to see me. "Well, isn't this convenient," he said. "Here you are at the first door I come to."

Henninger stuck his thumbs in his belt hooks; his sizable gut made this maneuver something of a challenge. Behind me, I heard Peanuts growl. He had no use for this guy either. Waving my hand to shut my dog up, I said to Henninger, "What's the problem?"

He stopped chewing his gum long enough to part his thin lips in a smile that revealed his small, even teeth. "Late night, McCauley?"

I repeated my question.

Henninger was enjoying this way too much to rush it. Releasing a dry chuckle, he said, "You look like death warmed over." He twisted his smile and added, "What can I expect? You're Irish, aren't you?"

"That's what I like about you, Henninger," I said. "You're a racist, but you're an equal opportunity racist."

Henninger's expression hardened. "You know you left your door wide open?"

"Gas leak," I said.

He regarded me for a moment like he was trying to figure out whether I was serious, then shrugged it off. "Well, I'll be out of your way if you'll just let us talk to Mrs. Wicklow."

Now I was confused. "Why should she be here?"

"She's not?" The wad of gum was bright pink against the yellow of his teeth.

"What's going on here?" Louise emerged from the hall, tying her robe sash.

"That's what I'm trying to figure out," I said.

Henninger nodded at her. "Mrs. Orwell, sorry to bother you at this hour."

She crossed her arms over her chest. "You'd be a bother at any hour, Otto." I could have hugged her.

Henninger shifted his feet. "I'm looking for Gina Wicklow. Witnesses put her with your tenant last night." He nodded in my direction.

"Well, she's not here," I said. She hadn't stayed with me last night. I'd have remembered. "Is something wrong?"

Amused by my ignorance, he said, "Figured you might want to tell me about that."

"Where is she?" I was angry with Henninger for toying with me and with myself for not figuring out what he was up to. I attributed my denseness to the wholesale slaughter of brain cells the night before. The combination of Scotch and gas must have been devastating.

Eyes narrowed, he studied me with something approaching disgust. "That must have been one helluva night you had."

"Is Gina missing?"

"Are you going to reach your point, or should I put on coffee?" Louise spoke with her stern voice—the one I imagined she had used on her students when she taught high school English.

Henninger heaved a beleaguered sigh and waited a couple beats before saying, "We got a call last night." He reached into his breast pocket and pulled out a small spiral notebook. "A woman in a red Ferrari was seen struggling to get out of the car, an act which was prevented by the driver who was holding her in the car." He flipped the notebook shut.

"Where was this?"

"Just a block south of Main on 35." He gave me a second to appreciate the fact that this was less than a mile north. "The witness gave us a partial on the plate and the description of the woman fits Mrs. Wicklow." Then he said, "Guess who the man sounds like?"

"That's ridiculous," Louise started. "Quint wouldn't do such a thing."

She'd probably have continued, but at this point I was worried enough about Gina to put up with some of Henninger's crap. "What time was this?"

"Around one-thirty. Why don't you come down to the station so we can talk about it?"

"Who was the witness?"

"Anonymous."

"Isn't that convenient," Louise interjected.

As much as I hated to cooperate with Henninger, I thought if anything had happened to Gina, I wanted to do whatever I could to help. At this point, Henninger's attitude didn't bother me; he was being a jerk because he was a jerk.

"Sure. I'll come down. I'll be down as soon as I change and let my dog out."

"I'll wait."

"Outside," I suggested, then remembered I wasn't home.

"How you planning on getting there?"

Shit. My car was back at the Dive Inn.

Amused by my dismay, Henninger said, "Well, you can't take the one parked out there now."

"What are you talking about?" I stepped out onto the porch. The place where I usually parked my Accord was occupied by Gina's red Spider. I'll say one thing. It cleared my head.

At the police station, I was taken to the "hard" interrogation room. No comfortable chairs; no coffee machine. Henninger told me someone would be along real soon to talk to me, then he left me to stew. Louise had offered to come down with me, but I told her no. She'd also offered to call Cal Maitlin. While I'd considered the advantage of having my lawyer here, I also figured that bringing him in now would only make me look guilty. At this point, no one was calling me a suspect.

I lit a cigarette and sat back in the chair, grateful that the zero-smoking tolerance hadn't made it to the interrogation rooms of Foxport.

I felt grungy and sour but the half dozen aspirin I'd taken were starting to work their magic. For that I was grateful. Between the gas and the booze, my head had been ready to split open. I'd lost count of the drinks I'd consumed last night. I remembered talking to Mick and anyone else who would listen to a drunk and then all of a sudden Gina was there. I hadn't called her. She'd driven me home, gotten me upstairs and left. I kept telling myself that as drunk as I'd been, I'd know if she had stayed. I remembered lying on my bed, the room swimming around me, Gina's face like an angel's looking down on me. I couldn't read her expression, but I do remember it was strange. I'd have understood if I'd seen disgust or maybe pity, but that wasn't it. I squeezed my eyes shut, thinking maybe I could erase the picture. Things just got worse. In the darkness came hideous images of what might have happened to Gina after she left my apartment. I wouldn't let myself believe that she turned on the gas and left me there to die. Whoever did it must have come along after she left. Or while she was still there.

Twenty minutes later the door opened and two detectives came in. Both wore white, short-sleeved shirts and ties. I recognized one of them, but knew him only by name. Martin Fick, a short, dark-haired man with a pale complexion and prominent eyes that seemed to pop out of his skull, had been on the force back when Ed was in charge. The other detective, younger than Fick by about ten years, I didn't recognize. He had short, blond hair and the kind of mustache you shouldn't bother with if that was the best you could do.

"Sorry about the accommodations," Fick said. "The other room was busy."

Sure it was.

"We've met, haven't we?" Without waiting for a confirmation, he continued, "This is Sergeant Clevenger."

I nodded.

"Can we get you anything? Coffee? Might be able to scare up a donut." Mr. Accommodation.

"I'd like some coffee."

He glanced at Clevenger and jerked his chin toward the door.

"Black, no sugar," I said to him on his way out.

Fick swung out the chair across from me and settled into it. He clasped his hands in front of him and stared at me. Just as I wondered if those eyes of his ever blinked, they did. It was a slow, lizard-like movement.

"Have you found Gina yet?" I asked, annoyed with the time they were wasting on me when they should be looking for her.

"We're working on it."

I waited. The sooner they finished with me, the sooner I could get out there and look for her myself.

"You want to tell me what Gina Wicklow's car was doing in your driveway?" Fick asked.

"I wish I could. She gave me a ride home last night."

"She drove?"

"Yes." I met his stare without blinking. "I wasn't in any condition to drive."

"Was she in your apartment?"

"Briefly."

"Then she left?"

I nodded.

"You sure?"

"At about two-thirty, I woke up to the smell of gas. Someone had closed the windows, put out the pilot light on my stove and turned on the burners. When I cleared out of the apartment, she wasn't there."

"So, you're saying Gina Wicklow tried to kill you?"

"No. I'm saying someone tried to kill me. I don't believe it was Gina."

"Why not?"

I couldn't answer that.

Leaning closer, he said, "You sure you weren't trying to off yourself?"

"Yes."

He stared at me for a minute. "Anyone else know about this?"

"My landlady, Louise Orwell."

"Did she smell the gas?"

"I don't know." She must have gotten a whiff of it as she stood at the bottom on the stairs.

"You're telling me someone tried to kill you, but you didn't call the police?"

"What could they do after the fact?"

He sucked in his lower lip as he stared at me. Then he shook his head and jotted something down in a notepad. "We'll check with Mrs. Orwell."

Still writing on the pad, he asked, "Where were you last night?"

I swallowed. "The Dive Inn." It embarrassed me to tell him that. It said more about my life than I cared to admit.

"Did you just happen to run into Mrs. Wicklow up there?"

"No. Well, yes. I mean, I didn't call her."

"Is that the kind of place where she usually goes?"

"I don't think so." Then I added, "It's not the kind of place I usually go."

He looked up from his notes. "Then why were you there?"

"I'm not sure."

Holding the pencil between his first and second fingers, he began tapping an uneven staccato on the table. "What do you think Mrs. Wicklow was doing up there?"

"I don't know."

"What kind of relationship do you and Mrs. Wicklow have?"

"We're friends." I paused, determining that he had no business knowing about the night Gina and I spent together. "I'd only met her a few days ago."

"Oh, really?" The pencil noise stopped and Fick's eyebrows shot up. They looked like two woolly caterpillars inching their way across his white forehead. "When was that?"

I thought back to that day outside my office when she'd dropped off the check. "Thursday."

"Thursday," he echoed, as though rolling it around in his head. "When was Kurt Wicklow reported missing?"

"Friday, I think." Like he didn't know.

"One of Mrs. Wicklow's neighbors said she spotted someone fitting your description snooping around her house. That you?"

"I was looking for her last night."

"Why?"

"I hadn't been able to get in touch with her. She was supposed to be at a reception at Campbell Street Gallery but never showed." I shrugged. At the time, it had seemed a reasonable thing to do.

"You were worried about her?"

"Yeah, I guess. A little."

"A little?"

"I figured she might have had a good reason to skip the reception and no obligation to share it with me."

He nodded. "You ask her why she wasn't at the reception?"

"I think I did." I rubbed my forehead. "I don't remember what she said."

He regarded me for a minute. "You have anything else you want to tell us?"

"No." It got harder to keep my anger to myself. "Look, why don't you put your efforts into finding her instead of harassing me?"

"Did you recently try to deposit a twenty-five hundred dollar check from Gina Wicklow?"

"That was money Kurt Wicklow owed me for a job I did for him."

He nodded. "A job."

"Surveillance. Someone was trying to sue him. You can check with his secretary, Karen Lassiter." As soon as her name was out of my mouth I knew what a great character reference she'd make.

"We'll do that."

"There are court records," I said and gave him the name of the guy who had been suing Wicklow.

Clevenger returned with my coffee. After setting it in front of me, he backed off and stood in front of the door, arms crossed over his chest.

"Are you denying that you and Gina Wicklow had a relationship?" Fick persisted.

I hesitated too long and tried to cover by taking a drink of coffee. "Whatever relationship I had with Gina Wicklow happened since last Thursday. She was fine when she left me last night. I'm not saying another word without my lawyer." At this point I wasn't worried about looking guilty. I'd already arrived.

"We haven't charged you with anything." Fick's eyes bugged out in mock surprise. "Why do you think you need a lawyer?"

I lit another cigarette. The smoke seared my lungs, but it gave me some focus.

Fick gave Clevenger an "I told you so" look, then waved me off as he washed his hands of me, acting like he really wanted to help but I made it impossible. "Get him a phone," he told Clevenger, disgusted with his prisoner.

Chapter 19

It was almost noon before Cal Maitlin could get to the police station. I'd turned down Fick's offer of a sandwich, but when Cal walked into the interrogation room with a bag that smelled like grease and potatoes, my salivary glands kicked in. I needed something in my stomach.

When he set it on the table, he said, "Thought you might want something besides the cardboard they serve here."

While I devoured the cheeseburger and fries, I explained to Cal what the cops had told me and what I knew to be true. Then I told him about the gas, adding that whoever took Gina must have tried to asphyxiate me. He listened, without interrupting. When I finished, he sat for a moment, resting his chin on his hand. Cal Maitlin was old enough to retire, but he'd never hear of it. Small and wiry with a penchant toward bolo ties and cowboy boots, he had the most expressive hands I'd ever seen on a man. He once played Atticus Finch in a local production of *To Kill A Mockingbird*. Type casting. There was something composed and elegant about the man, and he had one of the most analytical and fair minds I'd ever seen at work. I attribute this partly to the fact that he was a very spiritual man. Quietly spiritual. On the other hand, I'd seen Cal work an uncooperative witness or client with the craft and precision of a lion tamer. Now he removed his hat and pushed his hand through his sparse, gray hair.

"So you and Gina did have a relationship, but it was nothing more than one night?"

"That's right."

"How drunk were you last night?"

I felt my face getting hot. "I admit I was in bad shape. But, I remember it well enough to tell you that Gina was fine the last time I saw her."

Cal tapped a long finger on the metal table as he regarded me with some concern. "Before we move on, Quint, I have to ask. What in the hell were you doing at the Dive Inn?"

"Last night we seemed like a good fit."

He shook his head, but didn't pursue it. I had the feeling he was more disappointed about my choice of bars than my binge.

"Did anyone other than Gina see you come home last night?"

"I don't think so."

"We'll ask," he said.

He shifted in the hard chair and folded his hands on the table. "How did Gina happen to be at the Dive Inn?"

"I don't know. She was just there. I remember we talked." I shook my head. "I can't remember what about. She told Mick to get me some coffee."

"Did he?"

I vaguely remembered drinking something other than Scotch. "I think so. Like I said, she wanted to talk." I shook my head. "She seemed anxious. But then I think we just went back to my place."

Fick stuck his head in, directing his attention toward Cal. "You wanted to know when we got the warrant approved."

"What warrant?" I asked, as the ground beef in my gut did a flip-flop.

"A search warrant," Cal explained.

I jumped out of the chair, banging my knee on the table.

"What grounds do you have to search my apartment?"

"Quint." Cal motioned me to sit. I didn't. My knee felt like someone had stuck a knife in it. "Did you let Officer Henninger into your apartment?"

"I let him wait there while I got ready. But he wasn't supposed to be going through my drawers, for God's sake." Then I added, "Besides, I've got nothing there to hide."

"Henninger didn't have to go through your drawers," Fick said. "What he saw was in plain sight."

"What did he see?"

"A Walther .38."

"I don't own a Walther .38."

"We know," Fick replied. "But Kurt Wicklow did."

"This is ridiculous," Cal said. "I've known Mr. McCauley for several years. If you're suggesting what I think you're suggesting, then he's an idiot."

"Or a drunk." Knowing a good exit line when he delivered one, Fick started to leave.

Cal was on his feet. "I'd like to be present when you're searching my client's apartment."

"Suit yourself," Fick said, but the scowl made it clear he wasn't happy about it.

"Give me five minutes."

Fick just nodded and left.

I sank down in the chair, feeling like I was seconds from being pushed under in the quicksand.

"All right," Cal began, "assuming that is Kurt Wicklow's gun, what's it doing in your apartment?"

"How the hell do I know?"

"Work with me, Quint. If you didn't put it there, then who did?"

I shook my head. Nothing made sense.

"Gina?" he asked.

"No, not Gina."

"Who else do you know who had access to both the gun and to your apartment?"

"Whoever took Gina."

"Did you hear anyone else?"

"No. I was out of it. The army bugle corps could have marched through my apartment and I wouldn't have heard them."

Cal slowly closed his eyes and took a deep breath. When he opened them again, I saw the steel shades had come down and he was through being sensitive to my perceptions.

"Here's what I need from you, Quint. I need you to keep an open mind. Can you do that?" He waited for a response.

"Sure."

"Good. I see two possibilities. One is that Gina was abducted and the other is that she, like her husband, needed to orchestrate her disappearance. Think about that while I'm gone."

No one was more surprised than me when, two hours later they said I could leave. No explanation. I could tell from the way Fick avoided eye contact that the momentum had shifted.

I had to wait until Cal Maitlin hustled me out to his car, past two or three reporters, before my curiosity was satisfied.

"You can thank your friend, Otto Henninger," Cal said as he pointed a small device at his Mercedes. With a polite chirp, the locks opened.

"He must have screwed up." I sank into the leather seat. It smelled like a new car. It should. Cal traded for a new one every year.

"He sure did." A smile played at the corner of his mouth, and he flicked the end of his gray mustache before he turned the key. The engine started to hum. "Illegal search." Then he said, "If Abigail MacKenna had been here this morning I doubt any of this would have happened."

"Where's MacKenna?"

"She had to be in court. No doubt she'll be in the mood to lecture when she gets back to the station."

He continued, "When we got to your apartment, Henninger showed us the gun believed to belong to Kurt Wicklow—it was in one of your kitchen drawers."

"That's bullshit," I said.

"Well, that's what I assumed," Cal continued, "so I suggested that in order for the gun to be in plain sight, the drawer would have to be open, which it wasn't. Henninger said that you shut it before you left with him for the station." He pulled the car out of the lot. I could see the river in his rearview mirror. "I suggested that was a lie. Henninger insisted it wasn't. I could tell Fick was uncomfortable, although he allowed the search to continue. I told him I would challenge them every step of the way." He paused. "They know they're walking on thin ice with this search warrant so they're reluctant to use anything they found. They've also gone over her car. No evidence of your fingerprints on the driver's side. Without any of that," he continued, "nor evidence of foul play for that matter, they couldn't ask you to stay as their guest much longer."

"Is it Wicklow's gun?"

"It is." Then he added, "Three bullets had been used. A preliminary test indicates the bullet found in Wicklow's office was fired from his gun."

Great. "What did they find, other than the gun?"

"A note from Gina Wicklow." We waited for traffic to clear for a left turn; the car's directional punctuated the silence.

"Yeah. She left that for me on Sunday."

He pulled the car into the parking lot at the Dive Inn. My Accord, all by itself along the back fence, looked like it was being shunned by the cars lining the rows nearest the door. I'd be glad to get it home where it belonged.

He put the car in park and turned to me. The air conditioner was cranked up all the way and for the first time in recent memory I was cold. "Have you had time to consider Gina's involvement in all this?"

"Nothing but time," I said. "I still can't believe she tried to kill me."

"How well do you really know her?"

"Why would she try to kill me?"

"You think about it." He gave me a second. "Why would she?"

Instead of answering, I asked him a question. "What do you know about the Church of Everlasting Salvation?"

He gave me a dubious look. "Please don't tell me you're thinking of joining that group."

I had to laugh. "Not me. Kurt Wicklow was a member."

Cal twisted his mouth as he mulled over this new morsel. Finally, he said, "It's not so much a religion, as a New Age health club."

"What do you know about them?"

"Well, to all but the members, they're a joke. However, they've got quite a few well-heeled individuals as members."

"Like Wicklow?"

He nodded. "He'd be their favorite kind of recruit."

"Well, I think I've got them annoyed with me. I paid them a visit. Later I recognized one of their members as the bank teller who claimed to have closed Wicklow's account. Randall Lewis."

"Interesting."

"Wicklow's secretary, Karen Lassiter, is also a member.

She hates me." Then I said, "Ron Christopher, or Reverend Ron, head sheep, was a medic in the service."

"So?"

I explained my theory about the blood I found on Wicklow's carpet having been donated by Wicklow himself. "If someone did draw the blood from Wicklow, Christopher would know how to do it. Didn't have to be Ellie."

"Interesting," he said again.

We sat in silence for a few seconds before he asked, "What about Gina? Was she a member of this church?"

"According to Gina, no." I recalled the painting of their kingdom away from home. Definitely her style. Seemed easy enough to believe she did it as a favor to Wicklow. No reason she should mention it to me. "No," I said again, more to myself than anyone else in the car.

And then, because I seemed to have lost touch, I asked how Carver's case fared.

"Well, we did turn up something that might be useful." He opened his ashtray, which was full of toothpicks, and removed one, rolling it between his thumb and forefinger. "Wicklow had been making monthly cash withdrawals in the amount of five hundred dollars from one of his accounts for as far back as we've looked. Ten years now. It's kind of difficult to see that and not think about the cash Ellie Carver had in her suitcase."

"Blackmail?"

"It certainly makes one wonder." He stuck the toothpick in the corner of his mouth, and chewed its tip.

"I do know that Ellie and Kurt had been meeting for dinner on a monthly basis for at least a few years." I told him about my conversation with the bartender at Beaumont's.

"Interesting."

I nodded, stifling a yawn.

Cal slapped me on the shoulder. "You look like you could use some sleep. Why don't you get some rest and I'll call you after I talk to Abigail." I liked knowing he was on a first name basis with the lieutenant.

My car had been baking in the sun all day, and when I climbed in, the heat hit me like a blast from a furnace. I started it and turned on the air, then got out to give it a minute or two.

As I stood beside the car—its surface was too hot to lean on—the back door to the Dive Inn opened and Mick Jensen emerged carrying a bag of trash. He didn't seem to be aware of me as he walked across the back of the lot toward the dumpster. He wore a short-sleeved blue T-shirt over a pair of chinos.

From the dim recesses of my brain, I retrieved a memory of him filling and refilling my cup of coffee. Then I remembered Hal, the Dive Inn's owner telling me that not so long ago he'd let Ellie use his office phone because the pay phone was out of order. If I hadn't called Gina, maybe Mick knew who did. I walked toward the dumpster.

When he turned away from depositing the trash, he saw me. At first he seemed startled, then wary. Understandable. Hell, I'd scared myself when I looked in the mirror this morning. "Wanted to thank you for doing your best to sober me up last night."

His shoulders relaxed, and he shoved his hands into the pockets of his pants. I noticed his T-shirt advertised an oyster bar in Charleston, South Carolina. He had a tattoo on his upper right arm, but his sleeve covered most of it. What I could see resembled a thin worm. "I'd have done the same for any drunk." Then, "How you feeling?"

"About as bad as I should be."

An awkward silence followed as I searched for the question I wanted to ask. "When that woman picked me up last night, did she say anything at all?"

He shook his head. "Not really. The cops already asked me about that." He adjusted the lid on the dumpster. "She was trying to tell you something, but you weren't hearing."

He pushed a hand through his hair, making the frizzy red mass shift its stance.

"I didn't call her, did I?"

"No." He paused. "At least you didn't use the phone."

"Did you let anyone use the office phone last night?"

"Yeah, a drunk woman who wanted to call her husband."

"What did she look like?"

"Heavyset with short brown hair. Kind of a sloppy drunk." He shrugged. "Any help?"

"I don't know."

I thanked Mick for his time and retreated to my car, which now felt like you could store meat in it. Life was full of extremes. I sat for a minute, trying to figure out my next move. I didn't know where to start looking for Gina. Just like I didn't know where to find Wicklow. Maybe he was dead. Ellie had seemed convinced that something had happened to him. But if Wicklow was dead, then I could think of only one other person likely to have killed Ellie. And I was supposed to be working for him.

As I shifted into reverse and checked my rearview mirror, I noticed that, instead of returning to the bar, Mick had continued to walk through the lot and was just disappearing around the corner of the Foxhole Motel. I wondered if he was living there. Why not?

I lit a cigarette and my throat felt like sandpaper.

While waiting for traffic to clear so I could merge onto Main Street, I saw Mick backing out of a space at the Foxhole. When he had pulled his green Cutlass up to the street, I was still waiting. He nodded at me. A couple seconds later the traffic cleared and we both headed west on Main. As I settled in behind him, I noticed how the left side of the Cutlass' fender was mangled and drooping. I guess it was that sad-looking fender that made me think. I recorded his license number to memory and as soon as I got home, I dug in the glove box for my trusty spiral notebook, flipping it open to the page where I'd copied the license plates in the church lot. Once I'd identified Brother Randall as Lewis, the bank teller, I didn't think I'd need them. I love it when I'm wrong.

Chapter 20

I'd been dozing in front of the television, vaguely aware of the sitcom being played out, when a soft knocking roused me. I opened the door to Elaine standing on my small porch, holding out a square, brown paper bag in her upturned palms. I caught a whiff of ginger and garlic.

"I'm trying to bribe you into forgiving me," she said. Her smile, curling one side of her mouth, implied that she knew I'd cave. But her eyes harbored some doubt.

I was so happy to see her, I had to jam my hands into the pockets of my shorts to keep from taking her in my arms. "The bribe's not necessary," I said. "But it is greatly appreciated." I stood back from the door and she walked into my apartment, giving me a quick kiss as she passed.

"I've never hit a man," she said, turning so she faced me. "Or anyone, for that matter."

I rubbed my cheek. "You do pretty well for a neophyte."

"I still don't believe Ed did it." She swallowed hard. "I can't even let myself imagine that." Without giving me a chance to respond, she continued, "So, you have to do that for both of us, okay?"

"Sure."

She set the bag on the coffee table then stepped up to me and wrapped her arms around my neck. I held her for a minute until we drew away from each other. "No matter what happens," she began, "I don't want to lose you as a friend."

"You won't," I said, wishing I could promise her that.

"We're okay now?"

"We're okay."

McGee had been twining himself around her ankles and now she bent down to pick him up. "How's the little hero?"

I told her he'd wandered back about an hour ago, looking full of himself, his striped tail pointing toward the sky.

Once they finished their cuddling ritual, she opened the bag she'd brought and pulled out a small waxed paper sack containing an egg roll. She gave it to me, arm extended as she turned away from the smell. Egg rolls were one of Elaine's reasons for living. "No stomach for them?" I asked.

She shook her head. "Although, the news isn't all bad." She lifted a carton out of the bag along with a pair of chopsticks in a paper wrapper. "I've discovered I can eat barbecue pork fried rice in small amounts. Actually, I could go through one of the big cartons, but it would take me all day."

"Hasn't Ed noticed anything odd about your eating habits lately?"

"Hardly." She popped the tab on a ginger ale and a Coke and handed the latter to me. "I think I could be walking around seven months pregnant and he wouldn't notice."

"That's preoccupied," I said, then offered, "I guess I've got his lawyer pretty busy." I gulped almost half the can. The carbonation burned going down, but the cold felt good. I belched. That felt good, too.

After greeting Peanuts, Elaine settled onto the couch. I turned off the TV, sat in my yellow canvas chair and propped my feet on the table.

Elaine hadn't remarked on my disheveled appearance. I'd slept a little, but still felt like I belonged in a detox unit.

She pulled a carton from the steaming bag, smiling as she handed me the plastic fork. It was a standing joke between us for almost as long as we'd known each other. Elaine loved to eat with chopsticks. If she could manage, she'd use them with her corn flakes. I was neither coordinated enough nor patient enough. If I had to feed myself with chopsticks, I'd starve.

Elaine stabbed at her fried rice for a minute, finally eating a small bite.

After watching her nibble for a minute, I said, "How are you handling it?"

"I'm doing okay. In a weird way this baby has kept me going." She looked at me and I nodded. "I know there's something beyond this mess."

"Maybe Ed would feel the same way."

"Well, my initial reaction was not joy. It took some time to adjust. To like the idea. I don't want to throw this at him now." She planted her chopsticks in the rice. "Once he gets past this, I know he'll be supportive. Then we can both afford to be happy."

McGee had curled up next to her and she began to stroke his back.

Then she said, "I talked to Jeff. He says you're still working on Ed's case."

"I never stopped." The chicken was tender and spicy.

"I guess I knew you wouldn't." She paused. "Jeff's dying to talk to you, you know."

"Yeah. I talked to him about an hour ago. Didn't have much to tell him. No great quotes to use. But," I shrugged, "I did promise him an exclusive when this is all over."

"What can you tell me?"

I told her about the connection I believed there was between Ellie and Wicklow and my visit with Kathryn Stapleton and Reverend Ron. And I told her about Gina. She listened, stopping me only for clarification. Finally, I mentioned the note in Karen Lassiter's appointment book. "The only thing she had marked on it for this entire week was 'R.S.!!, 9 a.m.'."

"Two exclamation points?"

"Indeed." I swallowed a bite. "Maybe it's a long shot, but I don't trust her or the rest of that flock. I mean, what if all this investment money that's missing was some big and possibly final donation Kurt Wicklow gave the church? To ensure his place in the everlasting kingdom, wherever the hell it is."

"You think they might have killed him?"

"Someone tried to kill me."

"Are you sure Gina wasn't in this with them?"

I didn't answer for a minute. Objectivity didn't come easy for me when Gina was involved. Instead, I tried to adjust my focus: find her, then sort it out. Her disappearance had to be related to Kurt's. Once I found him, I'd find her. For better or worse. "No," I finally said, "but even if she was involved, who's to say it didn't happen the same way?"

"Where does Ellie fit into all this?"

I set down the carton and rubbed my face, pressing my fingers against my eyes. My head was starting to hurt again. "Damned if I know." I told her about my conversation with the bartender at Beaumont's. "If they were keeping each other company, there wasn't necessarily anything illicit going on."

"Maybe they were just friends. It happens, you know."

"So I hear." Retrieving the carton, I speared a piece of chicken and a water chestnut.

"Maybe she was blackmailing him," Elaine suggested. "That's where all the money in her suitcase came from. Really, that would be great. It makes him a terrific suspect. Unless, of course, he's dead. That'd make it tough."

I studied Elaine as I chewed the bite. In more ways than I could name, I'd let her down.

She appeared thoughtful as she ran her thumb down the

side of her soda can, leaving a path in the condensation. "I don't think Ed knew about the money."

"You don't?"

She shook her head. "What time is Karen's appointment with R.S. tomorrow?"

"Nine a.m." I had a distressing thought. "Let's hope that's not her hairdresser."

"Let's pretend it's not," she said. "What time do you want me to come by?"

"You don't have to." Elaine loved to get me into disguise for surveillance.

"I do. I need to be doing something. How about if I get here at six?"

I wanted to tell her not to bother, but I knew she wouldn't listen. "Sounds good," I said.

"We got our phone bill yesterday." She stared down into her fried rice, jabbing at it with the chopsticks. "There was a call to New Berne. Twenty minutes. I asked Ed about it. He claimed he didn't know. Said it must be a mistake." She looked up at me. "On my way over here, I stopped at a pay phone and called the number."

Didn't I know where this was going? "Kurt Wicklow?"

"His answering machine."

"Maybe there's a reasonable explanation."

"If there was, why didn't he tell me?"

"Maybe Brewster made the call."

She shook her head. "It was placed before he got here."

"You want me to ask Ed about it?"

"I don't know. Maybe." She tried to smile and shrugged as though it wasn't a big deal. "I don't seem to get anywhere when I confront him."

I watched her for a minute, putting up the brave front, loyal to the end and for what? "Elaine, I've got to ask you something. One time. I swear I won't ask again." She waited. "Why are you going through all this? I know you care for Ed, but you're taking one helluva lot on. Are you just in this because you happened to be there when it all started? And because you're pregnant now?"

I think if anyone else had asked the question, Elaine would have been offended. Maybe she figured I deserved some slack.

"I do love Ed. I really do."

"Are you sure he's worth it?" I'd been holding that one back for weeks. It slipped past me.

She didn't answer right away, but took a bite of the fried rice and chewed it slowly. Finally, she said, "About six weeks ago . . . before all this started . . . Ed took me to Door County for the weekend. We stayed at a bed and breakfast in Sturgeon Bay. We spent a lot of time walking along the rocks and talking about the future. He told me how he knew his prospects looked pretty poor right now, but he also knew he wasn't the kind of person to stay down for long. He had a few job possibilities and one of them would come through for him. He was sure of that. And it wasn't going to be the kind of job that took over his life because he had other plans too. We'd get a place west of town. I'd have my garden." She paused. "And we'd build a life there. He said he loved the idea of looking up from his coffee and seeing me out in the garden." She gave me kind of a sad smile. "You see, not only did he have plans for a future, but they included me. They didn't just include me, they featured me. And I want to be there with him."

"Okay," I said, nodding. "Asked and answered."

She reached for her purse and unzipped the nylon bag. "I found this in the trash."

"You sound like a reporter for the *National Enquirer*."

"I'm starting to feel like one." She pulled a wrinkled piece of paper out of her purse and handed it to me. It looked like it had been crumpled up and then an attempt had been made to smooth it out. "Tell me what you think of this."

> Plunkett:
>
> October 12th in the year of the rat. A long time ago. Do you remember where you were? What you did? I'm here to remind all three of you. One at a time. You probably thought you'd gotten away with it.
>
> Well, you were wrong.
>
> And it's payback time. Hell's fires are waiting.
>
> See you soon.

It wasn't signed.

I looked up from the letter. "More important than what I think of this, what does Ed have to say about it?"

She shook her head. "He doesn't know I found it."

"But he just left it in the trash can?"

"The one in the second bedroom we use as an office."

"You'd think if he really didn't want it found, he'd have burned it."

"You think he wanted me to find it?"

"Maybe." I examined the letter, which had been typed rather than run off on a printer. The a's and e's were filled in and the print wasn't real distinct. "Did you look for an envelope?"

She nodded. "Nothing."

"I'd sure like to know where this was postmarked."

"Me too." Then she said, "October twelfth is Ed's birthday."

"I wonder what year this is referring to."

"I think I know." She pulled an orange piece of paper out

of her purse. As she unfolded it and laid it on the table, I saw it was a placemat from a restaurant.

"So, this is why we're eating Chinese take out." In the center of the placemat was a triangle in a circle. Lines radiated out from the circle and divided the surrounding area into twelve sections. Each section was devoted to a different animal. Instead of buying into the zodiac, the Chinese had their own way of letting you know that, like it or not, your birth date defined your personality.

I read the description of those born in the year of the rat. "Hmm. Rats are charming. Who knew? Perfectionists. Self contained. I wonder if Plato knew he was a rat." I noted the dates Elaine had circled. "So, you figure whatever this letter refers to happened either twenty-eight years ago or sixteen years ago on October twelfth."

She nodded as she swallowed a bite of fried rice. "Before that would be forty years ago. Ed was just a kid." She shrugged. "I guess it's possible, but Ed didn't know Brewster then. The next time the year of the rat occurred was just a few years ago. Hardly a long time."

"Okay." I leaned back into the couch, closed my eyes and enjoyed the colors swimming on the backs of my eyelids for a few seconds. Then I opened them and said, "Twenty-eight years ago, Ed was in college."

Elaine nodded. "Douglas University."

"With Brewster Plunkett and Kurt Wicklow. Now Brewster's dead and Wicklow's missing. If the third person referred to here isn't Ed, it could be Danny who just died. What's his last name?"

"Morgan."

"Where did he live?"

"In Douglas."

"Ed went to the funeral, didn't he?"

She nodded. "He also helped Danny's mother go through his things. Ed brought some stuff home with him. Mrs. Morgan was going to move."

"Do you know where?"

"She's up here now. In one of those assisted-living places. After Danny died her daughter brought her up here. Ed's gone to see her a couple times. LaGrange or LaGrange Park, I think." She looked at me. "Are you going to talk to her?"

"Probably."

She waved a chopstick at the letter. "What could this have to do with Ellie?"

"I don't know."

She stuck her chopsticks into the fried rice, then set the carton on the coffee table. "This stinks."

"You don't really want me to look into this, do you?"

"You know how sometimes you're afraid to look under the rock."

"Like I said, I don't know what I'm going to find. Maybe nothing. But do you really want things to stay the same? Whatever's going on is eating him from the inside out."

"When did I become such a wimp?"

"You're no wimp. You're just too close to him to have any objectivity."

"Maybe." Then she said, "I really didn't come here to dump on you." She tucked a lock of hair behind her ear and said, "I picked up something for you." She pulled a videotape out of her purse and handed it to me.

"I had it narrowed down to this or 'Chinatown,' which I know you love, but I thought you might feel like you were living 'Chinatown' these days."

Smiling, I turned the tape over. "Will you stay and watch it with me?"

"You bet." She pried her sandals off with her toes and

propped her feet on the coffee table. She looked so natural sitting there. Like she belonged. McGee had moved his bulk to her lap and was enjoying a belly rub.

"Where's Ed tonight?"

"Home. I told him I'd be here for a while. He doesn't care." She shrugged and took the tape from me, peeling off the plastic wrap. "I think he's afraid I'll start asking questions he doesn't want to answer." Then she muttered, "And maybe I don't want to hear the answers."

We watched Yul Brynner, Steve McQueen and five other guys defend a sleepy little Mexican town from a sneering Eli Wallach and the rest of the bad guys. Too bad they weren't always that easy to spot.

Chapter 21

By the time Elaine finished with me, I made Eli Wallach look like he'd come to town to teach Sunday school instead of plunder. With my two-day growth of beard and the drooping mustache and sideburns Elaine adhered to my face, I was a cross between the bad and ugly. I had to admit, the tattoo/decal of a coiled rattlesnake, partially visible under the sleeve of my T-shirt, was an inspired touch. It reminded me of Mick's semi-visible tattoo. Now that I thought about it, the thin worm could have been a rat's tail. It could've been a lot of other things, too.

I wore a pair of old, faded jeans, the knees of which were reduced to white threads, a Waylon Jennings T-shirt and a DeKalb Ag hat with the flying ear of corn. A scrawny ponytail attached to the back of the cap and a pair of sunglasses completed my transformation. Even I didn't know me.

Elaine wanted me to put a patch over one eye, but I asserted my veto powers.

I got to Karen Lassiter's apartment complex by seven-thirty and found her red Cavalier in the lot. I parked on the street and rolled the windows down. After about an hour, Karen came out of her apart- ment. Alone. During that time, the heat of the day built steadily. I hoped sweat didn't cause the mustache's adherent to fail. Nothing blew a guy's cover faster than half a mustache.

Karen climbed into her car wearing a pair of shorts and a tank top. All she carried was a canvas purse. The first time she tried to start the Cavalier, it wouldn't turn over. The second time it fired but died. Finally, it caught and she wheeled the little red car out of the space and took off like she was punishing it for misbehaving. I gave her a block, then pulled away from the curb. A red car should have been easy to follow, but Karen drove like a maniac. I'd never seen her drive before so I didn't know whether she was running late or if she just liked to go fast.

She drove into Foxport and turned right after crossing the river. With two cars between us, I followed her as the river wound its way north, but kept losing her on the curves and had to floor it on the straightaway to compensate. Elaine and I had swapped cars for the day. I wasn't sure a bad ass guy like me would drive a Saturn, but I didn't want to risk the chance of Karen recognizing my car. It wasn't as responsive as my Accord. As we neared South Hadley, only one car separated us. I didn't want to lose her if she turned off Route 41. Unfortunately, as we came into Hadley proper, Karen ran a light which was turning red as she entered the intersection. With rush-hour traffic, there was no way could I follow. She turned west and I lost sight of her.

Impatient, tapping the steering wheel, I sat out the light. Fortunately, I got a green arrow when the light changed and soon was heading west on a commercial street lined with restaurants, shops and businesses. I took my time, slowing to check out the parking lots. Because of the heavy traffic, I couldn't see what was parked on the south side of the street so when, after a couple miles, the commercial strip turned residential, I turned around in a driveway and headed back east. About a half-mile down, I spotted a red Cavalier in the lot of a coffee shop called, simply, Dot's. I pulled in, verified her license plate and parked as far away from the door as I could, then walked into the restaurant. I saw her right away in a booth by the window. Alone. She glanced at me, then looked away. I sat at the counter and ordered a cup of coffee, leaving my sunglasses on. I checked my watch—ten to nine—and decided that Karen drove like a maniac simply because she was a maniac.

I really wanted a cigarette, but too much was distinctive about the way a person smoked. As I drank the black coffee, I got to thinking about Gina again. The police had impounded her car and circulated her description throughout the area. Since the "witness" called 911, no one claimed to have seen her. The cops had no clues as to her whereabouts and neither did I. All I could do was follow Wicklow's trail and hope it would lead me to Gina and to Ellie's killer.

I was spared further contemplation when a squat, dark-haired man in his thirties came in, looked around. When he saw Karen, he stopped looking, just stared for a second until she nodded. Then he sauntered over to her booth and said something. She nodded again and he slid into the seat across from her. So, this was R.S. with two exclamation points. His hair was so black it was almost blue and he wore it slicked back. He smiled at her and a gold tooth flashed. It matched the small hoop earring in his right lobe. Without being summoned, the waitress poured a cup of coffee for him. He didn't bother to acknowledge her, just started dumping packets of sugar into the cup. I counted five before he moved on to the cream. A lot of cream. Karen watched him doctor his coffee. The whole time he was working, he never took his eyes off her. She shifted in her seat and seemed to find something interesting outside the window. As R.S. stirred the concoction, he said something to Karen. I couldn't make out his words, but I did hear him take a slurp of coffee. Karen nodded and reached for her purse. Although she still had a half-cup of coffee, she didn't seem interested in it anymore. She slid a business-sized envelope toward R.S., which he slipped under the table. I couldn't see what he was doing, but when he took his eyes off Karen for the first time, I assumed he was checking the envelope's contents. Then he tucked it inside his jacket, removed a brown envelope and passed it across the table to Karen. She undid the clasp and opened it, peering into the contents. He said something, and she quickly stuffed the envelope into her purse. Smiling, R.S. leaned back into the seat and twisted so his legs were stretched out in the aisle. Karen crossed her arms over her chest. It looked like R.S. wanted some conversation, and Karen wasn't exactly interested.

I put a couple dollars on the counter and left. I wanted a photo of R.S. and I doubted he'd oblige me if I asked him to pose. In the car I had my Nikon with a 70-300 mm fitted to it. I bought the lens about a year ago after borrowing a friend's. It cost me an arm and a leg, but was worth it. Then I sat back and waited, hoping R.S. wouldn't be overly tenacious in his pursuit of Karen.

He wasn't. Ten minutes later, I got several shots of him as he left the coffee shop and got into the silver Cadillac he'd parked in one of the two handicapped spaces. Maybe I'd send a copy of the photos to the Hadley police department. If they couldn't get him on whatever underworld activities he was into, maybe they could ticket him for being a jerk.

I drove back to Foxport and took the roll of film to Art Kringle at Art's Photo Works. He was the best in the area. For an extra couple bucks, Art would develop the photos right away. By the time I went home, showered, shaved, let Peanuts out, and drove back to Art's, my photos would be ready.

I found Jeff at his cluttered desk at the *Chronicle* looking over this week's contributions to "Voice of the People." From the personal treasures on his desktop—a couple autographed baseballs, a signed copy of Asimov's *The Foundation Trilogy*, and a fifteen-year-old photograph of him and Mike Royko—it was easy to believe his life centered around this place. He looked up from the copy in front of him and said, "You might find one of these ravings kind of interesting."

Friday's "Voice of the People" column, in which the newspaper printed verbatim transcripts of anonymous calls from readers on various issues, was a source of constant annoyance to Jeff. The rules were lenient. As long as a caller didn't slander anyone and the message wasn't "incendiary," his or her message was printed. The editor and publisher insisted it brought local concerns to light, because calling was easier than writing and people were less afraid to state their opinions if they could remain anonymous. While it made for some lively public debate, Jeff loathed the feature, calling it "Voice of the Jellyfish." He insisted that if one were going to take potshots at public officials, make outrageous statements with no apparent validity, and generally bitch about things, one ought to be forced to demonstrate the courage of his or her convictions with a signature. While I tended to agree with him, "Voice of the People" was often the first thing I read on Friday.

I stepped behind him and read over his shoulder. A quick perusal of the entries showed Kurt Wicklow's name cropping up frequently. The one Jeff pointed to with the tip of his pencil was the shortest on the page:

> Kurt Wicklow is alive and probably reading this. Rats have a way of surviving the worst that life can throw at them. Except fire. Even rats burn.

"Does that qualify as incendiary?" I asked.

"In the true sense of the word," Jeff said. "It won't make the cut."

If Elaine hadn't sworn me not to show anyone the letter she found, I'd have asked Jeff what he thought about it. Instead, I asked, "Any way of telling who made the call?"

"No, that's the object. Jellyfish are shy creatures." With a flick of his wrist, he tossed the copy onto his desk. "I listened, didn't recognize the voice. He was barely talking above a whisper."

He glanced over his shoulder at me. "So, what brings you here? Please tell me you'll give me a quote now."

"Sorry, not yet." I walked around the desk so I could face him.

Leaning back with his ankle planted on his knee, he began tapping his pencil against the sole of his Nike. "Then what?"

"I wondered if you might be able to identify someone for me."

"I'll try."

I handed him the photos I'd just picked up. "This guy look familiar? His initials are R.S."

Jeff lined the six photos across his desk like he was dealing from a deck of cards. Then he folded his arms on the desk and examined each one. He stuck out his lower lip and shook his head. "No bells." He glanced up at me. "This got to do with Wicklow or Ellie?"

"Maybe both, maybe neither." I paused. "I'll tell you when I can."

"You've got a nice, clear shot of his license plate, you know. You getting lazy in your old age?"

"I'm on kind of a tight schedule," I said, chagrined, but only slightly. "Besides, I figured even if I knew his name, I wouldn't know who he was." I could tell from the way he leaned back, distancing himself from the photos that, if I expected his help, I'd have to give him more. "Wicklow's secretary met him at a coffee shop in Hadley called Dot's. I think it's one of R.S.'s places of business. She gave him some money and he gave her an envelope. I don't think it was drugs."

"You sure?"

"I don't think she does them."

"Then what?"

"I don't want you to be predisposed."

One eyebrow shot up as a smile crept across his face. "IDs for a dead man?"

I shrugged.

With renewed enthusiasm, he gathered the photos together and flipped through them one at a time. "Leave me a couple of these. I'll ask around and maybe look through our files." He plucked two out of the group and handed the rest back to me.

"What's the *Chronicle* got running on Wicklow?"

"I'm doing a piece on him for the next edition." He retrieved the pencil and started tapping it against the desktop. "I wish I could say I've got a lot of dirt on him, but I don't." Then he added, "Prior to his current state, that is. Looks like he clear-cut his way through his clients' money."

"That bad?"

He nodded. "What did Mrs. Stapleton have to say?"

"Like you said, she thinks Wicklow killed her daughter, but has no way of proving it. And she thinks he did it because her daughter couldn't have children."

Jeff thought for a moment. Then, "I'm not sure how—or even if—I'm going to mention this in the story on him, but Wicklow's religious background is kind of interesting."

I pulled up a chair and sat down. "How's that?"

Obviously pleased to have an audience, Jeff leaned back in his chair and laced his fingers behind his head. "I guess he was raised Lutheran but as a young man—early twenties maybe—he converted to Catholicism. This was after a brief stint as a Baptist toward the end of his college career. Strange. Usually people change faiths because they marry into a different one or, after a lot of studying and soul searching, they make an informed decision. Apparently none of that applies to Wicklow. Paula Stapleton was Protestant. His conversion to Catholicism was pretty abrupt. I talked to the priest over at St. Cletus. Of course, he didn't denounce Wicklow, but he said before Wicklow joined, he encouraged him to take his time with the decision. He said one aspect of the religion really intrigued Wicklow." He paused. "I think he wanted to say 'obsessed him', but probably figured it was too strong."

"Let me guess," I interrupted. "It was the absolution part. Confess your sins and gain absolution."

Jeff lowered his arms and wheeled his chair a couple inches closer to me. "How'd you know?"

"It follows with this new church he joined. I think all they require for absolution is a lot of money."

"Hmm." He drummed his fingers on the desk. "Well, that fits. Wicklow held the almighty dollar in pretty high esteem."

"I've noticed."

"Before he joined his current church, he tried a few other, kind of way-out-there churches. Some bordered on cults."

"Whatever he was looking for, he had a hard time finding it, didn't he?"

Jeff leaned over the desk. "What else have you got?"

"I'm not sure."

"What can you tell me about Gina Wicklow? And don't say 'nothing' because I know better."

"I can't tell you anything with any authority."

"Damn, Quint. You're not exactly working with me here."

"I will when I can."

"Okay." He sighed. "I hope it's good. I could really use a Pulitzer."

Chapter 22

When I called Margaret Morgan, she said she'd be happy to see me, but she'd be going down to dinner about the time I hoped to get there. I offered to take her out, but she said it was too hot. So, I suggested bringing something in. She couldn't remember the last time she'd had pizza.

I took I-88 most of the way to LaGrange Park, exited on Ogden and, after picking up the pizza, found Oakwood Manor without much trouble. It was set back off a busy road on a huge expanse of lawn with lots of trees and shrubs.

I'd bought a large pizza and she saw that a couple of her friends got a slice before we took it to her apartment, which wasn't much more than a bedroom and sitting room with attached bath. But it was filled, she told me, with her own furniture and mementos of her life. Photos, afghans, a thimble collection.

Margaret was a tiny woman with a pronounced stoop. Her hands trembled slightly as she lifted a wedge of pizza from its cardboard container. The backs of her hands reminded me of tree branches, darkened with purple veins and fingers like twigs with swollen knots for knuckles.

"I sure miss living downstate, friends and all, but I guess being up here is easier for everyone."

There were two parts to Illinois—Chicago and downstate. Didn't matter if it was just a few miles south or west of the Chicago area, it was still downstate. And there was a difference. You'd find traces of a drawl in the voices and for every Cubs or Sox fan, you were likely to find at least two Cardinals fans. I may be mistaken, but there seemed to be a tendency among downstaters not to take themselves as seriously as the rest of us. Margaret Morgan was a downstate kind of woman.

She daintily worked at a slice of pizza as she talked about her son, Danny.

"He wouldn't leave Douglas. Wouldn't hear of it. Even when he got so sick he could barely get out of bed. Well, Susan asked us both to come up here. She's my daughter, you know. Lives in Burr Ridge. Fancy home." She winked and added, "Fancy husband." Then she sobered as she continued to talk about her son. "But Danny'd hear none of it. He made Douglas his prison."

"Did he have any friends down there?"

"None you'd care to call friend. Ed Carver was his only real friend."

"But Ed's up here."

"I know." She spoke as though she'd never gotten a satisfactory answer to that either.

"Did Danny drop out of college when Ed did?"

"Yes, he did. He was such a good boy. Potential. But he never had any luck."

"Do you know why he dropped out?"

She shook her head. "I always figured it was because Ed did. Danny just worshipped Ed. He never had a brother and his father, well, he's been gone since Danny was an infant."

"Did Danny get drafted too?"

"Oh, no. He and Ed enlisted. Together."

This was news to me. I'd assumed Ed succumbed to the draft. I guess I had a hard time imagining anyone enlisting in that war. I sure hadn't.

A shadow settled over her eyes as Margaret continued,

"He came back changed. Had a whole string of jobs. None of them ever amounted to anything. And he was sad. Used to be a cheerful child. Hardly laughed anymore."

"Vietnam did that to a lot of men."

She shook her head. "Well, that was the thing. I don't think it was the war. He got that way before he quit school. He was so sad. That's the only word I can think of to describe him. Sad. Within a month, he'd joined up." She shook her head. "Suppose he'd 'a been drafted anyway."

When she asked me why I wanted to know about Danny, I told her about Ed's situation and how I had a feeling it was linked to something that happened back in college.

After listening to me, she shook her head. "I can't believe Ed would hurt someone, let alone kill his wife. He's such a nice man. Decent. When Danny was dying he asked me to call Ed. I did and he came right down. But not soon enough. Danny died the night before he came. But Ed stayed and helped me go through Danny's things. I encouraged him to take whatever he wanted."

"Did he take anything?"

"Just a few things."

"Do you remember what?"

She set down a pizza crust and licked some tomato sauce off her thumb, then wiped it with a paper napkin. "Some photographs. I insisted he take them. Then he took this book of old clippings Danny had."

"Newspaper clippings?"

"I think so."

"Do you know what the clippings were about?"

"Well, I know some were about fencing tournaments he'd been in. Both he and Ed fenced, you know. And then Danny told me once they were just news articles about old friends of his. But like I said, Danny didn't have many friends that I can recall. But I never pried, you know."

"You never saw any of them?"

She shook her head and then stopped, holding a crooked finger up as though testing the wind. "I remember once. Yes, I do recall seeing him tear out a page of the newspaper and then fold it all up. When he saw me watching, he said it was a help-wanted ad and he thought he might apply for the job."

"Do you think that's what it was?"

"Well, it looked more like a page of personal ads, you know." She smiled. "Lonely hearts and all. I just thought maybe he was going to answer one and was embarrassed to tell me." Then she added, "But nothing ever came of it if he did."

"Did Danny ever mention Kurt Wicklow or Brewster Plunkett?"

Her eyebrows came together. "That last name sounds familiar, but then it is rather colorful."

I nodded.

"Those last few days were hard for Danny. So hard." She clasped her hands together. "He wouldn't go in a hospital. Always so resigned to his illness. They suggested chemotherapy, but he wouldn't hear of it. But, it probably wouldn't have done much more than prolong the end." She paused. "He was as ready to die as I've ever seen anyone."

"How do you mean?"

"Well, there was that day he asked me to mail this letter. I remember because he never wrote letters." She paused again. "So strange. After that he asked me to call Ed. Seemed to be at peace. As I said, he died before Ed could come down."

"Do you know who the letter was addressed to?"

"No, I don't know. I mean, no one. It was to a PO box."

"Where was the PO box?"

"Why, I believe it was in Douglas."

"Danny didn't say anything about it?"

"No, he was very private. I never intruded." She stared past me toward the window and the late afternoon sun.

"Mrs. Morgan, did you keep anything of Danny's?"

"Well, of course." She seemed a little affronted at first, but softened. "He didn't have much, really. I've got a photo album and a few books he was fond of."

"May I see them?"

"Of course. There's a scrapbook of Danny's on the bottom shelf of that table next to the couch. And the three books on the top shelf of the bookcase are his."

I retrieved an old-fashioned scrapbook with black pages and pictures secured with those little black corners you stuck on the page. From what I could tell, Danny had been an enthusiastic, but sporadic photographer. There were pictures of various pets, mostly dogs, a couple cats, no pedigrees. Danny had been a small man with long hair and sideburns when most of the photos of him had been taken. In one he stood shyly next to a young woman in a long dress and a wrist corsage. He had his mother's eyes. As I moved on, I saw a few pictures of Ed. He was a little thinner and his hair a little thicker, but hadn't changed a whole lot since college. In one photo they stood side-by-side in their fencing attire. Mrs. Morgan talked about the photos as I turned the pages. Despite the fact that her son hadn't amounted to much, she'd been proud of him.

The phone rang and Margaret excused herself to answer it. I moved onto Danny's books. There were three of them, all hardcover: *Call of the Wild*, *Lord Jim* and a collection of short stories by Hemingway.

As I flipped through the first, I gathered from what I could make out from one side of the conversation, that the caller was Mrs. Morgan's daughter. I swapped Jack London for Joseph Conrad where I found, folded beside the back cover, a page of classifieds from a newspaper.

When I glanced at Mrs. Morgan, I saw she was reading a list of things she needed her daughter to bring the next time she came, so I had a couple minutes to read the page. When I got to the item, I knew why it had been saved. I copied the words verbatim on a notepad along with the name of the newspaper and the date. Then I reshelved the book.

When Mrs. Morgan got off the phone, I asked her if she remembered the PO box number on the letter she mailed.

"I'm afraid not."

"Was it 1728?"

"It might have been, but I don't remember. I'm sorry." She seemed genuinely regretful.

"That's okay. I'm sure I wouldn't have remembered either."

She wanted me to take the remainder of the pizza. We hadn't eaten half of it. But she had a small refrigerator in her room and when I suggested that cold pizza was a good way to start the morning, she stopped trying to push it on me.

As I headed west back towards Foxport, I called Jeff on my cell phone.

"Hold on a second." I heard voices in the background, some laughter.

"I wanted to get on my secure line."

I was never sure whether he was serious when he said that. Jeff was both paranoid and whimsical. Strange mix.

"This is good," Jeff said.

"Don't make me beg."

"R.S. is Ramon Santiago. Did a couple years for passing counterfeit bills. I guess he's not much of an artist when it comes to making money look real, but if you're looking for a new identity, he's your man." He paused, allowing me to fill in the blanks.

"Fake driver's license, social security and all that?"

"The works."

Damn.

"Karen Lassiter is Wicklow's secretary, right?" Jeff asked.

"Yeah."

"I'm going with this story."

"Wait," I said. "There's more going on here."

"How long do I have to wait for it?"

"Tomorrow," I said, and before he could tell me to go to hell, I asked, "Do you know anyone who works on the *Douglas Debate* in Douglas, Illinois?"

"Yeah. Marty and June Slade. They own it. Why?"

I told him about Danny Morgan and the newspaper I'd found among his clippings. "Do you know how long they've owned it?"

"Marty's around your age. But his dad owned it before him so it's been in the family a lot of years. Why?"

"Later. You think he'll still be at the paper?" It was almost six-thirty.

"Probably. But, I'll give you his home number too." He paused and I heard him tapping keys on his computer. "I got it right here." Then he added, "This better be gold, McCauley."

It took three phone calls, but by the time I got back to Foxport, I thought I had enough information to crack Ed Carver's shell.

Chapter 23

Looked like I'd have to wait. Carver didn't answer the phone. Elaine, I knew, was having dinner with a friend so he wouldn't be with her. No matter. I'd try him later. In the meantime I had someone else to see, although I wasn't optimistic about coming away with anything.

While it was possible that Karen Lassiter had employed Ramon's services because she wanted a new identification for herself, I chose to believe she was acting on Wicklow's behalf. If so, she knew where he was hiding. I had a hunch where that place might be, but that's all it was. I knew my chances of getting an answer out of her were slim to none. But if she and the bank teller, Randall Lewis, were as chummy as they seemed, maybe he could provide me with some answers. I hoped he wasn't as tough as Karen.

I'd written down the address of the ranch house I'd followed Lewis to a couple days ago, so finding it was no problem. If, as I suspected, Lewis lived with his parents, that could work to my advantage. If he was a good son, he wouldn't want his parents to know what I thought he was up to. On the other hand, parents, especially mothers, can act like bears when their cubs are threatened.

I rang the bell and, almost immediately, the door was opened by a trim, blond woman shrugging her way into a suit jacket.

"I'm on my way out," she said, hooking a purse strap over

her shoulder. When she finally looked to see who she'd addressed, I saw she had sharp gray eyes and a round face with a dimpled chin.

"I'm looking for Randall Lewis."

"Randy!" she called over her shoulder in no particular direction. "Someone here for you."

Stepping back into the small, black and white tile foyer which spilled into white carpeting and a living area, she adjusted her blouse under the jacket collar. The pale green suit had a long jacket and a short skirt. If I'd seen her from a distance, I'd have guessed she was no more than forty. But, up close, her eyes sagging under the heavy makeup and the spray of lines around her mouth suggested she was closer to fifty. Old enough to be Lewis's mother.

She regarded me with some curiosity as she bent to pick up a black leather briefcase propped against the wall. "Are you a friend of Randy's?"

"We've met."

As I stepped into the house, the residual smell of dinner hit me. Fish. If the critters are so damned good for you, why didn't they make a place smell as good as Bolognese sauce did?

I introduced myself and, just as she opened her mouth to, I assume, do the same, Lewis made his entrance with a dishtowel in one hand and a butcher knife in the other. He stopped when he saw me, looked me up and down for a second before tossing the towel over one shoulder and swiveling the knife slightly. The light caught the blade. This move was all the more impressive because he wore no shirt. Standing there, he reminded me of Elaine's refrigerator magnets—Michelangelo's David with various outfits she dressed him up in according to her whim. For Lewis, today's whim involved a pair of blue jean cut-offs and high-topped sneakers. And a towel and a knife.

The woman's face lit up when she first saw Lewis, but her features clouded over as she looked from him to me and back again. "Is anything wrong?"

Lewis dropped his gaze to the carpet long enough for his expression to relax. Then he smiled at her and walked toward both of us, never taking his eyes from her.

She seemed relieved she didn't have to bother with a crisis. Straightening her jacket, she said, "I've got to run. I'm showing the Durants three houses. I probably won't be home much before ten." And then she kissed him. It was not a motherly kiss. Protracted, straight on the mouth and accompanied with a caress to his bare, muscled shoulder. In response, Randall slipped his free hand between her jacket and her blouse. I'm not sure what it did once it got there. When she finally broke away and caught her breath, she said it was nice to meet me, and left.

When I'm wrong, I'm wrong.

For a minute, we both stared at the closed door as though her image were seared into the wood.

Lewis broke the spell. "What do you want?"

"I'm hoping you'll tell me where Kurt Wicklow is."

He snorted his amusement and shook his head. "Yeah, right." Sobering, he added, "How would I know?"

"Because Karen picked up Wicklow's IDs from Ramon Santiago this morning. Someone's got to take them to him."

"I don't know what you're talking about," he said after a hesitation. "Now, get the hell out of here."

"You're saying you don't know where he is."

"I'm saying that even if I did know, why the hell would I tell you?" He raised the knife. At its widest, the blade was three inches.

"Okay," I said, trying to focus on him rather than the knife. "If you're sure you can't help me then I guess I'll go to the bank first thing in the morning and tell them about these midnight withdrawals you've been making."

His eyes narrowed and for a second he seemed to lose track of the knife. "What are you talking about?"

"Wicklow's office account. He never took that money out."

"Yeah. He did. I handled the transaction for him." He pointed the knife in the direction of the door. "Out."

"Don't you want to know how I figured that out?"

"I don't give a shit." Glowering, he brought the blade around so it was less than an inch from my chest.

I told myself he wouldn't let me bleed all over this white carpet. "Kurt is either faking it or he's really dead. If he's faking it, he's got to at least act like he's dead. Dead men can't make withdrawals. But live ones who work at the bank can. Especially if he knows someone who's got access to Wicklow's signature stamp."

"You got no proof."

"All I need is a suspicion. Enough to pique the bank's curiosity."

He shook his head. "You got no proof," he said again and this time I think he believed it.

Nodding toward the door, he said, "Next thing I want to hear is the door slamming on your ass."

"Does Mrs. Robinson know about you and Karen?"

He looked confused. "Mrs. who?"

"The woman you live with."

A hesitation. "What's there to know?"

"I've got photos of you groping Karen in her parking lot." I gave that a few seconds to sink in before adding, "Made that good-bye effort by the door look pretty tame."

He moved the knife up to my throat. "I used this knife to slice tomatoes. It's really sharp."

"Don't be stupid, Randy." I refused to believe I'd be done in by a tomato knife. "What are you going to do? Cut me up? Shove me down the garbage disposal?" On the other hand, I didn't want to give him any ideas. "Murder is messy. Bloody. We're standing on a white carpet. Can you have me cleaned up before she gets home?" I was real uncomfortable arguing for my life and basing my thesis on how inconvenient it would be to kill me.

He clenched his jaw at the same time his grip on the knife tightened. I could almost read the debate in his eyes.

"Whatever it is, it's not worth killing over."

"Look, I'm telling you, I don't know where Wicklow is."

"What real estate company does she work for?"

"Look, I don't know anything."

"She's a beautiful woman. For some reason she sees something in you." I hoped my rampant use of pronouns didn't make it obvious that I didn't know her name. "You want to lose all this?"

"You wouldn't."

"I would. That's how bad I want to know where Wicklow is."

After smoldering silently for several moments, Lewis lowered the knife. "They wouldn't tell me."

"Who's they?"

Reddening, he shook his head. "I don't know."

"Reverend Ron and who? Karen?"

When he turned away, I decided it was time to play my hunch.

"It's that cabin up in Wisconsin, isn't it? The one that belongs to Karen's folks."

I could tell by the way he went rigid that I'd guessed right.

"You didn't hear that from me," he said.

"Where is it?"

He didn't answer.

"Once I find it—and I will—I'll tell them you sent me."

He turned, stricken and brought the knife up again. "Now, why would you do that?" His face was the color of watermelon pulp.

"You tell me how to get there and I won't."

He took one look at the knife and then, apparently disgusted with it for being of no help to him, hurled it across the room. It impaled one of the couch cushions.

Exasperated, he pushed his hand through his hair. "Look, I'm not even supposed to know where he is."

"So much the better for you. They won't think it was you who told me." Then I added, "If you draw me a good map, you can go about your life like we never met."

He mulled that over and seemed to like where it took him. "Yeah," he said, nodding. "Okay." He kept talking as he walked into the living room and dug a piece of paper and a pencil out of a drawer in a low table. "Look, I barely know Wicklow. Just from the bank. I don't know what's going on. I heard Karen and Reverend Ron talking one time. That's all."

"What about Gina Wicklow?"

He shook his head, pleading with his eyes. "I swear. I don't know."

"Did Karen take her?"

"Really. I don't know anything about that."

I dropped it. Once I found Wicklow, I'd get my answers.

"You a friend of Mick Jensen?" I asked.

He looked up from the map he was drawing. "Yeah, I guess. What about him?"

"What's he got to do with Wicklow?"

He gave me a blank look. "Nothing. Why?"

"Is he a member of your church?"

"Yeah."

"When did he join?"

"I don't know. A couple months ago I guess. What of it?"

"Never mind. Keep writing. Remember, if I get lost all bets are off. Karen and Ron will be calling you Brother Rat, and your roommate will be looking for a new house boy."

As much as I dreaded a confrontation with Ed, I was relieved to see a faint light flickering in one of the windows. But after pounding at the door for five minutes, I almost walked away from it all. If it hadn't been for Elaine and Gina, I might have. Finally, after almost ten minutes, I guess he figured that wishful thinking wasn't going to drive me away. He opened the door and, without a word, walked back into the living room.

He looked bad. He'd given up shaving. Worse, he looked like he'd given up. Slumped on the couch, he gripped his coffee mug like it was the only thing keeping him grounded. The curtains were drawn and the room's only source of light came from the TV screen where Vanna White smiled and flipped letters. When I glanced into the dining room, I saw that someone had given up on the flowers. The vase sat empty except for an inch of dirty water in its base.

Ed had resumed watching TV as though I weren't there. Again, wishful thinking will only get you so far.

I took the letter Elaine had given me out of my pocket, unfolded it and stuck it in front of Carver's face. "What's this about?"

He didn't take it. In fact, he tried to look around it as though he was really interested in the puzzle on the screen. Vanna flipped over three n's.

"The Brandenburg Concertos," I told him.

When he focused on me, his jaw tightened. Despite the air conditioner, the room felt close and stale. "Where'd you get that?"

"Elaine."

"This is none of your business. Or hers. It's got nothing to do with Ellie." With one hand, he snatched it from me, crumpled it up and tossed it on the floor.

I retrieved it before he decided to shred it. "But it does have something to do with Brewster's death, doesn't it?"

He didn't answer me.

"And it's got to do with Wicklow disappearing."

Still no response. The television audience applauded.

"And you're the third person this letter refers to."

He glanced at the letter.

"Then who? Danny?"

Nothing. Behind me, the music from a commercial for a pain reliever blared. I picked up the remote and pushed the "Off" button, then tossed it back on the coffee table. The silence was so abrupt and complete, I almost reached for it again. Instead, I sat on the edge of a chair facing Ed.

"Whatever's going on here, it's eating you from the inside out."

"Maybe I should just let it."

"What about Elaine?"

"Elaine would be a hell of a lot better off without me."

"We finally agree on something."

Ed smiled grimly. "You'd like nothing better than to have things back the way they were."

Carver really made it hard. "I'm not here for a debate. Choices were made and now we're all living with them. Or most of us are trying to. One of us seems to be on a fast train out of here."

"You go to hell." He reached for the remote.

"Okay." I pushed myself up from the chair. "I'm going to talk to Kurt Wicklow. He can't afford not to give me some answers."

It took several long seconds to register, but when he sat back again and turned toward me I knew I had his attention. "You know where Wicklow is?"

"I think so."

"Where?"

"About three hours north of here. Near the Dells."

"How do you know that?" Then he shook his head like he didn't care and looked down at the mug in his hand.

"Maybe you've also got a few things to ask him."

"I wish I'd never met the son of a bitch." His voice sounded real tight.

"You two might want to talk about old times. Maybe Tracy Mitchell will come up."

He kept staring at that mug. I pulled out the piece of paper on which I'd copied the ad from the *Douglas Debate* and read aloud, " 'Anyone with information regarding the death of Tracy Mitchell on this date in 1972, please reply to PO box 1728. Reward.' The paper was dated October twelfth. That's your birthday, isn't it?" He didn't move. "We've got a long ride together. One of us has got to do the talking."

Chapter 24

"What do you know about Tracy Mitchell?" Carver asked.

We'd been driving for two hours with probably another to go and, so far, Ed had little to say. I'd done most of the talking, explaining how I came to learn where I thought Wicklow was hiding out, waiting for his new identity so he could get on with his new, sin-free life.

"I know how she died." Then I added, "And I know someone's been running the same ad in the paper on October twelfth for the last twenty-six years."

"That was my twenty-first birthday." He stared out the side window, toward the woods that lined this side of the divided highway. I recalled my own twenty-first. Some of it. A rite of passage that, for some college students, was right up there with graduation.

It was several minutes before Ed continued. "I don't remember much about the night. Started drinking in the afternoon. By the time we hit the bars that night I was pretty wasted. We were at this place called Rudy's. It was packed. I remember the way the place smelled like spilled beer and smoke." He paused and added, almost reflectively, "Everybody smoked back then." Then, "Wicklow pulled me aside and said he had a birthday surprise. Told me and Danny to be outside in fifteen minutes. He'd pick us up. So, we drank another beer and went outside. Sure enough, he pulled up. He and Brewster were in the front seat. Wicklow was driving.

Brewster had his arm around this girl sitting between them. Danny and I got in the back and Wicklow introduces her as Tracy and says she wants to party with us, but she's only eighteen so she can't drink in the bars." He stopped then and adjusted the air conditioning vent.

I waited.

After another minute, he took a deep breath and started again. "I didn't really see her until we got to where we were going. It was the middle of nowhere. Way out in the country. This big old barn out there all by itself. No lights except the stars. It was cool that night so we sat in the car drinking for a while. Tracy got drunk pretty fast. Wicklow'd gotten her a bottle of Peppermint Schnapps. I remember she was kind of plain. Brown hair she wore straight, kind of stringy. Hadn't gotten rid of her acne yet. A little on the plump side. She giggled a lot. Didn't say much. Kept looking up at Wicklow. Must have figured he was some kind of a god. Big football hero. She was what we called a townie. Lived in Douglas.

"After a while, Wicklow, Brewster and Tracy get out of the car. Wicklow comes back and sticks his head in the window. Tells me Tracy's my present but he wouldn't think of giving her to me unless he knew she worked." He paused. "That was how he put it."

"But, you knew what he was talking about."

"I did. Drunk as I was. And I guess I figured if she was up for it, then so was I." He shook his head. "Don't know what I was thinking. In my state, I doubt I could've gotten it up.

"Anyway, Wicklow and Brewster took her into the barn. I remember how clear it was that night. Clear and the stars—God, there were so many of them. Me and Danny got out and lay on the hood of the car, drinking beer and smoking cigarettes and just looking up." He paused. "I wish we'd all spent the night doing that." Sighing deeply, he continued. "I think maybe I dozed off. Next thing I know, Wicklow and Brewster are back and saying something about Tracy falling out of the loft. Broke her neck, Brewster said. Wicklow seemed real scared. Shaky. Kept pacing back and forth, rubbing his hands together. Well, that sobered me up fast. At least I thought it did."

"Didn't anyone think about taking her to a hospital?"

"I did. I mean, I said we should. But Brewster kept saying she was dead. Said he was sure there was no pulse. If we took her to the hospital we'd all be in deep shit. We had to stick together on this."

"Then what happened?"

"I guess we were just going to, you know, leave. But then Brewster started talking about all the evidence we'd leave behind. We were both majoring in law enforcement." He stopped.

"So, you burned down the barn?"

I felt him turn so he could look at me. "That was Brewster's idea. Cover our tracks by burning the barn. He kept saying we had to destroy the evidence. I don't know. It made sense at the time. It'd been a dry fall. The barn was old, hadn't been used for years. Figured it'd go up real easy."

I couldn't see the expression on Ed's face. "Didn't that bother you?"

"Hell, yes. Still, I figured she was dead. Whatever we did wouldn't change that. I was drunk." He shrugged. "No excuse."

He didn't say anything then, just stared out the window at the dark shapes of the trees. I prompted him. "But she didn't die from a broken neck."

"I know," his voice sounded ragged. "I think I saw her. I don't know. Maybe it was my imagination. I looked up and saw that loft window. Flames were coming out and then I thought I saw a figure in there. Dark against the orange. Just for a second. And this scream. You ever hear a rabbit scream?"

I shook my head.

"Well, that's what it sounded like. High pitched. Keening. Brewster said it wasn't human. Was probably the wood giving out. I don't know."

"If you saw her in the loft, that meant she didn't fall out of it like Wicklow claimed."

"You think I haven't figured that out?" he snapped.

I waited.

"I ran for the barn. Don't know what I was thinking. Hell, I didn't want to die. If that was her up in the loft, there's no way I could've gotten to her."

"What happened?" I asked when he stopped.

"Danny tackled me. I remember lying there . . . this weight on top of me. He was screaming at me. I don't remember the words. I lay there and breathed in the dirt. The smell of smoke and the orange sky . . . it was like a big bonfire. I can still feel it, smell it."

I wondered if either Wicklow or Brewster would have stopped him.

Finally, he said, "There wasn't anything in the paper for a couple days. Took them that long to find her. Big investigation, but they never turned anything up. Wicklow was real careful when he picked her out and set everything up. When they finally did an autopsy, it showed she hadn't died of a broken neck. Her jaw was broken. She burned to death."

I could think of nothing to say.

"Burned to death," he repeated. "Brewster swore she was dead. Said he checked. Wicklow said she wasn't moving."

"Was Brewster mistaken?"

After a moment, Ed shook his head. "I don't think it was a

mistake." Then, "Strange, he's the only one of us who never had any trouble living with it. Maybe that's why I could stand to be around him. Watching him act so normal, I could almost believe it never happened."

"But Brewster didn't have much in the way of a conscience."

"None at all."

"What about the letters?"

"I never got one. I think it must have been Danny who answered that ad in the paper. All this started happening after he died. It got to Danny worse than the rest of us. He couldn't even function."

"When Brewster showed up at your doorstep, was that the first you knew about the letter?"

"No. Brewster called me after he got it. And then when I went to Douglas for Danny's funeral, I saw the ad in all these clippings he'd saved. It was weird. He'd saved them all except for one. Starting in '73. I counted one missing. Must've been the one you found. I think his mother figured they were just Danny looking for a job. Or a love life." He paused. "She'd never see anything bad in Danny. And there really wasn't. He didn't have a mean bone in his body." He paused. "Once I saw all those pages from the newspaper, I knew something was going to happen. Like walking through a mine field. You know one with your name is out there, but you don't know where or when it's going to get you. Brewster got the letter first. Then Wicklow."

We drove in silence for a few minutes. Then I asked, "Does it make sense to you that Wicklow might have used all this money to buy himself forgiveness?" I explained about the church.

"That fits," Ed said after I finished.

"Would you have done the same?"

"You bet I would." He shifted so his arm rested on the top of the door. "You know, there are some days I'll wake up and won't think about it right away. I'll just lie in bed, listening to the morning sounds and it feels so damned peaceful with Elaine there and all. I feel good. Then it comes flooding back and I think some days if I had a gun next to the bed, I'd swallow the barrel." He paused. "If I thought money could buy me peace, I'd do just about anything."

"Did Brewster come out here to try to get to the bottom of all this?"

"Yeah. Brewster figured Wicklow ought to be able to tell us something. Never got the chance to ask."

"He never saw him?"

"No."

"Did you know Tracy Mitchell had a brother?"

"No." I felt him watching me. "None of the papers said anything about him at the funeral."

"He wasn't there. He was finishing up his tour in Vietnam."

"How do you know?"

"I talked to the editor of the *Douglas Debate*. He remembered. Said his name was Michael."

"Did he place the ad?"

"He doesn't know. That was anonymous. Paid in cash or a money order."

"Nam," Ed murmured. "I might have replaced him."

Chapter 25

We'd gotten off 90 about forty-five minutes earlier and taken Route 60 to a two-lane paved road. It was almost two a.m. Flashes of light in the west heralded a storm. I hoped it didn't hit before we found the cabin.

While we'd made good time on the interstate, the rural stretch of road had lots of bends and curves and I had to slow considerably. According to Lewis's instructions (which, depending on how seriously he took my threat might or might not be accurate), we stayed on this road for six miles, then we'd turn off on a gravel road called Milton and take that west for another three. "Remote" was a good adjective for this hideaway.

"There. Up ahead on the right." Carver had been navigating and apparently he had keen eyes. I slowed, not sure what he saw. Then, like a wide patch of snow, the gravel road appeared in the headlights. I took the corner doing forty-five. The car's rear end fishtailed and Carver grabbed the dashboard.

"This isn't a high-speed pursuit, for God's sake."

I flashed back to driving lessons with my dad, then quickly shoved the picture aside as I concentrated on the road, which deserved all the focus I had. A fairly steep incline slowed the car some, which was fortunate because I'd never have made the sharp left turn which followed. Who'd mapped out this road? Beyond the bright beams was nothing but pitch black. I couldn't go much faster than thirty. Thick clouds had moved in, obliterating the moon, and the air felt heavy with moisture. A crack of thunder followed a flash of lightning. The storm was closing in on us as we closed in on the cabin. Despite the muggy night, I had the window down. I guess I figured my senses would stay sharper. The road was barely wide enough for one car. I checked the mileage. We'd come only about a mile on the gravel.

When I thought about Gina, I imagined two scenarios. One, she was a part of all this. Deep down, I felt she wasn't, but I didn't know if that was my gut or my heart talking. If she had been abducted, for whatever reason, I didn't know what her chances of staying alive were. Maybe it depended on whether Wicklow thought he'd given enough money to pay for two souls.

Damn, but this road was a twisty sucker. As I eased the car around another curve, the headlights caught the eyes of some animal—a raccoon maybe—and I slowed as it waddled its way across the road. Beside me, Ed grunted.

Since he'd told me about the incident in college, we hadn't exchanged more than a few words. I sure as hell didn't know what to say. I doubted he was looking for absolution from me. I tried to imagine myself as a drunken twenty-one year old in the same situation. I wanted to believe I'd have behaved differently, but I'm acquainted well enough with my own character flaws to realize that there's a possibility that I'd have done the same thing Ed did. Nothing.

"There. On the left."

I'd seen it about the same time he spoke. Lights in the woods. I pulled the Accord off onto the narrow stretch of grass separating the road from the woods. Branches scratched the door and snapped at me through the open window. I cut the lights.

Set back about a hundred feet off the road, the cabin looked like it had sprung out of the forest without disturbing a twig. I guessed that even in the daylight, not much of it was visible from the road. Had it not been for the lighted windows, we'd have missed it. From where we sat we had a view of the back of the cabin. According to Lewis, the cabin itself overlooked the Pine River, and across the river was another cabin. As far as Lewis knew, that was the only neighbor.

Ed opened the glove box, removed his SIG Sauer and handed me my .38 Smith and Wesson. We were both breaking rules, but neither of us mentioned it.

I had to climb over the gearshift and slide out on the passenger side behind Ed. After clipping the .38 to my belt, I went around to the back and dug a flashlight out of the trunk. The wind had picked up some but, so far, the rain held off. We stood at the narrow dirt drive which led to the cabin and tried to get our bearings. Two cars were parked next to the cabin, one behind the other. I couldn't see the one in front, but the other looked like a Cavalier.

"Karen Lassiter's here."

"She the one bringing his IDs?"

"Yeah."

We walked beneath the dense pines and poplars, which provided a thick canopy and filled the air with their scent.

Windows on the lower floor were illuminated.

"Wonder if he's waiting for us," I remarked.

"Maybe he's getting ready to leave."

Then I saw a light in one of the windows flicker. At first I thought fireplace, but it was way too bright.

Shit. "That's fire."

I started running and as I neared the cabin, the window in the back door blew out and flames licked into the night, sending embers flying. Hoping the main entrance would still be accessible, I ran past the cars parked beside the cabin and around to the front. I heard Ed coming up behind me.

A long porch ran the length of the cabin with a big, heavy wooden door in the center. The flames hadn't reached the front windows yet. The door felt warm, but not hot. It was locked. I kicked it once. Again. Nothing. I pulled my gun and was about to put a bullet in the lock when it occurred to me that there might be someone alive on the other side. I glanced at Carver who'd come up beside me.

Without exchanging the thought, we simultaneously gave the door our best kick. Wood cracked as it gave. "Again."

With our third try, it flew open. Smoke billowed out. We reeled back. The heat seared and the smoke nearly overwhelmed us. The smell of gasoline was strong. I pulled my handkerchief out and clamped it over my mouth. Once the smoke cleared some I could see into the cabin, which, from what I could make out, was one large room with an open balcony. The fire had engulfed what looked like the kitchen and eating area—the black skeleton of a chair and table were barely visible through the flames. It had climbed the stairs and the balcony blazed. There must have been rooms up there, but I couldn't see through the flames.

"Gina!" I tried to raise my voice above the breaking glass and cracking wood. Nothing. The air feeding into the fire made it howl and rage like a beast.

She could be in one of those rooms off the balcony. I started to move toward the stairs, without any idea how I'd get up there. The heat intensified. A shard of flaming wood dropped at my feet. I looked up and saw that the rafters had caught fire. Ed grabbed my arm.

"Jesus," he said at the same time a banshee wailed. As I looked up at the balcony, I saw a portion of the flames had moved, taken life, split off from the rest. Appendages flailed as it plunged from the balcony to the floor then rolled toward us like a burning log. I looked around and saw that Ed had grabbed a large Indian rug by the door. I helped him throw it over the body. As we patted it down, I heard a loud crack; and a fiery length of rafter hit Carver square on the shoulder. As he buckled under it, I kicked it off him. The air seethed with embers. Breathing hurt. Carver, his face a dark mask of concentration, barely acknowledged the blow as we wrapped the blanket around the body and dragged it out the door.

This had to be Wicklow. It couldn't be Gina. We set it on the ground and I lifted the rug; the body smoldered.

"Jesus," Ed said. "Oh, Jesus."

I thought it was a man, but I couldn't be sure. "Wicklow?"

Carver shook his head. "Wicklow's bigger than this."

I saw the fire had crept to the cabin's door. Now I prayed for rain. With the wind feeding the flames, if it didn't rain soon, we'd have an inferno on our hands.

Then I heard the sound of a car engine. It cranked, but didn't turn over. I saw the glare from the headlights as I heard the engine grind again.

"Wicklow!" I called out like I expected him to wait. I took off and as I rounded the corner, the engine caught and the Cavalier started to backup. "Wicklow!" Drawing my gun, I ran past the first car. The Cavalier had made it halfway down the driveway when I shot out its left front tire. It retreated a few more feet, then limped to a stop. Squinting into the headlights, I started toward the car. Then the brights flicked on, blinding me. As I shielded my eyes, the gravel crunched beneath the tires and the dogged little car inched forward, the wheel with the flat wobbling like a weak ankle. Then the engine revved and the Cavalier lunged at me. I dove toward the woods, rolling as I landed. A bullet buried itself in the earth near me. I fired at the car as I gained my footing and scrambled back into the shelter of the dark and the trees.

An explosion sent flames billowing up from the cabin in a fiery cloud, igniting a tall fir tree. One end of the cabin collapsed, and chunks of flaming wood and embers filled the night with fireworks. Another tree caught.

My shelter amounted to a few tenuous birches. I'd have to go deeper into the woods if I wanted more. Fifteen feet separated me from the driveway. Where the hell was Carver?

The Cavalier crawled forward then backed up so it was in front of the other car. Its headlights lit up the area I called shelter. I hugged the ground.

"Forget that," someone yelled. Wicklow? "Get her in the Taurus." Wicklow.

He fired two shots. One hit way to the right and the other behind me. He couldn't see me. If he could, I'd be dead. Come on, Carver.

Muffled voices. A car door opened. I couldn't see for the brights. Footsteps on gravel moved toward me. I fired into the glare. Just as I could make out a silhouette in the brights, two shots came from the direction of the cabin. The shadow dropped to the ground. Thank you, Carver.

"Kurt!" A woman screamed.

Wicklow got up and scuttled back to the Cavalier. "There's two of them."

The woman in the passenger seat fired twice in Carver's direction. "Move everything to the other car," she yelled. "I'll cover you."

I recognized Karen's voice. She fired again. This time the shot hit the trunk of the birch six inches from my head. I bolted. Two more shots, one close enough to count in a game of horseshoes, and I was out of the headlights' glare.

I crouched beside a tree about twenty feet from the cars. The Cavalier blocked the Taurus so I couldn't disable it. I assumed Ed couldn't get a shot at it either. In the orange light from the fire, a head bobbed into view as Karen crawled out of the Cavalier on the driver's side.

Using the Cavalier as a shield, Kurt and Karen made their transfer to the Taurus, firing into the dark at us as they climbed into the newer car. I got a look at Wicklow as he ducked into the driver's seat. The car started like a champ and they took off down the driveway.

I ran for my Accord, hugging the edge of the woods for cover. By the time I reached my car, Wicklow had swung the Taurus around and it spit out gravel as he headed back toward the main road. Using the driveway, I executed a sharp three-point turn and jammed the gear into first. The tires spun when I floored it. Then they caught and I nearly wound up in the back seat as the car lurched forward. As I edged my car up to forty, a crack of thunder shook my bones. Then, as it dissipated, another sound picked up. Sirens?

Even with the brights, it was all I could do to keep the car on the road. Trees loomed up out of pitch black. I had less than three miles to catch up with them. After that I'd have only a fifty-fifty chance of following in the right direction.

I stared straight ahead, scouring the dark for a glimpse of taillights. Sweat stung my eyes. The road took a sharp turn and as I downshifted, the Accord's back end swung violently on gravel. I edged the car up to forty again. I hoped the blaring siren belonged to a fire truck. It was getting closer.

I heard Wicklow's words in my head. "Get her in the Taurus." He had to mean Gina. Did they have time to move her? I prayed she was anywhere but in the cabin.

According to my gauge, I had less than a mile before I got to the paved road. My jaw ached from gritting my teeth. A few raindrops smacked my windshield. Then I saw the lights. Two white beams not more than thirty feet ahead. I coaxed a little more out of the car and closed the distance some. Damn, the sirens were closing in. It occurred to me that this road was way too narrow for two cars to pass, let alone a car and a fire truck. Wicklow was trying to beat the truck to the intersection. The drops grew fatter and then a sheet of rain blinded me. Flipping the wipers on high, I pressed down on the accelerator.

I recognized the right angle curve coming up. We were almost to the paved road. Next would come the hill which spilled out onto the highway. Ahead of me, the Taurus's rear end slewed as Wicklow made the turn. He had less than ten feet on me when his brake lights went on. But he wasn't slowing. I downshifted to second and the Accord's engine howled in protest as the tach needle jumped into the red. But it responded. The Taurus shot down the hill and at the last second it looked like Wicklow tried to veer off the road. But the car skidded into the intersection directly in the path of the lead fire truck. Metal on metal screamed. The truck's breaks screamed. I screamed.

Chapter 26

The fire engine pushed the Taurus almost twenty feet before careening into the road abutment. A ball of fire shot up, defying the torrent of rain, then dwindled and receded. I eased my car the rest of the way down the hill until I could see Wicklow's car, which was recognizable only as metal accordioned between the truck and the wall.

I sat there for a minute, watching the emergency lights flashing as the vehicles accompanying the fire truck closed in on the accident. Through the rain-swept windshield their movements resembled a strange, impressionist ballet. Then I turned the car around and headed back up the hill.

I drove as fast as the rain and the road would allow, latching onto the notion that I'd find Gina in the Cavalier and I clung to it like a dying man clings to God. I'd find her in the back seat. Or maybe the trunk. Yeah, the trunk. Or in the cabin. No. Even Wicklow couldn't do that to two women.

As I pulled in the driveway, I saw that the rain had contained the fire. While the cabin still burned, the trees had won the battle. I pulled up beside the Cavalier. Its back door was still open and the car was empty. I dug a crowbar out of the Accord's trunk.

The rain came so hard and fast I could barely see as I wedged the tool below the trunk's lock and with a few solid efforts managed to pry the lid open. The trunk's light went on as it swung up revealing nothing but a blanket and some pieces of rope. I stared into the empty space, the rain stinging the back of my neck, and couldn't believe I'd lost.

"A key works better, you know."

I looked up and saw Carver standing beside me in the rain, dangling a ring with two keys on it from one finger. A flash of lightning illuminated the area.

"Gina?" I had to yell to be heard above the thunder.

"She's fine."

Slumping against the car's frame, I could practically taste the relief.

Carver palmed the keys and dropped them into his pocket. "She helped me get Mick over to a shed on the other side of the cabin." He waved a flashlight in the general direction.

I tried to wipe some of the rain from my eyes. "Mick Jensen?"

He nodded. At this point, I guess that didn't surprise me.

As we started to walk toward the shed, I thought I could make out a white shape standing in its door.

"Wicklow?" Carver asked.

"He ran into a fire truck."

He turned to me, eyebrows raised.

I shook my head. "I don't think he had enough money left over for a miracle."

Ed spoke as we walked. "Mick was able to talk some." He paused, staring down at the ground for a few steps. When he looked up again, he was blinking rain from his eyes. "Tracy was his sister. Danny wrote him just before he died. He named Wicklow and Brewster. Mick said he killed Brewster. Tried to burn him to death, but Brewster put up too much of a fight." Then, "I'm not sure, but I think Mick's dead. He hasn't moved or spoken in a while."

Gina met us a few feet from the shed. She gave me a hug and whispered in my ear, "I knew you'd figure it out."

I crouched beside Mick Jensen who lay on the Indian rug. Carver knelt beside me and turned the light on the body. It was real hard to look. His face, neck and chest were black and charred. His shirt had been mostly burned off. A blackened, curled up piece of T-shirt clung to his shoulder. One arm was black and the other had a few patches of white. Then I saw it on his upper right arm. Part of it was burned, but there was enough left to recognize the tattoo. That thin, worm-like appendage I'd seen before did belong to a rat's body.

"Mick?" I barely breathed the word.

His eyes blinked open. They were red slits buried in the charred black of his skin. I wasn't sure if he could see me. When he opened his mouth it was like a piece of raw meat. "Wicklow," the word hissed out of him.

I couldn't believe he was alive, much less talking.

"He's dead."

"You're sure?"

"Yeah," I said. "He went up in flames."

He looked up toward the roof of the shed. "All of them. We got all of them, Tracy." Then he closed his eyes.

I touched the skin of Mick's throat, feeling for a pulse. Nothing. I wasn't sure it could be felt under the burns.

I glanced up at Carver. His thumb and forefinger were pressed into his eyes. He looked like he was praying.

Chapter 27

For once this summer, we had a storm that actually cooled things off—low eighties and just enough humidity so you knew you weren't waking up in Phoenix. It was past noon by the time I pulled into my driveway. I felt twitchy, but not tired. Past tired. I'd offered Ed a cup of coffee and he'd accepted.

Ed, Gina and I had been up in Comstock, Wisconsin until seven a.m., answering questions and explaining how we all happened to converge on this cabin. Ed didn't say anything about being involved in the death of Tracy Mitchell. Mick was dead by the time an ambulance arrived. Both Wicklow and Karen had died in the accident.

Gina told us and the police that two nights ago Karen Lassiter had called her and told her Kurt was up at the Dive Inn and wanted to talk. When she'd gotten there, she'd found only me. She saw how drunk I was, and after feeding me some coffee, she'd poured me into her car and taken me home. Then she'd been abducted at gunpoint from my apartment by Karen, who forced Gina into the trunk of her Cavalier, and then tried to gas me to death. She'd driven Gina up to Wisconsin where, eventually, Gina would be disposed of. "Someplace where I'd stay buried for a long time." Apparently it was all part of an elaborate plan to set up Gina as the ruthless wife who got a love-smitten sap—that would be me—to kill Kurt, and then disposed of me when I was no longer useful to her. The object was for Kurt to be considered missing and presumed dead, instead of just missing.

"We played right into it," Gina said. "They didn't even have to set us up as lovers."

Kurt kept Gina tied up in one of the bedrooms until last night when Karen returned with another man. "I never saw him," Gina said, "but from what I could hear, he'd forced her to bring him." This man was, of course, Mick, who had come there for a single purpose: to kill Kurt Wicklow. But somehow Wicklow managed to get the upper hand because shortly after Gina smelled smoke, Wicklow came for her. "He threw me over his shoulder like I was a sack of dirt and carried me past this man lying on the balcony. I could tell he wasn't dead. I saw him try to get up." Kurt poured gasoline down the steps and all over the kitchen. "The smell made me gag." She put her hand over her mouth and took a few seconds before continuing. "He lit a match and dropped it in the puddle of gasoline." As he carried her outside, she saw the fire climb the steps. "They must have seen your headlights or something because he threw me in the trunk and left me there for a few minutes before they came back and tried to leave."

If they hadn't had to change cars, Kurt and Karen would probably have beaten the fire engine. But they'd still have Gina and I considered it a just exchange.

Our next stop was Foxport PD where we spent another two hours being grilled by Lieutenant Abigail MacKenna and company. She found the theory that Ellie had been blackmailing Wicklow worth considering. No one knew what Ellie had on him, but since the monthly five-hundred dollar withdrawals from his account could be traced back fourteen years, almost coinciding with the death of his first wife, Paula, it was possible that Ellie knew something more about her death. So, Ed wasn't off the hook yet, but Cal Maitlin was feeling optimistic.

While we were there, Abigail sent a couple of her people to the Foxhole to check out Mick's room. Among the things they found were files on Brewster Plunkett and Kurt Wicklow and a smaller one on Danny Morgan. A photo album displayed pictures of Mick's family with his sister, Tracy, featured prominently. She was prettier than Ed had remembered. Or maybe it was just that she looked so young. There were also shots of several men in army gear. From the background, I'd guess they were taken in Vietnam. In one photo five guys stood front to back so their sides faced the cameras. Each of them had yanked up the sleeve of his T-shirt to show off a rat tattoo.

When I dropped Gina off at her house, I walked her to the door. Other than some nasty rope burns on her wrists, she'd come through this physically unscathed.

"I feel numb," she'd said. "I can't believe what he did. Any of it. That young girl. Thinking he could buy his own salvation. Set us up. Crazy, isn't it?"

We stood on her porch, holding onto each other for a couple minutes. I didn't want to let her go, but I had to talk to Ed. And it couldn't wait.

When I got back to the car, he had my cell phone to his ear. After a minute he pushed the disconnect button and said, "Can't get hold of Elaine. I'll try her again from your place."

Now he sat, hunched over my dining room table, staring into his laced fingers.

Somebody had to bring it up. "Maybe you need to put this behind you, Ed. Almost thirty years of guilt—maybe that's enough." I stood at the kitchen counter, smoking a cigarette as I drank my coffee which wasn't nearly strong enough.

"I don't deserve to get away with it. Nobody else did."

"What purpose would be served in coming for- ward?"

"Justice."

"Maybe you could call the last twenty-eight years you've spent sorry to be waking up justice." Then I added, "Anyone who knew you were there when Tracy Mitchell died is dead. Let the guilt die too. Get on with your life."

"It's not that easy."

I smashed out my cigarette and went into the dining room where I pulled out a chair and sat across from him at the table. "This isn't about Tracy anymore, is it?"

He looked up at me.

"Wicklow didn't kill Ellie, did he?"

"How do you know?" It wasn't a challenge, merely a question.

Once I told him, I couldn't go back. Hell, I couldn't go back anyway. "Ellie was as surprised by his disappearance as anyone. Wicklow left his old life behind. Including the baggage. Including Ellie. No reason to kill her."

Staring past me, Ed took a drink of coffee.

I gave him a minute and then said, "You killed Ellie, didn't you?"

When he locked his eyes on mine, I knew I'd guessed right. I saw pain there, but I also saw relief.

"Why?"

He shook his head slowly and lifted his hand in a helpless gesture. "It just happened."

I waited.

"I got mad. She . . . she wouldn't sign the papers. Didn't want to see Elaine and me together." He shrugged. "I got mad. Hit her. She fell. Hit her head on the hearth. I didn't mean to kill her. Even to hurt her. It just happened."

I waited. Some Canada geese flew overhead. They sounded like professional mourners. I got up and poured us each more coffee.

"You know what I don't get," I said. "Ellie had been

blackmailing Wicklow for—what?—fourteen years. That's the most civilized case of blackmail I ever heard of. I talked to one of the bartenders at this restaurant in Richton. She said Ellie and Wicklow had been meeting every month for as long as she worked there. Three years. Have you ever heard of the guy who was being blackmailed buying his blackmailer dinner every month when he makes his payment? Talking and laughing like they're old pals?"

Carver shrugged. "It's a weird world."

I stopped. "How old is Dee?"

He looked up at me, but didn't answer.

"She's fourteen, isn't she?"

"Leave it alone." His voice was low and his tone ominous.

"She's Wicklow's daughter, isn't she?"

"You heard me. Leave it alone."

"I can't leave it alone. Whatever you tell me won't go past this room, but you've got to tell me. I know you didn't hit Ellie because she ticked you off. I can't believe you'd do that. But maybe I can believe you hit her when she told you Dee wasn't your daughter."

He pushed the mug of coffee aside and buried his face in his hands. He sucked in and exhaled three deep breaths, then dropped his hands to the table. His eyes glistened as he shook his head. "It wasn't that either."

"What was it?"

I heard the kitchen clock ticking and McGee crunching hard pellets of cat food. Outside, the sky was blue and a pleasant breeze stirred the trees.

Finally, Carver shifted in the chair and retrieved his coffee mug, wrapping his hands around it. "When I got to the house I saw how she was packing. I asked where she was going and she said Tahiti first. Then, who knows? I said what about the kids. She said, 'They're yours. You want to play house, you see how your little friend likes raising teenagers.' I told her that was fine with me." He shrugged. "I think that made her even madder."

I waited.

"Then she took this photo off the mantel—from the high school homecoming—and she wiped off the glass part. I guess she was going to pack it. I've always hated that picture. You know, she'd use it against me. Say stuff like this was when she was happiest. Even the football hero wanted her." He rubbed his hand across his mouth. "Then things got real nasty."

"What happened?"

"I told her she lived in the past. Her glory days were high school. Life never got any better for her. Kurt Wicklow wouldn't give her the time of day if he saw her on the street. Then her mouth kind of twitched like she does when she's about to smirk, and she nodded like she'd been waiting for me to say that. She said, 'Yes he would. In fact he gave me more than that.' She picked up another frame from the mantel and handed it to me." His voice caught. "It was Dee's eighth grade graduation picture. At first I didn't get it." He shook his head like he still couldn't believe it. "But then she said, 'She has her father's eyes. His coloring.' and I knew what she was saying." Ed looked at me, his features contorted in anguish. It was all I could do not to turn away. "All that money," he said. "Almost a hundred grand. She called it child support. Dee never saw any of it. And then—"

"What?"

He burst out of the chair and began pacing, his hands jammed into his pockets as though he were still trying to contain his rage. I could hear it in his words when he spoke. "She said she was going to write Dee a letter and tell her I wasn't her *real* father. That's how she said it, too. She stomped on the word. I lost it. I mean, it's one thing to tell me, but why tell Dee? I knew why she was going to tell her. She wanted to get to me. Anything to make it harder for me to raise Dee. But God, it was an awful thing to do to her own daughter." He stopped and put one hand to his forehead as though trying to contain some excruciating pain or thought. He continued, his voice barely above a whisper. "I hit her. I don't remember doing it. I guess I hit her hard. I didn't mean to—" He shook his head and dropped his hand to his side. "I knocked her down. The next thing I know, she's on the floor. There was blood. It killed her. She didn't have a pulse. Her eyes were open. Wasn't breathing. I left her there." He squeezed his eyes shut. "I did it again."

Neither of us spoke for a couple minutes. His words hung in the air, their echo drowning out the sounds of a late summer afternoon.

Finally, I asked, "What are you going to do?"

Slowly, he opened his eyes, then fired the question back at me.

"Nothing," I said. For a number of reasons I couldn't go to the police with this. The fact that Elaine was part of the equation was only the beginning.

He looked at me like he was trying to decide whether to believe me or not.

"One thing," I said.

"What?"

"You've at least got to tell Elaine. She's got a right to know."

He nodded as though that seemed like a reasonable request. Then he stared down at the floor, weighing his choices, I assumed. Possibly wondering how his decision would affect his next twenty-eight years.

He walked over to the table, picked up his coffee mug and

drained it. "Mind if I use your phone?"

"It's in the kitchen."

On his way, he stopped to refill his mug, draining the pot. When he picked up the receiver, he looked at it like he'd never used one like that before. But then he punched in some numbers, put it to his ear, stuffed his other hand in his pocket and waited. I had the duration to speculate as to who would be picking up on the other end. Elaine or Cal Maitlin? The lady or the lawyer?

Chapter 28

"I should know better than to ask for your help."

I looked over my shoulder and saw Elaine standing in the doorway leading to the Jaded Fox. It had been more than a week since Ed Carver pleaded guilty to involuntary manslaughter in the death of his estranged wife, Ellie. Sentenced to two years, he'd probably serve one.

I hadn't seen Elaine since then. She looked good. Pale, maybe a little drawn, but composed and calm. Her arms were crossed over her chest and the loop of the jade necklace she wore over her pale green T-shirt rested on her wrist. In one hand she held a letter-sized envelope. She walked into my office, stopping beside my desk and picked up a small calendar I'd gotten from some insurance company. Each month featured a different quote. Even though we were deep into September, I hadn't bothered to tear off August yet.

Elaine said, "Who was it who said to be careful what you wish for, you may get it?"

"I believe that was Mr. Spock," I replied. "But he may have been quoting a human at the time."

To my great relief, she smiled. Then she sat in the chair across from my desk.

"I was mad at you, you know," she said.

I nodded.

"I had no right to be mad, but I was. I'm sorry."

"It's all right."

"I guess you're just too good at what you do."

"That explains why I'm so rich."

"Right." She smiled politely. "Really, I guess I thought you wouldn't let it turn out bad. That wasn't fair of me."

"We're okay now?"

"If you are."

"I am."

She looked down at the calendar. "It's not August anymore, you know."

"Thank God."

She lifted the calendar's top page. "May I?"

"Please."

She peeled the page off, tore it in half, then quarters, and dropped it in the wastebasket.

"Good riddance," I said.

"Amen," she agreed, then read off the calendar: " 'Always do right. This will gratify some people and astonish the rest.' Mark Twain." She replaced it on my desk.

Along with the unpleasant events, August took with it the heat and humidity, leaving behind warm days with bright blue skies and cool nights. I'd switched from lager to stout.

"Have you been to the doctor yet?" I already knew the answer to that; Louise had served as a go-between during the last few weeks.

"I have." This time her smile showed all over her face. "My due date is March twenty-eighth."

"A good day."

"I think so."

"How's Ed?"

"All right. I mean, as well as can be expected. His kids are with his folks. I guess they're doing pretty well."

"What did he say about the March event?"

Instead of answering, she said, “I guess I was kind of surprised you didn’t tell him about me that day he told you everything.”

“You asked me not to.”

She nodded.

“Do you wish I had?”

“I don’t know. I wonder if he would have confessed if he knew he was going to be a father.” She quickly shook her head as though rejecting the notion. “No, this is for the best. I know it is. He’s happy about the baby. I think he’d be happier if he knew I’d be waiting for him when he gets out. But he said he wouldn’t blame me if I moved on.” Then she said, “He also told me about Tracy.”

“He did try to go back in for her. Did he tell you that?”

“He did?”

I nodded. “Danny stopped him.” In a way, Ed’s omission of that detail made perfect sense. He may not be inclined to cut anyone any slack, but he was no easier on himself.

She pushed a lock of hair behind her ear and picked up the penguin Louise had given me. It had been occupying the corner of my desk, warding off depressing thoughts. “You know, I really can’t believe myself. If this were a friend of mine in the same situation I’d tell her to run like the wind. He killed his wife—or caused her death—and was complicit in another death. But, it’s not so easy.” She stroked the penguin’s smooth surface with her thumb as she shook her head. “What am I thinking?”

“He’s not a bad person.”

“I know that. And I can’t turn off my feelings for him.”

“You’ve got time to think it through.”

She nodded. “No one came out very well, did they?”

“No.”

Then I asked, “Do you want your cat back?”

"Do you mind?" She tried real hard to sound sincere.

"Really. I don't."

"You're sure now?"

"Absolutely." I paused. "You can't be changing the litter, you know." I'd heard somewhere that pregnant women weren't supposed to change litter boxes. I hoped she would tell me that this warning, like cats sucking the breath out of infants, was part of the feline myth.

But she said, "You're right. You'll be visiting me at least once a week, won't you?"

"Oh, probably."

Then she stood and began to pace in front of my desk, still petting the penguin. "I feel like I've been so selfish about all this. Lots of people got hurt. What about Wicklow's clients? Will any of them see any of their money?"

"It's possible. I talked to Gina this morning. She said once they unravel the church's dubious finances, there might be some compensation. Who knows? I may even get my twenty-five hundred dollars."

"You deserve more."

I wasn't sure whether I deserved more, but I sure as hell needed more. If I didn't stop working as a pro bono private detective, I'd soon be a full-time shopkeeper. Nobody would want to see that. I'm lousy with customers.

"What was the name of the guy who heads the church?"

"Reverend Ron Christopher. He's doing a lot of explaining these days. His own flock is getting edgy. Wolf in the fold, you know. As it turns out, that immaculate retreat wasn't nearly finished. Although, they had the pool in and the tennis courts were partly done."

"Where was the place, anyway?"

"Some remote area in northern California."

Elaine's eyebrows drew together as she frowned. "I didn't

think there were remote areas in California anymore. Not where you'd want to live, anyway."

"Yeah, I wondered about that too. But here's what really had me confused. Once the end comes, and these people are convinced it's on its way, what state do you think will be the first to go?"

"Good point. One big thunderbolt and the whole west coast slides into the ocean."

"Exactly."

She'd come around my desk to the opposite wall where my new purchase hung. Now she stopped to examine it. "This is nice. Local artist?"

"Gary Niebuhr. Retha Burt assures me it'll be worth three times what I paid for it in as many years."

"I see. So, it's an investment."

"No. I just like it."

She gave me a quizzical look. "This isn't in character, is it? Next thing you'll be buying a chair for your living room."

"Don't hold your breath."

"Gee," she smiled, teasing, "I thought you'd have one of Gina's paintings hanging somewhere."

"Actually, I think she is painting one for me. The other day she was out at the house taking pictures of Peanuts and me. Action shots—a Frisbee was involved."

"How's Gina doing?"

"All right. Working with the investigators to figure out how much Kurt embezzled. At this point it looks like more than a million."

"Louise told me Gina might be going back to Paris."

"It's a possibility."

"Day at a time?"

I nodded.

She perched on the edge of my desk, still clutching the

penguin in one hand and the letter in the other. She seemed a little uneasy. Like she wasn't sure where her place here was anymore. "Um, Louise said she and Albert are going up to that place in Burlington for dinner tonight. She asked if we'd join them."

"The chicken fried steak place?"

"I think that's the one."

"Yeah. Sure. Sounds good." I stopped. "They usually eat around five, don't they."

"Four thirty. But, Louise said to tell you she'd hold him off until six."

"She's all right."

"Ed asked me to give you this." She stood and thrust the envelope at me. "I don't know what's in it."

When I leaned forward and took it from her, she dropped her hand to her side and said, "But I've got to tell you I'm dying to know."

Printed in Carver's small, precise hand was "McCauley." Nothing else. I couldn't think of an appropriate response. Frankly, I was speechless.

"Well," she said. "I'd better go. Louise has some errands to run." She replaced the penguin on my desk.

"You may want to hold onto him." I nodded in the direction of the Jaded Fox. "The lady you work for says penguins always make you feel better. She swears by them."

"Do they?"

"They may," I conceded.

She picked it up again and wrapped her fingers around it. "Guess it's worth a try." She gave my shoulder a small squeeze. "I'll see you tonight." Then she left.

As I slit open the envelope with my pocketknife, I decided if this was a thank-you note I'd treat myself to a Guinness.

Quint,

I'd like to believe Elaine will wait for me, but I've got no right to expect it. Please keep an eye on her and, when it comes, the baby. Whatever it takes.

I appreciate what you did. I don't suppose it was easy for you.

Ed

I read it again. Close enough, I decided.